**Praise for Manda Collins' Studies in
Scandal series**

DUKE WITH BENEFITS

"A delight to see a classic Regency hero so smitten with
a truly unusual heroine. Driven by multiple passionate
scenes and the hunt for a murderer, it's a swift and intense read. A bluestocking Regency romance of unusual
intensity."
                                        —*Kirkus Reviews*

"Intense romance."   —*Publisher's Weekly*

"The romance is lovely, with both hero and heroine falling into love the way people do in life outside of books—
in a slow tumble and a sharp drop, all at once."
                              —*New York Times* bestselling author
                                        Sarah MacLean

"This is a terrific historical romance . . . I definitely
have to recommend."
                              —*Night Owl Reviews* (Top Pick!)

"A delightful book full of romance, intrigue, and mystery, *Duke with Benefits* should be on your to-buy list
for July!"   —*Romance Reviews Today*

"A delicious romance with a curious mystery thrown in
to spice things up!"   —*Fresh Fiction*

Also By Manda Collins

Wallflower Most Wanted

MANDA COLLINS

St. Martin's Paperbacks

This is a work of fiction. All of the characters, organizations, and events portrayed in this novel are either products of the author's imagination or are used fictitiously.

WALLFLOWER MOST WANTED

Copyright © 2018 by Manda Collins.

All rights reserved.

For information address St. Martin's Press, 175 Fifth Avenue, New York, NY 10010.

ISBN: 978-1-250-10990-3

Our books may be purchased in bulk for promotional, educational, or business use. Please contact your local bookseller or the Macmillan Corporate and Premium Sales Department at 1-800-221-7945, ext. 5442, or by e-mail at MacmillanSpecialMarkets@macmillan.com.

Printed in the United States of America

St. Martin's Paperbacks edition / February 2018

St. Martin's Paperbacks are published by St. Martin's Press, 175 Fifth Avenue, New York, NY 10010.

10 9 8 7 6 5 4 3 2 1

For Janga, whose support in those early days of drabbles and Bon Bon fanfic is a big part of why I'm published. Our mutual love for a certain author's work sparked a friendship that's withstood kerfuffles, drama, and real life struggles and I look forward to decades more.

Acknowledgments

As always, huge thanks to my editor Holly Ingraham for steering my crazy plots in the right direction, and trusting me to go off the map sometimes; Holly Root, agent extraordinaire, who keeps me focused on the business side of things and is always there when I need a voice of reason and a read on this crazy publishing world; my friend and now third set of eyes, Lindsey Faber, who makes sure my timelines don't go off the rails and my word echo problem is under control; the art and production departments of St. Martin's Press who give me gorgeous covers and lovely typesetting; Vanessa Kelly who listens to me whine and shares my love of this discrete corner of English history; my pets for keeping me company during long days at the laptop; my family who keeps me afloat when the vagaries of everyday life threaten to consume; and last, but not least, my readers, whose appreciation for my mystery/romance mashups will never cease to amaze me. Thank you all for keeping this writing gig weird and fun.

Chapter 1

Consumed by the need to capture the scene in front of her before the light changed, Miss Sophia Hastings didn't notice the newcomers until it was too late.

She'd struck out early that morning—an unusual occurrence for her—carrying her own equipment to her favorite spot at the edge of the Beauchamp House property, atop the chalk cliff overlooking the sea.

The desire to capture the morning light dancing over the waves had been building in her for days. It was always thus with her artistic motivations. Every painting she'd ever completed had begun as the kernel of an idea: a hint of color, a flicker of light, a touch of shadow. And slowly, over time—while she worked at other tasks—the idea would grow from thought to need. And she would give in to the impulse that made her try—however fruitlessly—to capture what she saw on canvas. Sometimes what she saw was a scene she'd crafted with models and costumes and props. But other times, like today, the scene was one that nature had provided for her. And that meant bringing her tools to the spot that nature herself dictated would give the best view.

Having removed her slippers so that she could feel the

solid earth beneath her stockinged feet, she dashed her brush across the canvas, blending grays and blues and a hint of white in an energetic frenzy. Her arm arced in wide sweeps, mimicking the movement of the waves below and the wind that whipped around her. She'd been working for almost an hour, and was in that otherworld where her awareness of her own surroundings was dimmed by the vision before her, when several things happened at once.

A deep male voice sounded from somewhere in the trees behind her.

Footsteps crunched on the pebbled beach below.

And she lost her balance in the middle of a particularly energetic brush stroke, tumbling over the edge of the cliff.

The fall itself seemed to happen in an achingly slow unfurling of time, though in actuality it took only seconds for her to drop the ten or so feet from the precipice to the rocky beach. And somehow she managed to twist in such a way as to land on her feet and not her head.

Unfortunately, one of those feet landed on a rather sizeable stone that twisted her ankle.

She'd no sooner hit the ground than a large male form knelt beside her on the beach.

"My God. Are you hurt?"

Sophia blinked, and looked up into the alarmed face of Lord Benedick Lisle, vicar of Little Seaford. With a visage that was almost too fittingly angelic, his clear blue eyes and unruly brown curls had set every female heart in the vicinity into a flutter since his arrival some months earlier. And as an artist, with an eye for beautiful forms, Sophia couldn't help but notice that the vicar was almost perfectly made. That he possessed an innate decency and sense of humor was perhaps gilding the lily.

Now, however, his usual good humor was replaced with real concern.

"Of course you're hurt." He didn't seem to need a reply, which was good because she'd lost her breath from the fall. "No one can fall that far and remain unscathed."

He waited a moment, just taking her hand in his, watching her with a mixture of concern and wonder. Shoving away her response to his gaze, she began assessing herself for damage. Her arms and upper body seemed fine. But her right ankle was throbbing and when she gave it an experimental flex, it made her cry out in pain.

"It's my ankle," she said through gritted teeth. It was mortifying to be in this situation. Not only because the vicar—who was undoubtedly the most handsome man in the county—was seeing her in such a vulnerable state, but also because he'd likely think this was some sort of ruse to get him to notice her. Not that he was vain—quite the opposite—but the unmarried young ladies of Little Seaford had all but turned vicar hunting into a sport. Why should he think she'd be any different?

But Lord Benedick didn't seem to be overly concerned about his hide, for he gave a grim nod. "I'm just going to feel for broken bones, Miss Hastings," he assured her solemnly. "Let me know if something pains you."

Moving back so that he could get to her foot—which was bare but for her stockings—he very carefully slipped his large hand beneath her heel and lifted it. Sophia bit her lip to keep from voicing her pain at the movement, and when he probed the joint with steady fingers she nearly levitated.

For a moment, all she felt was white hot pain.

"Easy," he soothed, lowering the offending extremity gently to the ground. "There's no sign of a break. At least not that I could feel. I think you'd better get Dr.—"

He broke off at the sharp bark of a shout from the clifftop above them.

Sophia's eyes flew to his as she recalled the man's voice she'd heard right before she fell.

She opened her mouth to tell him when Benedick raised a finger to his lips. Realizing that it might be best if they weren't discovered, she nodded.

"Damn you," the man cried. "I knew I should have seen to this business myself. You're far too soft to deal with our problem. Can you be relied upon to eliminate our little stumbling block if necessary?"

The other man's voice was too low for them to hear, but it seemed to be placating, because the first man's next words were calmer. Something about their location allowed his utterance to float down to the beach below with amazing clarity. "See that you do," he said in the tone of a man who has little patience with excuses. "If this scheme doesn't work out, I will hold you responsible. And I am not kind to those who disappoint me. You've been loyal enough so far. I hope you won't allow yourself to be weakened by your loyalty to people who don't care about you. I am the one who truly understands you. Only I can help you rise above your circumstances and achieve the success you deserve."

There was something familiar about the man's voice. But Sophia was still too shaken from her fall to concentrate on it.

Once again, they heard the low mumbling of the second man. Then, the sound of footsteps shushing over the dead leaves of the little wooded copse indicated that the two men were leaving.

Sophia and Lord Benedick were silent for a few minutes more, just to be sure the men were gone. The sound of the sea, battering into the shore again and again, punctuated their breathing while they waited. The sun, which had been wan when Sophia first came out that morning, had gone behind a cloud, and Sophia shivered a little.

"Who was that?" she asked glancing up at the cliff, almost afraid the two men would climb over. "Even only hearing one side of their conversation I know it was not about their plans for the village fete."

"I'm not sure," Lord Benedick said, following her gaze upward. "Perhaps it's best if we forget we heard that. It was clearly not intended for public consumption. And the louder man did not sound like the sort of person who would take kindly to having interference in his business."

Sophia turned to him in surprise. "I should have expected that attitude from other men, Lord Benedick, but I should think as a man of God your first responsibility is to help people. And clearly someone is in grave danger. We just heard one man tell another that he must be prepared to eliminate someone."

"I am aware of what we heard, Miss Hastings," he said stiffly, "but you are in no condition to look into the matter. We must see to getting you back to Beauchamp House. Whatever we overheard can wait for that at least, can it not?"

As if the conversation were over, he rose easily to his booted feet and put his fists on his hips. He rather looked like an avenging angel, now, Sophia thought sourly. An avenging angel who was urging caution.

She knew very well when she was being fobbed off. Still, she was determined. Her own sense of justice insisted. "Very well, Lord Benedick. It can wait. But do not think to dissuade me from learning more about those men. If someone is truly in danger we must do something to protect them."

At her vehemence, something in his gaze softened.

"Very well, Miss Hastings. I will commit to learning more. But for now we must get you to the house."

She nodded, and was about to ask him for a hand up when he bent and gathered her into his arms, lifting her as if she weighed no more than a feather.

The jolt to her injured ankle, however, soon replaced any shyness at being lifted bodily from the ground. Her head swam a little as the chalk cliffs spun by her as she was propelled upward. Closing her eyes against the disorientation, she concentrated on getting past the painful moment. When it had abated some, she took a deep breath and became aware of the warmth of the hard male chest against her side, as well as the bergamot mixed with pure male scent of him.

"I'm sorry," he said, and she realized she must have made a noise at the pain. "I'll do my best not to jostle you as we go up the sea stairs, but it will be impossible to avoid some bumping. It is the nature of stairs, I'm afraid."

She looked up into his eyes, which were once more creased with concern. She needed to be careful or she'd find herself enjoying this sort of tender care a bit too much. "Thank you, my lord," she said with a firmness that was as much for her as it was for him. "I will try to keep my cries of pain to a minimum."

Sophia was only half-joking.

"Good girl," he said with a nod. "Let's get you home."

Lord Benedick Lisle, vicar of Little Seaford, had been on his morning walk along the seashore when Miss Hastings had quite literally fallen from the heavens. Or at the very least from the clifftop.

One minute he'd been studying the crumbling stone sea wall that marked the boundary of the Beauchamp

House property, and the next a female body was hurtling down from above.

He'd been too far away to do anything but watch in shock as he tried to make sense of what he was seeing. Then, he broke into a run. When he reached her side, he realized it was Miss Sophia Hastings, one of the four Beauchamp House heiresses.

She was an exceptionally lovely young woman—he might be a vicar, but he was still a man, and he doubted the Archbishop of Canterbury himself would be able to resist the pull of Miss Hastings' ample charms—but it was her spirit that made her truly beautiful. Whereas other young women with her looks might have gone to London and taken the *ton* by storm, or searched for a wealthy husband, Sophia was a painter of some skill and she was determined to make her mark. Which meant she spent a great deal of time in her studio, or painting outdoors. And when she wasn't working, she was surrounded by a cadre of young men from the village. She hadn't, so far as Ben could see, given any of them an indication that she was interested in more than flirtation, but she somehow managed to handle them without allowing them to get too competitive over her.

Ben had considered entering the fray himself, but with his own duties in the parish he hardly had the time for friendship, much less anything more serious. And, if he were being honest, as a vicar, he needed a certain sort of wife. He had watched his brothers Archer and Freddie fall in love and marry, and he certainly wanted the sort of partnerships they enjoyed with their wives. But he also had to be pragmatic when it came to choosing a bride. A vicar's wife would need to be content with sharing him with the parish. A vicar was never off duty. If someone were ill, or suffering, he had to be ready to leave at a moment's notice. And his wife would need to be someone who shared his dedication to caring for the people of his parish. Who wouldn't worry about getting her gown a bit dirty when she visited the homes of people who worked the land. Who could converse with all sorts of people, be they noble or commoner. He wasn't sure that Miss Hastings possessed those qualities.

Of course, that was putting the cart before the horse. But he was a sensible man, and he was perhaps a bit too prone to overthink things. And if truth be told, he was unlikely to find Miss Hastings in a quiet moment to assess whether they could even be friends. She was always chatting with someone or working on one of her paintings.

If he'd wished for a few minutes of uninterrupted conversation with the lady, however, he hadn't wished for it to be while she was in excruciating pain.

He tried to be as gentle as possible while he climbed the sea stairs, but it was impossible to be as smooth as a well-sprung carriage, and by the time they reached the gardens behind Beauchamp House, he was panting from exertion and Miss Hastings' face was white with pain.

As they neared the fountain, he heard a shout from the house and Lady Serena Fanning, who served as chaperone to the heiresses, came hurrying out followed by the Duchess of Maitland—Lady Serena's sister-in-law and one of the four heiresses.

"What's happened?" Lady Serena asked as she reached them. Her strawberry blond hair was coiled tightly around her head in a rather severe style, but Ben knew she was fond of her charges. "Sophia, my dear, are you hurt?"

"I hurt my ankle," Sophia said through clenched teeth.

"But how?" Daphne, Duchess of Maitland, asked, her

brow furrowed. "I thought you were painting this morning."

"Perhaps we can discuss this inside?" Ben asked. Sophia wasn't heavy per se, but he wasn't exactly Gentleman Jackson either and he didn't want to drop her.

"Come," Serena said and he followed her through the gardens toward the terrace where two French doors opened into a drawing room.

It was a comfortably appointed room with warm rose walls and a pair of overstuffed sofas before a low fire.

"Here is fine," Sophia said indicating one of the sofas. Ben lowered her as carefully as he could onto the cushion and inhaled the lemon scent of her hair just before he pulled away from her.

Stepping back, he found himself clasping his hands behind his back to stop the impulse to reach for her again.

"Perhaps you can ask Greaves to send for the doctor, Daphne dear," said Serena, who was obviously in caretaking mode, putting a pillow behind Sophia's back, and bringing her a light blanket.

"Stop fussing, Serena," the patient protested. "I'm perfectly fine."

"You are not fine," her chaperone corrected her. "But I will leave you be for a moment. I'll see if someone can find your sister. There's no telling where she's got to looking for her rocks."

Without waiting for a reply, Serena turned to Ben. "If you'll wait here a moment, I'll go get some ice for Sophia's ankle and ask cook to send some refreshments."

And then she was gone.

The urgency of the need to get Sophia up to the house had erased any awkwardness between them during the long walk, but now there was a tension between them.

Not liking to loom over her, Ben lowered his tall frame onto the sofa across from her.

"You're in good hands, I think," he said, breaking the silence. "Lady Serena seems quite competent."

Sophia ignored his small talk and got right to the heart of the matter. "Thank you for rescuing me, my lord. I don't know what I'd have done if you hadn't happened along." Her blue eyes were bright with sincerity. "Not to mention what would have happened if those men on the bluff had discovered me."

At the reminder of the conversation they'd overheard, Ben's gut tightened. He didn't like to imagine that scenario. "I want you to promise me that you'll concentrate on healing and not try to investigate the matter on your own. I'll handle it."

She tilted her head. "You'll investigate it? I thought you said it was best to leave it alone?"

"As you said, someone is in danger." He wasn't sure what exactly he would do, but he knew he had to keep her away from the matter. There had been menace in the man's voice. And he sounded like the sort who would not take kindly to prying eyes in his business. "I'll ask a few questions."

Her pretty lips pursed in frustration. "It's not fair that I'm injured. I would like to know what they're up to."

He was entirely unsurprised that she was already chafing at the constraints of her injury. And it had only just happened. For her sake he hoped it would heal quickly.

"What if I promise to tell you what I learn?" he offered her. He didn't add that this way she could remain out of the matter, which would ensure her safety. He had a sneaking suspicion that she wouldn't give a fig for her own safety if it meant protecting someone else's.

Like a queen accepting a favor from a serf, she gave a

regal nod. "I suppose that will have to do," she said with a moue of distaste. "Though I do wish I could go with you. Who do you intend to question first?"

He was saved from response by the arrival of the butler Greaves carrying a laden tea tray. "Miss Hastings," he older man said gravely, "May I say how unhappy I am to hear of your injury?" He gave a deep bow.

"Thank you, Mr. Greaves," Sophia said with a sweet smile for the butler. "It is an annoyance, but these things happen in the pursuit of one's craft."

Ben rather thought most artists avoided tumbling over seaside cliffs, but kept his own counsel on the matter.

He watched in amusement as the butler, who clearly had a soft spot for Sophia, handed her a cup of tea and a plate of biscuits. "Lady Serena told me to serve you, Miss. She is fetching your sister from upstairs."

"Thank you, Greaves," Sophia said, sipping her tea. "You may go. Lord Benedick will keep me company while we wait for Gemma and Serena."

Ben wasn't positive, but he thought he saw a flicker of disappointment cross the man's face before he gave a brisk bow and left the room, closing the door behind him.

"He's a sweet man," Sophia said, "but overly solicitous at times."

"He certainly holds you in some affection," Ben remarked. He might as well have been invisible for all that the butler noticed him.

Sophia gave a slight shrug, but didn't comment on the matter. Instead she changed the subject. "I wonder if you might do me a favor, my lord."

He nodded. "Of course. Whatever I can do to make you comfortable."

"It's just that my canvas and easel and paints are all still on the bluff," she said sheepishly.

Of course. She hadn't exactly carried them down to the beach as she fell.

Ben stood. "I'll go retrieve them for you." She obviously cared about her materials and wanted them to be in good hands.

"I could ask a footman," she added in a low voice, "but I thought maybe you could look in the little wooded area and see if our arguing men left any traces of themselves behind."

Ah. Not a bad idea, actually. "I'll be off then. I've got about an hour until I'm to meet with the altar guild."

"Oh." She looked a little guilty. "I don't wish to take you away from your work. I'll send a footman."

But Ben was already eager to get to the copse to look around for himself. "I have the time, Miss Hastings," he said, crouching beside the sofa where she reclined with her ankle elevated. He took her hand and squeezed it. "I will bring your things back, though I may not have time to come in and report to you. But I'll send a note round if I find anything."

Her dark lashes lowered as she looked down at their joined hands. When she looked up and met his gaze, her smile was one of relief. "Thank you for keeping me apprised. I know you'd rather I stay out of this business, but I can't help but feel responsible for whomever it was they were discussing."

"You can only do what's in your power," he said, trying to reassure her. "But I share your concern. They were rather rough customers."

Stroking his thumb over the back of her hand, he reluctantly let her go and stood.

"Wish me luck," he said with a crooked smile.

"Just don't tumble over the edge," she said wryly. "I won't be there to rescue you."

Chapter 2

As it happened, Dr. Holmes was unable to come that afternoon because he was attending to another patient in the next county.

Lady Serena was concerned, but Sophia was convinced that it was only a sprain, and once she'd been helped to her bedchamber by two sturdy footmen, she allowed her maid to tuck her into bed with ice for her ankle and agreed to rest.

"I know you must be disappointed about missing Mr. Morgan's ball this evening," Ivy said, from where she perched on Sophia's bedside. "Of all of us, you're the lady most likely to be found dancing the night away."

She, Daphne and Gemma had come to check on her after luncheon. Only the sisters, Sophia and Gemma, had known one another before their arrival at Beauchamp House. But since then, the four ladies had built strong friendships. They each had expertise in separate disciplines, but they all appreciated the difficulties of being a female in the arts and academe, so offered one another support not only as friends, but also as fellow pioneers. And when both Ivy and Daphne had found themselves in danger thanks to tasks given them by their benefactor, Lady Celeste Beauchamp, they'd grown even closer.

Sophia frowned at her offending ankle. "I'd forgotten about the Morgan Ball," she said.

She'd been looking forward to the entertainment at the industrialist's newly refurbished country estate, which he'd bought for what was rumored to be a ridiculously large sum from a deeply indebted nobleman. It would be the neighborhood's first chance to see what was purported to be one of the most expensive renovations in Sussex history. According to local gossip, Morgan had chosen the south coast for his country home because he claimed to have a fondness for history and the location was near to Hastings—where William the Conqueror had claimed victory.

No one quite knew what to make of the self-made man who had made appearances in Little Seaford and the surrounding towns occasionally over the past year or so. By all accounts he was brash and a bit rough, but Sophia wasn't really concerned with his manners. She would really like to discuss his textile mills in the north, the conditions of which she'd learned about thanks to a letter from her Aunt Dahlia in Manchester.

If my sources are right, Peter Morgan is in Sussex for no other reason than to buy himself a seat in the Commons without having to face a local population who has suffered from his dangerous factories. He stood by and did nothing while the women and children working in his factories fell ill from cotton lung, and what's more, were torn limb from limb by his wicked machinery. And now he would flee from Manchester, where his perfidy is known far and wide. He seeks to whitewash his reputation in the waters of the sea.

It can hardly be a coincidence that a little bird in-

forms me one of the local members in that same vicinity has recently decided to give up his seat in the Commons. You must do all you can, my dear, to keep this awful man from what will be nothing less than theft. It is bad enough that the working men who give their lives and labor to make England great are kept from the vote, but to also ensure that government positions are handed out to the very industrialists who crush those same workers is monstrous.

Be vigilant, dear Sophia! And pray urge that stubborn sister of yours to do so as well. I know I taught you both better than to sit by while the weak are bullied by the strong!

Sophia had, of course, promised her aunt to learn all she could about the man, and if she had to miss his first entertainment, she'd lose her chance. Not to mention she was as curious as anyone else to see the spectacle of the newly embellished interiors of Morgan's house. Aunt Dahlia would likely be disappointed in her, but she was human after all, and liked to be dazzled as much as the next person.

She mentioned none of this to Gemma, however, who, as Aunt Dahlia had said, was stubborn and if truth be known, was far less interested in the workings of the political system than in her own pursuit of knowledge.

"You may have forgotten the ball," Gemma said tartly, "but I cannot imagine that your usual little coterie of admirers has. They will be cast into despair when they arrive to find you are not there. A shame, really, since it is one of my chief pleasures in life to watch them persist in the face of your polite indifference."

Tugging at one of Sophia's locks, she added with a saucy grin, "I can't imagine why they are so taken with you. You've always got paint in your hair."

Sophia made a face. "At least I don't have dust from dirty old stones under my fingernails," she retorted. "And besides, my gentleman callers can hear about my accident from me. I'm going to the ball."

All three of her companions gasped.

"You can't!" Gemma said, her mouth agape.

"Sophia," Ivy said with a sigh. "I don't see how, unless you wish to bring Thomas and Walter in the carriage with us so that they might carry you around on a litter like the king in his younger days."

"You won't be able to dance," Daphne said, looking puzzled. "What would be the point?"

"Oh ye of little faith," Sophia said with a wave of her hand. "I will simply use the walking stick we found in the attic during our initial explorations of the house. I'm sure with the sturdy arm of some strong gentleman, and the walking stick, I'll be able to hobble along quite nicely."

"I never met a more stubborn person in my life," Gemma said with a shake of her head. "You're worse than Aunt Dahlia."

"It's because of Aunt Dahlia I must go," Sophia protested. Then, she explained what her aunt had told her about Mr. Peter Morgan and his possible political aspirations. "So, you see, I need to find out what he's about. And what better place to do that than his first large entertainment in the neighborhood. How a man entertains says a lot about him."

"Why didn't Aunt ask me to look into Morgan?" Gemma asked with a frown. "I care about women and children."

How to explain that one's sister had a bit of a one-track mind? To one's sister?

Daphne, who was not known for either her tact or propensity for biting her tongue, saved her the trouble.

"Gemma, you'd never be able to concentrate long enough. You'd start daydreaming about one of your fossils and would lose track of the conversation."

Gemma looked offended and looked to Ivy then Sophia for support. "Am I really that bad?" she demanded when they only gave pained shrugs in response to her questioning look. "I'm not that bad."

"Dearest, you were so lost in thought about some issue with your research," Sophia said not unkindly, "that you tried to put on a hat *while you were already wearing a hat*."

"That was one time!" Gemma protested. "And it was a very thorny issue."

"It's nothing to be ashamed of," Ivy assured her with a kind smile. "You're very dedicated to your work. It's quite admirable. But even you must admit that you aren't precisely interested in anything quite as much as fossils and the possibility that giant lizards once roamed about the countryside."

Gemma shook her head, her light brown hair a little frizzy as it escaped its pins. "I don't mean to do it. It's just that I'll start thinking about something and then everything disappears."

"It's the same for me and maths," Daphne said with a nod of agreement.

"We all do it," Sophia assured her. "I fell from the chalk cliff because I was so absorbed in my work, for heaven's sake."

That diverted everyone.

"I thought you tripped walking on the shore," Gemma said with a frown. "You didn't tell me you fell from the cliff. Sophia, you might have been killed."

She gave her sister an impulsive hug. "Thank goodness you weren't hurt worse."

"How did you come to fall?" Daphne asked. "If you stay far enough from the edge, it's safe enough."

Quickly Sophia explained how she'd been startled by a man's voice behind her, and how Lord Benedick had come upon her.

"Who was it you heard?" Ivy asked. "That's Beauchamp House land. If there are trespassers we should let Kerr and Maitland know." The Marquess of Kerr and the Duke of Maitland were nephews of the bluestockings' benefactor, and more importantly, the husbands of Ivy and Daphne.

Sophia frowned. It hadn't occurred to her that the men they'd overheard were trespassing. But it was also possible that one or both of them had some association with Beauchamp House. The idea gave her a chill.

Mistaking her shiver for a more general fear, Ivy tried to reassure her. "Since both Daphne and I were accosted here, Kerr is quite firm about ensuring the safety of the house. He and Mr. Greaves have made sure that all the footmen are trustworthy, and there are new locks on all the doors. Even if someone were to wander onto Beauchamp House land, there's no way he could get into the house without someone knowing."

Sophia nodded. She had to tell Lord Benedick about her new insight into the quarreling men. He hadn't sent round a note, which she assumed meant he hadn't found anything in the copse. But she could speak to him tonight at the ball.

To Ivy she said, "I trust Kerr. Whoever the man was, I don't think he meant me any harm. He was speaking with someone else and they were far too involved in their own conversation to notice anything else."

"I'm just glad that Lord Benedick happened to be walking on the beach when you fell." Ivy's eyes behind her spectacles were wide with concern. "You might have been stranded there for hours."

"I wish I'd been there to see him carrying you from the shore up the sea stairs," Gemma said with a wink. "It must have been quite romantic."

"I was far too busy trying not to cry out every time my ankle was jolted," Sophia said wryly. Though she had noticed just how very muscular the vicar was on their journey. And she'd been tempted to snuggle her face into his neck more than once. But she wouldn't admit that now.

"Then how on Earth will you manage to go to the ball?" Ivy asked. "You're being stubborn to the point of lunacy, Sophia."

"I will manage," Sophia assured them with a calm she didn't feel. She was still determined to go. Though she wasn't quite as sanguine about her ability to withstand hours on her feet as she let on. But Aunt Dahlia needed her. And she'd made a promise.

"Now, you should all go and let me rest so I can look my best."

When Daphne and Ivy had gone, Gemma came and sat beside her sister on the bed.

"You weren't too distracted to notice the vicar's strong arms," she said with a sly look. "I've seen the way you look at him. He's the only unmarried man in the village who doesn't dance to your tune. And you like that."

"He's a handsome man," Sophia said blithely. "I'd hardly be human if I failed to notice. And between us, he's quite strong."

"You do like him," Gemma said with a grin.

"Of course I like him." Sophia refused to be baited. Whatever attraction she might feel for the vicar was not nearly as important as finding the identities of the men they'd overheard. And there was the matter of Peter Morgan and his political ambitions. She had plenty to keep her occupied without adding a *tendre* to the list.

"Now, please go find some old rocks to examine so that I may rest."

Gemma gave her a disappointed look, but took herself off.

Ben had been unable to find anything in his search of the little wooded area where their mysterious arguers had been hidden. He had quite easily found Miss Hasting's easel, canvas and supplies. The painting was still a little wet, and promised to be intriguing when it was finished. The way she'd captured the light and colors of the sunrise on the sea was impressive. He'd never been particularly artistic himself, but seeing work like this made him wish he had that sort of talent.

He reflected on the matter that evening as he drove his gig to the country estate of Mr. Peter Morgan, where the industrialist was set to hold his first public entertainment in the neighborhood. It hadn't occurred to him to ask Miss Hastings if she'd planned on attending, but given the state of her injury, he had little doubt that she'd have to send her regrets. Which was a shame. He'd enjoyed her company, and had hoped to reassure her that she shouldn't worry overmuch about what they'd overheard. But that could wait until later.

The line of carriages in the gently curving drive of Morgan House was impressive. Clearly the rest of the residents of Little Seaford were just as curious to see the inside of the mansion as he was. Having handed over the reins, he was greeted by a few parishioners as he made his way to the receiving line.

"Good evening, Vicar," said Mr. Josiah Almond, a

member of the local gentry, whose estate was just on the other side of Beauchamp House. He was a widower of middle years, whose children were grown, and a regular church-goer. He was also a bit of a gossip. In a lower voice, he said with a wink, "I see you've come to see what this Morgan fellow is about just as the rest of us have. I don't mind telling you I hope his refreshments live up to the promise of his taste in building materials."

Almond gestured to the marble beneath their feet. And if Ben's memory served from when his mother had been refurbishing the Pemberton ducal residence, the gilt molding and fabric-lined walls of the Morgan entry hall were quite expensive.

"I have a feeling you won't be disappointed, Almond," Ben assured the older man. If his assessment was correct, Morgan was intent upon impressing his neighbors. Everything about his home seemed to promote the idea that Peter Morgan was a rich, successful businessman. Was it a bit over the top? For Ben's tastes, yes. But then, he'd grown up in a ducal household that was built for similar purposes, and had long ago come to see the finery for what it was, a show of power. He had no need for such flummery. But the powerful did. And it would be hypocritical to take his father's show of wealth as a given while criticizing Morgan for doing the same thing.

Further discussion was stalled when they reached the place where Morgan, his wife and sons stood greeting their guests. Morgan himself was a large man, whose large belly was as much a show of wealth as any bit of gold in his home. His wife, on the other hand, was rail thin. She was pretty enough, with guinea gold hair that was still unmarred with gray. While Morgan greeted Mr. Almond, Ben took Mrs. Morgan's hand.

"Thank you so much for the invitation, ma'am," he told her sincerely. "I am always grateful for the chance to get out in the evening."

Mrs. Morgan smiled at him. "You are quite welcome, my lord. I'm sure our little home isn't what you're used to, but I hope you will be comfortable."

The description of what must be thirty rooms at the least, as a "little home" might have had Ben spraying his beverage, if he'd been unlucky enough to be drinking at that moment. As it was, he had to tamp down his natural response for the easygoing expression he'd perfected over the years of being the recipient of odd confidences from his flock. "I'm quite sure I will be most comfortable, Mrs. Morgan. But let us discuss the most important thing. I hope you'll reserve a set for me?"

The bit of flirtation did the trick and she blushed. "You rogue," she said without heat as she batted him on the arm with her fan. "You know I'm past the age for dancing, but if I were not, you may be assured I would not be able to turn down the most handsome man in the village. Aside from my Peter, of course."

"What's this?" said the man himself as he turned from Mr. Almond, who was moving along the line to the younger Morgans. "I hope you're not trying to lure my wife away, Vicar."

There was no menace in the man's tone, but Ben could hear a slight thread of pique, as if he didn't take the matter seriously but couldn't help but be a little annoyed. Whether because Ben was younger, or higher born, he couldn't say.

"Of course not, Mr. Morgan," said Ben smoothly. "Only inquiring if your dear wife was dancing this evening. But alas, she has informed me that she is not."

"She would make all the young ladies green with envy if she did," Morgan said putting a proprietary arm around his wife. "I don't blame you a bit for asking."

Then, obviously considering that matter behind them, he changed the subject. "What do you think of Morgan Manor, eh? I don't mind telling you I'm quite proud of it. Designed the place m'self, did you know that? From the ceilings to the floors. No expense spared, I can tell you. I wanted it to be a jewel on the coast, and so it is."

Ben blinked at the boast. "It's quite a sight to see," he said truthfully. "And I can tell that you put a lot of thought into every detail."

Morgan beamed. "I knew you'd understand. I'll bet it rivals your father's place in the country, eh? Of course it does. His place must be a hundred years old at least. And has none of the modern conveniences we've got here."

The Duke of Pemberton had actually had modern plumbing installed several years ago, but Ben wasn't about to get into a competition with Morgan over whose home was better. "It is indeed over a hundred years old," he confirmed. "And nowhere near as modern as this. You are to be congratulated."

Before Morgan could use the pause to add more comparisons to his father, Ben continued, "I was just telling Mrs. Morgan how thankful I was for the invitation. I'm looking forward to this evening's entertainment. Thank you, sir."

The industrialist looked a bit frustrated at being unable to continue his explanation of how he had bested the Duke of Pemberton, but the person behind Ben diverted his attention then, and with an over-hearty handshake, he sent the vicar on his way.

After exchanging greetings with the Morgan sons,

who were typical young men, with shirt points and hair that were higher than advisable, Ben stepped into the ballroom, which was already teeming with guests.

To his surprise, however, his eye was captured by a familiar head of auburn-tinged dark hair amongst the chaperones and wallflowers.

He couldn't see the lady's face, as she was at the moment surrounded by a circle of young men, but it was most certainly Miss Sophia Hastings, holding court. No doubt having taken to the side of the ballroom thanks to her ankle injury, but here at the Morgan ball nonetheless.

"Evening, Vicar," said a male voice from beside him. He looked up and the Duke of Maitland handed Ben a cup of watery-looking punch. So much for Mr. Almond's hopes for lavish food and drink, he thought wryly. "It tastes better than it looks."

Since Ben had performed the duke's marriage ceremony not long after his arrival in Little Seaford, he and the other man had become friendly.

"Why aren't you dancing with your bride?" Ben asked, taking the cup and sipping. It did indeed taste better than it looked. Perhaps Mr. Almond wasn't to be disappointed after all.

"She's over there lecturing the schoolmaster, Mr. Pinter, about something having to do with maths," Maitland said with a shrug. "I don't pretend to understand half of what she says about all that business. But it makes her happy, and that's enough for me."

Ben had known as soon as he met the couple that they were fond of one another, despite the circumstances that had led to their hasty marriage. And though they seemed on the surface to be a mismatch, given that the duchess was one of the most gifted mathematicians in the nation, and the duke . . . was not, they made it work. And Maitland had even agreed to live the rest of the year in Little Seaford, away from his own properties, so that his wife might fulfill the requirements of her inheritance at Beauchamp House. Of course, the duke was also the nephew of the former owner of the home, Lady Celeste Beauchamp, so he already felt at home in Little Seaford. But Ben didn't know many men who would adjust their lives in such a way simply to please their wives. And considering that Maitland's cousin, the Marquess of Kerr, had done the same thing, it was clear that the men in that family doted on their wives.

Ben looked across the room to where the blond duchess did indeed seem to be explaining something to Pinter, using her hands to sketch figures in the air. "Pinter looks a bit nonplussed," he said to the duke.

"Probably because she knows more about the subject than he'll ever forget," Maitland said with a shrug. "But he'll be all right. He likes her. And is far better at accepting a woman as his superior in an academic subject than most men in his position would be. He's a good fellow, Pinter."

The two men were quiet for a moment as the musicians began warming up, and the buzz of conversation around them picked up. It was unusual for Ben to remain unmolested by the female population for so long, but he supposed it was because they were slightly afraid of the duchess, and he was currently standing next to her husband.

"Heard you rescued Miss Hastings from the shore this morning," Maitland said, turning to give Ben a curious look. "I didn't know you were in the business of rescuing damsels in distress. Though I suppose being a vicar and all, it's part of the job."

He felt his ears redden at the other man's teasing tone.

"I'm sure if anyone else had come upon Miss Hastings, he too would have done what he could to help her."

"But how many men would have carried her a quarter of a mile—up treacherous sea stairs no less—to help her?" Maitland asked. "I'm quite fond of the chit, but I don't even think I'd have tried it."

"I couldn't leave her there," Ben argued. He didn't add that they'd just overheard a man threatening murder, so leaving Sophia on the shore would have been dangerous in more ways than one. "And it wasn't as difficult as all that."

His aching biceps told him differently, but he wasn't going to admit to it here and now. The less emphasis he put on the physical exertion it had taken to get Sophia from the shore to the house, the better. He didn't want the duke or anyone else at Beauchamp House thinking he'd helped her out of some sort of *tendre*. As lovely as Miss Hastings was, she was not the sort of lady he should be associating with. He would need to, when the time came, marry someone who would make a good vicar's wife. Nothing he'd seen of Miss Hastings had indicated that she was so disposed.

"You do know there's a secret passageway from the shore that leads into the house, don't you?" Maitland asked with a raised brow. "I should have thought Sophia would have told you. It has stairs as well, but it's a damned sight shorter than all the way up the outer stairs, across the lawn and through the garden."

Ben blinked, not sure what he was hearing. "Are you telling me Miss Hastings might have saved my back by telling me of a shorter route? Why didn't she tell me?" He thought back to the long trek from the beach to the house. He had a sudden inclination to give Miss Hastings a lecture—complete with gesticulations rivaling those of the Duchess of Maitland.

"I daresay she was too overset by pain to remember it," Maitland said thoughtfully. "She's not the sort to keep something like that to herself on purpose. She's a good 'un, is Sophia."

Good 'un or not, Ben thought with a frown, he was going to have a word with her about it. If for no other reason than to assure himself that he'd not been hood-winked into helping her. The ladies of the village had tried all sorts of machinations to get close to him. He had difficulty believing someone like Sophia, who obviously had her own ambitions, would do such a thing, but who was he to claim knowledge of the female brain?

He was about to excuse himself to go speak to her, when Peter Morgan stepped onto a small dais at the front of the room, which he hadn't noticed before. It wasn't unusual for a host to say a few words at the open-ing of a ball. But something about this felt different.

With a gesture to the musicians, indicating they should be silent, their host began to speak.

From her seat at the side of the ballroom, Sophia wished for the hundredth time that she'd listened to her sister and stayed home. Her ankle was throbbing, and the circle of young men around her, rather than distracting her from her pain, were only annoying her with their competi-tion to see who was willing to do more for her. She could only drink so many cups of punch, and she flatly refused to let them carry her about the room like a pasha. It had been lowering enough to hobble into the room with her walking stick.

She'd had visions of holding court from her perch

with the matrons and wallflowers, but hadn't actually thought through the grueling process of getting from the carriage to said perch.

Fortunately, the sound of the musicians warming up signaled that her suitors would have to go soon and dance with those young ladies who hadn't fallen from the cliffside that morning. Her injury could be counted a benefit in that instance at least.

"Your attention, ladies and gentlemen," came the sound of their host from the front of the ballroom. And fortunately, Sophia's young gentlemen had the sense to move so that she could see where Peter Morgan had taken a position at the dais situated near the musicians.

Sophia wondered, a little thrill of electricity running down her spine, if as her Aunt Dahlia had predicted, Peter Morgan was going to announce his intention to run for the vacant seat in the Commons.

"Thank you all for coming tonight," said Morgan with a broad smile, which he made sure to beam over everyone in attendance. At least the ones in the ballroom at the moment. "It is with great pride that my wife Millie and I welcome you into our new home away from home. Our little jewel on the coast. As most of you know, I've made my home for most of my life in Manchester, but since our arrival in Little Seaford, we've been most cordially welcomed by you and the rest of the villagers. I've met with Mr. Givens, the mayor, and have listened to his concerns. And I've made it my business to become involved in local activities, like the upcoming art exhibition, the board of which I am now a member. I mean to make it clear to you, the residents of Little Seaford, that I will put as much effort and energy into the wellbeing of our village, as I have done with my businesses."

There was a smattering of applause from the room at large, but from one side of the room, where the two Morgan sons and their friends had gathered, came a raucous cheering. Obviously, the man had brought his own audience, which could be counted on to cheer in the right spots.

Sophia glanced around the room, and noticed that with the exception of the cheering lads, the rest of the guests looked puzzled. And in some cases, troubled.

When the cheering had died down—at the behest of Morgan, who gave a gesture in his sons' direction—he continued. "It is my great pleasure to announce that I intend to run for the vacant seat in this district for the House of Commons. And I hope all of you will give me your support!"

Once again, the cheering group erupted into huzzahs. And there was a bit more applause from the main room. It was more polite, however, than genuinely enthusiastic.

Since she'd been forewarned by her aunt, Sophia wasn't surprised, but she was puzzled at Morgan's decision to make the announcement at what was ostensibly an entertainment for the upper echelon of Little Seaford society. If he had wished for a large cheering crowd, surely a more public celebration would have been far more conducive to that.

"Now, without further ado, I shall allow you to get on with what you've come for," Morgan said, beaming out over the room. "Let there be dancing."

He gestured to the musicians, and they began playing, and Morgan, looking as pleased as if he'd just delivered a New Year's infant, led his rail-thin wife, Millicent, out onto the dance floor in the first dance.

"I suppose that is what Aunt Dahlia was speaking of,"

said Gemma from where she'd come to stand beside Sophia's chair.

"Indeed," Sophia said. "Only I didn't expect him to make the announcement tonight."

"I'm not sure anyone did," Gemma said with a nod to the guests, who were slowly making their way onto the dance floor. But there were several small groups of gentlemen who seemed to be in deep conversation. "It seems to have set some of the local tongues wagging, that's certain."

One thing their host had mentioned, however, had caught Sophia's attention and it was far more personal for her than her aunt's request to keep an eye on Morgan. "What do you suppose he intends, getting himself a seat on the art exhibition board?" she asked her sister. "What can he possibly know about art?"

But Gemma gave her a speaking look. "What does anyone in this village know about art, excepting you and the Primbles with their group of artists at Primrose Green? Isn't the owner of the livery stable on the board?"

"Yes, but Mr. Essex has a very keen eye," Sophia argued. The man had chosen very complimentary colors for the exterior of his establishment, after all. "And besides, I know that all of the board members—Mr. Morgan excepted—have the best interests of the village at heart. And they will judge impartially. We don't know what sort of motives Mr. Morgan has for affiliating himself with the art board."

"One would imagine he simply wishes to ingratiate himself with the local populace," Gemma said. "Though it is difficult to know what any man will do. They are fickle creatures to be sure."

Sophia supposed her sister was close to the truth. Still, since she intended to enter the exhibition this year, she was concerned that the entry of Morgan onto the board of directors would affect her chances of having her pieces shown. "You're likely right. He will simply sit on the board and let the others take charge. It is no doubt his intention to use the meetings to solicit support from the other business owners in the group."

"Are you afraid that he will try to keep you out of the show?" Gemma asked, her eyes narrowing. "Sophia, your work can be a bit controversial, but no one in Little Seaford is the least bit interested in censoring you. This is hardly the wilds of Yorkshire. Most of the gentry hereabouts spend their springs in London and summers on the road between here and Brighton. They are quite sophisticated."

But Sophia wasn't sure that Morgan had the purest of motives. Her aunt had seemed to think he was going to run his campaign with a view toward capitalizing on the populism that had grown stronger in the years since the Peterloo massacre, where fifteen people had been killed when cavalrymen stormed into a crowd demanding parliamentary reform in St. Peter's Fields, Manchester. For many years now, a growing contingent of the population had been protesting the inequities of the voting system, the cutting—by industrialists like Morgan—of wages when the market shifted, and the Corn Laws, which imposed a tariff on foreign grain, and meant the people were forced to buy more expensive British grain. It was quite canny actually, Sophia thought, for Morgan to choose to run for his seat in Sussex, where he was relatively unknown, as opposed to in Manchester, where his reputation as a factory owner would hardly do him any good.

"He could make quite a name for himself as a reformer if he were to come out against the scandalous paintings of an upstart young lady who would do better to stay at home embroidering," Sophia told her sister. "It's what I'd do if I were in his position."

"Well, I think you're being far too suspicious," Gemma said with a shake of her head. "You're seeing plots where none are there."

Before Sophia could respond, she spotted a couple of her usual cadre of admirers headed their way.

"Don't go," she hissed to Gemma, as her sister gave her a pat on the arm, then hurried away to where Daphne was speaking to the local schoolmaster.

But it was too late.

"Ah, Mr. Walsh, Mr. Ellis," she said with more enthusiasm than she felt. "What a delight to see you again."

Chapter 3

A few minutes later, she was wishing desperately that Gemma would return.

Or Daphne.

Or anyone who could get her away from the utterly tedious pair of young men who were currently monopolizing her attention.

"If you don't mind my saying so, Miss Hastings," said the Honorable Mr. Toby Walsh, handing Sophia a glass of punch, "you aren't at all what I expected when the mater told me about the bluestockings up at Beauchamp House back when you first arrived."

"Nor me," said his friend Walter Ellis, making use of the quizzing glass that looked ridiculous in the hand of such a young man. "I never knew it was possible for pretty chits to be smart." Perhaps realizing his words were not exactly flattering, he colored a little and added, "That is to say, I'd never . . ."

Needing to get out of the ballroom before she said something she'd regret to her two remaining hangers-on, she stopped Ellis with a hand on his arm. "I wonder if I could trouble the two of you for a favor?" she asked, showing none of the irritation she felt with the two young men on her smooth visage. "I see the Vining sisters there by the potted lemon tree looking a bit down pin. They're quite shy, you know, and I know they would simply fly into the boughs with happiness if two handsome young fellows like yourselves would ask them for the next set."

When Mr. Ellis looked as if he would object, Sophia added with a speaking look, "I believe their marriage portions are quite generous, and I cannot imagine your Mama would object to your at least making an effort in that direction."

Since the young man's mother had complained to Sophia earlier that she despaired of young Walter ever showing an interest in a suitable young lady, she knew that was an understatement. And Walter, perhaps realizing the truth in what she said, exchanged a look with his friend. "Perhaps one dance won't hurt, eh Walsh?"

Calculation in his eyes, Walsh turned from his friend back to Sophia. "One dance. But you must promise to give me a personal viewing of your paintings in the exhibition next week."

Not wanting to be outdone, Ellis echoed, "And me. For you must know I am interested in your painting above all things."

Since Sophia doubted young Mr. Ellis had ever contemplated art or its creation in all his one and twenty years, she wasn't convinced. Even so, if she were going to get out of this ballroom and off her aching ankle, she had to concede. "I'll give you both a tour of my studio, but you must hurry before the Vining girls abscond."

With promises to seek her out later, the two men hurried over to where the well-dowered Vining sisters stood whispering to one another.

Freed from the last of her coterie, Sophia breathed a sigh of relief and rose carefully from her chair to make her escape. Like her fellow heiresses, she'd been chosen to inherit Beauchamp House because of her renowned intellect and skill. In her case, it was her talent as a painter and her knowledge of art in general. Her work had been shown all over England, and she'd gained a reputation for art that both pushed the boundaries of what ladies were expected to depict on the canvas and called attention to those issues that might better, in some opinions, be hidden from view. Now, however, she wasn't thinking about her work, or anything but getting out of the ballroom before she was besieged again by young men looking for flirtation and a bit of scandal.

"I don't suppose you'd like a steady arm to help you get to wherever you're going," said a male voice from behind her.

A frisson of awareness ran through her as she recognized the voice of Lord Benedick, whom she'd spent far too much time thinking about since he'd rescued her from the shore.

Of course he'd be here at the most talked about social event to happen in Little Seaford in months. As the local vicar, he was practically required to attend. And as one of the town's most eligible bachelors, his absence would likely have caused a revolt amongst the village's unwed— and even some married—female population.

Sophia herself was not immune to the clergyman's charms. Certainly not after he'd carried her against that broad chest as if she weighed no more than a feather. And she'd had more than one improper dream about the man since his arrival. And yet, she knew all too well that a woman like her had no business with a man like him. Not only was he, as a duke's son, far above her reach socially, but he was also a man of God. And she and God weren't precisely on good terms.

Still, a supporting arm, when her ankle was aching from having all the blood rush to it for the past hour, was something she couldn't pass up. "I must confess, my lord, that I would accept the arm of the devil himself at this moment if he were kind enough to offer it."

Taller than her by at least a head, Benedick stepped closer and with courteous expediency, slipped an arm around her back and let her rest against his solid form for a moment. It was no more intimate than the waltz that had already been performed once that evening, but it was closer than Sophia had ever been to him and she could feel the warmth of his body through the barrier of their clothing.

Even so, the throbbing of her ankle overrode any feelings of euphoria or attraction she felt at the contact.

Unable to stop herself, she gave a sharp intake of breath when she accidentally put weight on it.

"Easy there," he said, his blue eyes shadowed with concern, "I think perhaps you might better sit down."

But she shook her head. "I have to get out of this room before I'm trapped again."

He didn't bother to ask who would do the trapping, only said, "Where to?"

"Somewhere less crowded," she said through clenched teeth, her painful ankle threating to make her cry out.

It had really been beyond foolish for her to attend tonight's festivities.

"Your wish is my command, my lady."

Giving up control of their destination to her companion, Sophia concentrated instead on maintaining her composure.

Fortunately, they were near a door leading into a side corridor, so they were able to slip away without being waylaid. And before she knew it, Sophia found herself seated on a long settee with her offending ankle propped on a fluffy cushion.

"We must stop meeting like this," Benedick said as he took a seat in a low-slung chair near her. "One could almost accuse us of taking a tour of the couches of lower Sussex."

"I imagine the Pavilion at Brighton has much better settees than this," Sophia said, with a look of mock disdain for the piece of furniture upon which she currently lounged. She should be mortified at being forced to accept help from the vicar again, but instead she felt a sort giddy excitement at seeing him again.

Quite a dangerous thing, really, if she allowed herself to dwell on it.

Which she most certainly would not.

Benedick didn't seem to mind. "I can assure you, Miss Hastings, that the Pavilion also has far less gilt." He accompanied the remark with a comical wide-eyed glance around the room, which did indeed look as if it had been decorated by King Midas himself.

After they shared a laugh, he leaned forward, his elbows on his knees. "I had thought you would forgo tonight's entertainment given your injury this morning. Has no one ever told you to take better care of yourself?"

It was certainly what her sister and friends had said to her before they set out this evening, but Sophia was hardly going to admit that in the face of a gentle scold from the man who'd come to her rescue twice in the same day now. "What is the fun in staying home while everyone else is out dancing?" she said with a toss of her head. "Besides, I came at the request of a dear relation who needed me to be here for our host's announcement tonight."

His brows rose. "Someone who knew that Morgan would announce his political campaign?"

Deciding, given their shared experience that morning, that he was a safe person to share her aunt's information with, Sophia nodded. "My aunt works with a group in Manchester where Morgan's factories are located. She heard from her contacts there that he'd decided to run for the seat here, far from where his business dealings might sour the local people on him. She asked me to do what I could to stop him. Which meant attending the ball to-night."

"But surely she'd have understood if she knew you'd injured yourself," he said not unkindly. "One must admit to human frailty from time to time, Miss Hastings."

"Of course she would have done," Sophia said with a frown. "But some things are more important than personal difficulties. And besides, I wanted to hear what he had to say for myself. There will be plenty of time to rest tomorrow."

"One cannot help but admire your determination," he said. His blue eyes were warm with what looked like appreciation, though Sophia suspected that was just her imagination. "What did you think of Morgan's speech, then?"

Thankful to be off the subject of herself, Sophia leapt at the conversation thread. "It was remarkably short," she said. "I suppose I'd expected something more elaborate, but he must be saving that for when he talks to the villagers. He will certainly need the support of those in attendance tonight, but it will be the more skeptical farmers who own their own smaller plots of land he'll need to convince."

"Then I should think an assembly ball would have been more suited to his political needs," Benedick said. "But that would not have allowed him to show off his magnificent palace."

"Precisely," Sophia said with approval. "He must re-assure everyone of his wealth and power, so that they will put their lot in with him. Aunt Dahlia mentioned in one of her letters that his speeches in Manchester before he made the decision to come south were very focused on shifting the balance of power back to the people. Un-fortunately his treatment of those same people in his factories—particularly the women and children who work in them—made it impossible for him to gain any sort of support in the north. Nearly everyone had a friend, or a neighbor or a relation who had suffered thanks to cuts in wages, or injuries on the job, or worse."

"You don't suppose the conversation we heard this morning might have had some bearing on the announce-ment tonight?" Benedick asked, his face darkening.

It hadn't occurred to Sophia, but thinking back to what the men had said, she nodded. "It's possible. Po-litical intrigue is certainly one interpretation to put on the matter." In fact, the more she reflected on the one man's vehemence about "eliminating a stumbling block" the more this explanation made sense. She was already composing a letter to her aunt in her mind, when Benedick's next words penetrated her fog of concen-tration.

". . . so, you must agree with me now that this is not something a young lady should be involving herself in," he said in a placating tone. "The men we heard were quite serious. I hope you will allow me to look into the matter. I have friends who work with the Home Office who may be able to . . ."

"Certainly not," Sophia interrupted him. "I do appreciate your concern for me, Lord Benedick, but I'm hardly a frail young thing to be wrapped in cotton wool. If you intend on doing any sort of investigation into the conversation we overheard, I must insist upon being a part of it."

"With all due respect, Miss Hastings," said the vicar, looking as if he'd like to tug on his hair in frustration, "you are injured, and you must know that men are far more likely to divulge secrets to other men than they are to a beautiful young woman whom they are trying to impress."

She tucked away the fact that he'd just called her beautiful to be examined at another time. "Are men so weak that they cannot manage to speak sense in the presence of a lady?" she demanded. "If that is the case then I believe we should immediately cease spouting the fiction that women are the weaker sex. For I am quite certain any woman of sense can say what's on her mind no matter how many men are looking on."

"I was merely making a general observation, Miss Hastings," said the vicar, his color rising a little at the retort. "In my experience, men, especially powerful men such as our host, have a tendency to put their best face forward in the presence of ladies. It is human nature. And you cannot deny that such things happen when ladies are in the presence of men they wish to impress too."

Thinking back to the antics of Mr. Walsh and Mr. Ellis earlier, Sophia relented. "I suppose there is some truth in what you say. But I do wish there was some way to remove the silliness of vanity from such important matters. Can we not simply talk sense without constantly being concerned about how we appear to the opposite sex?"

At that Benedick relaxed a little and grinned. "My dear Miss Hastings, what you are asking is the impossible."

His smile was infectious and in spite of her determination to "talk sense" Sophia found herself smiling back.

He continued, then, his blue eyes meeting hers in amusement. "I should certainly think you've become accustomed to having men make cakes of themselves in an effort to win your approbation."

"No more than you have, Vicar," she said with a raised brow. "Unless I've imagined the bevy of unmarried ladies who linger after church every Sunday in hopes of gaining a kind word from you."

"Touché," he said softly. "So, we are agreed that both gentlemen and ladies are prone to making fools of themselves when it comes to impressing one another. Where does that leave us?"

"It leaves us with the fact that I insist upon being a part of whatever you intend to do to find out what those two men were talking about this morning," she said calmly. "And while I admit that I might need to give myself a few days to recover from my injury, I will not allow you to pat me on the head and send me on my oblivious way."

The vicar shook his head at her vehemence, and leaned back in his chair, stretching his long legs out before him. "Miss Hastings, has anyone ever told you you're stubborn?"

"I believe you implied it not five minutes ago, my lord," Sophia responded with a sweet smile.

Chapter 4

He'd only meant to see Miss Hastings comfortably seated, but Ben found himself taking the chair across from her as soon as she'd got comfortable on the settee.

It had been impossible not to be aware of her all evening as the crowd of men—ranging from young men just home from university to wealthy friends of their hosts, men of a certain age on the lookout for a pretty paramour—ebbed and flowed as she flirted and dismissed them. He'd discussed Mrs. Brown's rheumatism while Sophia accepted punch from a young man with high shirt points. He'd assured Mr. Stevens, the local butcher, that he'd greatly enjoyed the side of beef the man had gifted him while she laughed at some quip from the Northmans' steward. Then, when finally the last man had gone, he'd made his way to her side for the first time that evening.

Only to find her mouth tight with pain as she tried to stand on the ankle that had made it impossible for her to dance.

He could have told her it would be a bad idea to attend a ball on the injury she'd sustained that morning, but he was now more sure than ever that Miss Sophia Hastings made up her own mind about things.

Now, he was forced to admit the fact again, since she'd just effectively backed him into a corner over allowing her to help him look into the contretemps they'd overheard that morning.

"I suppose you've left me with no choice but to work with you," he admitted with a rueful shake of his head. "You drive a hard bargain, Miss Hastings."

"I learned from my Aunt, my lord," she said with a grin. "Aunt Dahlia is quite good at getting what she wants from a negotiation. And so am I."

Clearly.

Just then, the clock at the end of the gallery began to chime.

Had they really been here alone for so long? Ben should have felt panicked at the notion, but instead he felt only a protective urge for Miss Hastings' reputation. "I'll just go find your sister, now, shall I? You've stayed long enough to make an exit without comment."

He watched as she stared down at her slippered foot for a moment. When she looked up at him, it was with a slight frown of frustration. "Yes, all right. I disliked making the others leave before they were ready, but it's been a few hours now."

It was on the tip of his tongue to remind her that her sister, with whom he'd danced earlier, had been ready to leave hours ago, but he stopped himself. Instead, he stood, and glanced down at her. "Is there something I can do for you before I go look for one of your party?"

But as he'd expected, she shook her head. "Go. The sooner we can call for the carriage, the sooner we can leave." For a moment he saw just how much of an effort it had been to keep up the pretense that she was not in pain.

He laid a hand on her shoulder. Nothing more than a show of support. Then headed in the direction from which they'd come.

And almost collided with Miss Gemma Hastings as he reached the door leading into the ballroom.

"Lord Benedick," said the brunette, who while she shared some resemblance to her sister, wasn't nearly as breathtaking as Sophia. At least, not in Ben's opinion. "Have you see Sophia? The last I saw her she was surrounded by her usual coterie, but she disappeared while I was dancing and though she insisted that her ankle was merely strained, I know it must be hurting like mad."

Though Sophia hadn't asked him to, once he'd sent Gemma to where she could find her sister, Ben went in search of either the Marquess of Kerr or the Duke of Maitland. He found Kerr and his wife, unfashionably conversing with one another, at the edge of the dance floor.

"I knew she was fibbing," said Ivy, Marchioness of Kerr with a shake of her head. "Of course we'll see she gets home safely. Thank you so much for looking after her, Lord Benedick. I doubt any of those cloth heads who pester her every time she sets foot out of the house would have done so."

Since his assessment of those men was similar, Ben didn't argue. Instead he said, "Why don't I see that she gets to the driveway safely, while you see that the carriage is readied. If you're not quite ready to leave yet, I can see her home. I know her sister is with her so it would be perfectly proper."

But the marchioness, who was looking rather pale, demurred. And Kerr agreed. "I was ready to get Ivy home an hour ago, so this simply gives us a good excuse. But I do appreciate you getting Sophia to the carriage. Maitland and Daphne came in their own rig so there's no need to worry about them."

Relieved that plans for getting Sophia away from there were in hand, Ben turned to go back to the gallery when he was waylaid by his host.

"Lord Benedick," said the nascent politician. "I hope you'll give your father, the duke, my best."

Since to Ben's knowledge, his father, the Duke of Pemberton, had never met Morgan, it was an odd request, but hardly the first of its kind. People were always trying to ingratiate themselves with his father. And Ben was just a means to an end.

"I will, Mr. Morgan," he assured the man. "And I thank you very much for this evening's entertainment. I've been told balls are rare in this neighborhood, and from what I've seen of the dancing tonight, everyone is very much enjoying it."

Morgan preened. "I invited a number of people from town as well, you know. Thought I'd bring a bit of town polish to the rustics, don't ye know?"

Since the neighborhood boasted any number of members of the *ton,* Ben thought that was rather stretching it a bit, but he didn't correct the man.

"Well, I thank you, but now I'm afraid I must be on my way. I've a sermon to write and . . ."

When the industrialist stayed him with a hand, Ben fought the urge to remove it. "I hope you'll tell me something, my lord," Morgan said in a low, confiding voice. "What do you make of the ladies up at Beauchamp House?"

At the mention of Beauchamp House, Ben stilled.

"What of them?" he asked silkily. He might not live

in the pockets of the Beauchamp House ladies, but he'd performed the marriage of the Duke and Duchess of Maitland and he counted them as friends. And there was the matter of Sophia, whom he found far more attractive than was prudent. Something about Morgan's tone told him that the man had nothing positive to say about them.

"Well, I mean to say," said Morgan with a shrug. "It's not right, is it? Ladies wasting their time with pursuits that are better suited to men? I'm not one for book learning at the best of times, but I see it's something that must be done. But it don't seem natural for ladies to do such things. My Millie certainly would never think to read poems in English, much less in that heathen Greek. And I've heard from some friends in London that the painter, Miss Hastings, I think, well, she paints things that aren't fit things for ladies to be dwelling on."

It wasn't the first time Ben had heard such sentiments about the inhabitants of Beauchamp House. Indeed, he most often heard the complaints from other ladies in the neighborhood who didn't know what to make of the unconventional lady scholars, who were also better than average—and Sophia's case, much more than average—looking. But he wasn't in the mood for such piffle and he was within an inch of telling his host so, when Morgan continued his speech.

"I understand that Miss Hastings will have a couple of her works in the art exhibition next week," the man said his eyes narrow with judgment. "I was hoping you'd lend your voice to mine as well as a few other concerned citizens who'd like to make sure that whatever she brings is fit to be seen by our wives and daughters."

It was something that was better discussed in private, not in the middle of a crowded ballroom where anyone might overhear them. And Ben was already late getting

Sophia down to meet the waiting carriage. But as there was no way on earth he'd ever agree with this man's narrow minded attempt to censor Sophia's work—work he'd seen and admired in the months since making her acquaintance—he simply said what he was thinking. "No, Mr. Morgan. I will not lend my voice to this effort. I believe Miss Hastings is a talented artist—one of the best I've ever seen—and I look forward to seeing her work in the exhibition."

With a short bow, he continued, "Now, if you'll excuse me, I must be off. Thank you again for a pleasant evening."

He felt the other man's gaze on his back, but he didn't much care at the moment. His desire to get Sophia out of this house had only increased with Morgan's words. Not glancing behind him, he made his way back to the gallery.

To Sophia's mortification, her slow progress from the gallery to the ground floor made it necessary for Benedick to lift her up into his arms and carry her most of the way down to the carriage. So, for the second time in twelve hours, she found herself being bodily carried by the vicar.

It was the stuff that village gossips dreamed of.

And it would make her an object of scorn for every unmarried young lady in the county.

"It's only a bit farther," she protested, when Benedick stopped and made the suggestion. She wasn't sure why, but she knew that while allowing him to carry her would indeed spare her ankle, it would prove uncomfortable in a more personal way. "You see," she said, biting back a gasp of pain as she limped along past her sister and the vicar down the stairs, "I can do it."

"And you'll damage your ankle," Gemma chided, "perhaps irreparably. What if it's broken, Sophia? Do you wish to become an invalid?"

Since the offending joint had swollen more in the time since they'd arrived that evening, Sophia feared her sister might be correct.

"Come, Miss Hastings," Benedick said with a kind smile. "I won't bite. And you must admit that at the rate we're traveling now it will be next week before we get downstairs."

"Oh I do wish you would dispense with Miss Hastings and call me Sophia," she said crossly. "It seems non-sensical given the frequency with which you're compelled to carry me about like a sack of potatoes."

She felt as well as heard his laughter. "I suppose that's acceptable," he said, "Sophia." He said her name a few seconds after, as if savoring the taste of it on his tongue. "And you must call me Ben."

"Very well, Ben," she said, with a brisk nod, almost hurrying over the syllable, as if to prove to him that she wasn't feeling a little thrill at the small bit of impropriety.

Then, before she could continue, the vicar had lifted her into his arms with an ease that was surprising to her despite the evidence of his strength when he'd carried her from the shore. He was much stronger than his lean build had led her to believe. Especially when one considered that she was not the sort of fashionable waif favored in the fashion plates these days. Despite her pain, she couldn't help but feel the hard muscles of his arms and chest where she cradled against him. And her relief at having her weight off the ankle almost had her sagging against him. Still she managed to keep some modicum of decorum.

They were almost to the second landing when they

were met by their hostess, who gasped when she saw them. "My dear Miss Hastings, whatever has happened?"

"Only a sprained ankle, Mrs. Morgan," Sophia assured her, wishing the woman away. Though he'd not shown any signs of flagging, she didn't wish to test Lord Benedick's—Ben's, she mentally corrected herself—strength farther than necessary.

"Oh dear, I am sorry to see you in such pain, Miss Hastings," said Mrs. Morgan, a lovely, if not terribly intelligent woman, whose sweet nature seemed at odds with her brash husband. "I've suffered from sprains myself and they do get worse before they get better."

Then her face turning serious, she asked, "Have you passed my husband on your way down? I thought he was having a little chat with Mr. Penn in the library, but no one seems to have seen them."

Mr. Barnaby Penn was a local art dealer whose shop was the sponsor of the upcoming Little Seaford Exhibition. Could it have been Penn she and Ben had overheard in the gallery? It was impossible to get a good look at the vicar's face in her current position, but she felt him stiffen at their hostess's words.

"I'm afraid we haven't seen him, Mrs. Morgan." Sophia could feel his deep voice reverberate through his chest. "Now, I'm afraid I must get Miss Hastings to her carriage."

At the reminder of his burden, the matron flushed. "Of course, of course. I hope you'll feel better soon, Miss Hastings."

There was no opportunity for conversation about what their hostess had revealed since Gemma was with them, and it was minutes later when he was lifting her into the spacious Kerr carriage that Ben told Sophia in a low voice, "I'll call on you tomorrow and we'll talk."

She felt the tickle of his breath against her ear, and breathed in the clean hint of bayberry and warm male as he pulled away and gave her a nod. "I hope you'll be feeling more the thing tomorrow, Miss Hastings," he said in a more normal tone that might be overhead by the others. "Do take care of yourself."

Alone in the carriage, she listened as he exchanged a few pleasantries with the marquess and Ivy. While they were still speaking, Gemma was handed in by a footman. Settling into the seat across from Sophia's she said wryly, "I'll wager that was more adventure than you were expecting from this evening."

Now that she was out of view of Ben and the rest of the ball-goers, Sophia felt a mantle of exhaustion fall over her. "You have no idea," she told her sister, leaning her head back against the plush squabs of the carriage. "It was foolish of me to go to the ball. I'll admit it now. But only to you."

"Stubborn to the end, I see," her sister said with a snort. "But don't try to change the subject. You know very well I was talking about your rescue at the hand of the most handsome vicar in three counties."

"Since I know very well you've not met all the vicars in three counties, I will have to respectfully disagree." Sophia raised a brow but didn't raise her head. "I will admit he's good looking though. But there's no need to weave some romantic tale about it. He was simply being a gentleman."

"A gentleman who saw to your every comfort and looked as if he wished to ride home with us to see you safely tucked up in bed." She knew without looking her sister was wearing her I-know-I'm-right expression.

At that moment, Lord Kerr handed Ivy into the compartment, and Sophia was saved from replying to her sister's absurdity. It took a minute for them to get situated, what with Sophia's foot propped on the cushion where Ivy would have gone. They ended up riding the short distance with the marchioness seated rather improperly on the marquess's lap.

Sophia might have hoped this would mean they'd not wish to converse, but in that she was sorely mistaken.

"I believe you've got a champion in our vicar, Sophia," said Ivy with a grin once Kerr had given the coachman the signal and the carriage began to move. "He seemed quite attentive, did he not, Kerr?"

"Far be it from me to cast any man's behavior in a certain light," the marquess said with a hint of amusement in his voice. "But I do agree that Lord Benedick seemed to be more concerned for our Sophie's injury that he might have done with, say old Mrs. Mason."

"You're all, as Maitland would say," Sophia said from where she'd settled into her corner of the coach, "dicked in the nob."

"We'll see," Gemma said sweetly.

Not wanting to hear more, Sophia closed her eyes and feigned sleep the rest of the way home.

Chapter 5

Ben only had a couple of servants at the vicarage, which was a tidy red brick house with a pretty walled garden at the back and, as he'd learned not long after his arrival, a secret passageway leading from the cellars into a series of smugglers tunnels that opened out onto the beach just below Beauchamp House. His predecessor had been severely injured thanks to a miscreant's misuse of the passageway, and Ben had been happy enough to see that door sealed to prevent mischief.

Since he didn't keep a carriage of his own, he'd accepted a ride home from the Morgans in the coach of the local magistrate, Squire Northman, and his wife. It had been a brief drive, but he was grateful to step down and bid them goodbye thanks to Mrs. Northman's incessant chatter. He was also fairly suspicious that she'd felt his thigh for one moment when the conveyance hit a rock, but perhaps he was simply imagining it. It had been a strange evening. And there was no denying his senses were on high alert thanks to the moments spent cradling the luscious Miss Hastings against him.

The lantern at the door to the vicarage was flickering

merrily when he shut the gate behind him. Though he'd instructed his manservant Jeffries not to wait up, that fellow was still conscious of the harm done to his previous master on his watch, and kept his own conscience on such matters that related to caring for the new vicar. And sure enough, the door opened wide when he stepped up to it.

"My lord," Jeffries said bowing. "I hope you had a pleasant evening."

Ben peeled off his gloves and handed the man his coat and hat. "It was well attended, and though I suspect Morgan wished for a crush it was hardly that."

"My lord, I must inform you that while you were gone you received a visitor."

Ben stopped just as he reached the stairs leading to his rooms. "Who—"

Before Jeffries could respond, an all too familiar voice spoke up. "I hope you'll excuse the late hour, Ben, but it couldn't be helped."

Arrested, he turned to see his younger brother, Lord Frederick Lisle, lounging against the door jamb of the front parlor.

With a cry of surprise, Ben pulled the other man into a hug, which quickly devolved into their childhood habit of wrestling for the upper hand.

"Hah," the vicar taunted when he'd managed to get his elbow around Freddie's neck, "I still have it!" He knocked his knuckles on his brother's head before turning him loose.

When he'd been set free, his younger brother shook his head, straightening his cuffs and cravat. "One would have thought that your years in the church would have taught you a sense of decorum."

"Oh, I have plenty of decorum in the right company," Ben said with a grin. "But you're my little brother. I had to greet you properly."

Dismissing Jeffries for the evening, he led Freddie upstairs to his study, and once they were settled in front of the fire with glasses of brandy, he waited for an explanation. While it wasn't unheard of for one of the Lisle brothers to visit another unexpectedly, Freddie had only recently celebrated the birth of his second child and it wasn't like him to leave his wife, Leonora, on her own at such a time.

They chatted a little about news from their parents, and their brother Archer, whose wife was expecting. "And I suppose you've heard that Cam is giving a paper at the royal society this week. One of his bits about bones or fossils or whatnot." Freddie, nor indeed any of the other Lisles, had never been able to understand where Cameron, the second to last of the brothers, had got his love of all things ancient. It wasn't as if the family were Philistines. They appreciated history and knowledge, but Cameron needed to touch everything he learned about. And spent his days digging into the earth in search of artifacts from the past.

"I'm glad for him," Ben said, taking a sip of his drink, "but better him than me."

"Amen to that," Freddie agreed. "I'm quite sure I'd nod off before the first presenter finished a paragraph."

"What of Rhys?"

Their eldest brother, Rhys, Viscount Lisle, heir to their father, the Duke of Pemberton, had, the last time Ben had spoken to him, been considering an extended stay on the continent. Since their father was in his prime, and needed little assistance in the running of the various Pemberton estates, he was a bit restless with life in the country. And London was far too full of matchmaking mamas for his comfort.

"On an extended stay at the hunting box in Scotland," Freddie said with a frown. "I had given him any number of contacts in Paris when he was making plans, but at the last minute he changed his mind. If you ask me, there's some trouble with a woman, though you know how tight-lipped he is about such things."

Rhys had never been one to discuss his affairs with his younger brothers. Perhaps since their father had instilled his position as the eldest, and therefore the role model, from the time he was small. Ben remembered quite well how in awe of his brother he'd been when they were children. It was as if he could do no wrong. No high spirits. No misbehavior. He was the perfect child. And as they'd grown, he's continued to be the one who pleased most everyone. There were lapses, of course—he was human. But Ben had often thought it must be very difficult to show so little weakness all the time.

Freddie's theory that a woman might be involved was not without merit. The few times they'd seen their eldest brother act out, it had been over some affair of the heart. Or some other, less romantic organ.

"I'd say we'll find out soon enough," Ben said wryly, "but it's Rhys. He might blurt it out in his cups at Christmas, or we'll never know."

"True." Freddie raised his glass. "To the brothers Lisle. Wherever they may be."

They drank deep, and sat in companionable silence for a moment.

Then, no longer able to hold back his curiosity, Ben said, "Speaking of locales, I don't suppose you wish to tell me that brings you here with no advance warning so soon after little Libby's birth?"

At the mention of his new daughter, Freddie's face softened, and Ben was reminded once again of how much his brother had changed since his marriage to Leonora. Once the most eligible bachelor on two continents, Freddie had settled into life as a husband and father as if he'd been born to it. And in a way, if their father was anything to go by, he had been.

"You know I wouldn't have left them without good reason, Ben," he said, his expression turning serious. "It's important, and I thought worth a quick trip down here to speak to you in person."

Setting his glass aside, Ben leaned forward, his elbows on his knees. A listening posture.

"You remember Mainwaring does a bit of work for the Home Office from time to time?"

"I do," Ben replied. The Earl of Mainwaring was one of Freddie's oldest school friends and was well known to all the Lisles.

"Well, his man in the Home Office has some concerns about some dealings in this area, and Mainwaring immediately thought of you when he heard of the locale."

It wasn't exactly routine for a minister with the Church of England to become involved with the affairs of the Home Office, but nor was it entirely out of the ordinary, Ben knew. He'd never been asked to do so before, however, and was a little surprised that the earl had thought of him so readily. It wasn't as if they were as close as he and Freddie.

As if hearing his questions, Freddie explained, "I'd just given him a rundown of family news and mentioned that you'd accepted a position in Little Seaford. So, it must have been in his mind when the fellow from the government spoke to him."

There was something else, however, that made the

hairs on the back of Ben's neck stand on end. That conversation he and Sophia had overheard was still fresh on *his* mind. And it was far too coincidental to imagine that there was more than one conspiracy at work in their little village.

With a quick nod, he indicated that his brother should continue.

"According to Mainwaring, your tiny Sussex village has over the past year or so been flooding the homes of the newly rich and shall we say, artistically unfamiliar, with forgeries of valuable and coveted paintings."

Immediately, Ben thought of Sophia, though it pained him to do so.

How long had it been since her arrival at Beauchamp House?

Almost nine months exactly.

"What makes them think that the culprit is in Little Seaford?" he asked, careful not to reveal what he was thinking.

"They've traced the origins of the forgeries to one of the two galleries in the village," Freddie said, his mouth twisted in amusement. "Who would have thought a tiny village like this would have more than one gallery? I'd say it barely has enough inhabitants to sustain one."

"There's an artist's colony at Primrose Green," Ben said distractedly as he tried to recall if Sophia had ever sold her paintings through the local galleries. He wasn't as familiar as he might have been with her work because most of his time since arriving in the village had been spent getting to know his parishioners and ministering to the poorer families of the area. He'd attended a few social gatherings at Beauchamp House and the other gentry residencies, but he was hardly so well acquainted with Sophia that he knew the details of her business transactions.

To his frustration, Freddie noticed his shift in attention. "You've thought of someone," he said with a sharp gaze.

Ben cursed himself for a fool and despite his instinct to protect Sophia, he decided to trust his brother.

"There is a local artist." He leaned forward with his elbows on his knees, looking down so that Freddie couldn't read his expression. "She's been here for about the same amount of time as you've indicated. But I have no notion of whether she sells her work through either of the local galleries. I don't know enough about her art to assess whether or not she'd be able to create the sort of copies you're talking about."

He looked up and saw that Freddie's expression had turned sympathetic. "That's the way of things, is it?"

Unable to remain still, Ben stood abruptly and began to pace. "Don't make assumptions," he said, rubbing the back of his neck. "I barely know the lady. But I have found her to be a pleasant enough companion and I suspect she is quite talented since she's one of the four Beauchamp House heiresses."

This had Freddie cocking his head. "Is she indeed? Of course we'd heard about Lady Celeste's unusual bequest, since Leonora runs in intellectual circles—the sort that welcome ladies, I mean. But I don't think I knew there was an artist amongst them."

"A classicist, a mathematician, an artist and a naturalist," Ben said. "But surely she would have no reason to do paint forgeries now that she's safely in Beauchamp House." He didn't add that he wasn't convinced that she had the sort of questionable morals necessary to pass her own work off as someone else's.

"Isn't there some sort of contest amongst them?" Freddie asked. "Whoever remains longest gets to keep the house?"

"Yes," Ben said, waving his hand in dismissal. "But I think they've agreed at this point to simply share the house amongst themselves. Two of the ladies have married peers, and have no need of the house as a domicile, and the other two, Miss Hastings the artist, and her sister Miss Gemma, the naturalist, would be content to share, I think. As far as I can tell, she has no need for funds."

"It is difficult to know what goes on beneath the surface with some people, Ben," Freddie said gently. "For all you know the lady has gambling debts or dressmakers bills or some other sort of financial troubles."

But Ben couldn't see it. Then, something occurred to him. In context of what Freddie had said about the forgeries, he ran back through the conversation he and Sophia had overheard at Morgan's.

"Would people who trade in forged art be the sort to eliminate a conspirator who no longer pulled his weight in the scheme?"

Freddie's gaze sharpened. "Absolutely."

Quickly, Ben related the details of what he and Sophia had overheard.

When he was finished his brother gave a low whistle—something their mother would have skinned him for if she'd been there to hear it. "I'd say you stumbled onto the very men Mainwaring is looking for," he said with a slight shake of his head. "What are the odds?"

But Ben was lost in his relief that Sophia was no longer a suspect. His gut had told him she couldn't possibly be the person Mainwaring hunted, but it was calming to know that was true.

"And you have no idea who these two were you overheard?" Freddie asked. "There was no hint of an accent? Or perhaps a phrase someone you know uses?"

"No, neither Sophia nor I could decipher who they were. Their voices were simply too low."

"Sophia, is it?"

Dash it. Ben knew better than to speak to Freddie when he was fatigued. His brother was a master at reading his weaknesses.

"Miss Hastings," he corrected himself. "I misspoke."

"Did you, indeed?" Freddie didn't seem convinced. "So, it was the Beauchamp House artist you were secreted with when you overheard our schemers? That is fascinating. Tell me more about this lady, whom you know so little about."

"Freddie?"

"Yes, Ben."

"Shut up."

Chapter 6

Sophia spent a restless night, both because of her ankle and plagued by memories of the conversation she and Ben had overheard. Though ice from the icehouse helped with the swelling, the next morning it was still paining her enough that she welcomed Serena's suggestion of sending for the doctor again.

"At the very least he can feel if anything is broken," Serena said, her blue eyes dark with sympathy. "And perhaps give you something for the pain."

Having managed only to move from her bedchamber into the adjoining sitting room, Sophia sighed. "You know I detest being ill," she said, "but it is time to call Dr. Holmes. I thought perhaps when he was unavailable yesterday that I should be well enough, but it's time for him to look at it."

"Good girl," Serena said with a nod of approval. "I'll go send for him at once."

The chaperone left her alone, and Sophia slumped back against the settee.

If she didn't have such a fear of becoming like her mother, who took to her bed at the slightest hint of illness, she'd have agreed more readily to calling in the doctor.

But though she loved both her parents, she had no wish to emulate either of them. Her father, the younger son of a Yorkshire baronet, made a prosperous living for himself as a solicitor in York, and had married as much for social standing as for affection. The former Miss Laetitia Gorham, now Mrs. Hastings, was a beautiful but rather spoiled beauty, whose wealthy parents had indulged her every whim. And her husband had continued doing so, allowing her to take to her bed with smelling salts at the least provocation. That Sophia and Gemma had gained any sort of standing in their chosen fields of study was entirely due, Sophia was convinced, to their Aunt Dahlia, the eccentric younger sister of Mr. Hastings, who lived with them.

It was from Dahlia that Sophia first learned to hold a paintbrush, and Dahlia who taught both Sophia and her sister that though they'd been born female, they were entitled to use the intellect they'd been gifted with to better themselves and the world. If it hadn't been for their aunt, Sophia strongly suspected she and Gemma might have developed into the same sort of empty-headed young ladies she'd seen on the ballroom floor last evening.

Theirs had been an unconventional upbringing, to be sure, but it had led them to be chosen by Lady Celeste Beauchamp to be her heiresses, and for that she had to be grateful.

She did wish, at this moment, however, that she'd been a bit less enthusiastic with her painting yesterday. Though, she reflected crossly, if it hadn't been for the mysterious men on the bluff she'd not have gone flying over the edge.

Sophia wasn't left long to brood, however.

Only moments after Serena's departure, Ivy, Daphne

and Gemma crowed into her cozy sitting room, followed by a maid carrying a tea tray.

"We thought you might need a bit of cheering up," Ivy said from where she'd settled onto an overstuffed chair beside the tea table. "And tea always makes things better."

"But you said we were going to quiz her about her *tête-à-tête* with Lord Benedick." Daphne's nose crinkled in confusion as she perched on the arm of the sofa where Gemma sat. "I do so hate it when I'm disappointed like that. Maitland has some very interesting theories about how they passed the time and I wished to prove him wrong."

Gemma and Ivy groaned at their friend's words, but Sophia simply sighed and rubbed the spot between her eyebrows, which was suddenly feeling tight.

"Daphne," Gemma chided, her wide mouth quirked with frustration, "that was the part we weren't going to talk to Sophia about, remember?"

"No, no," Sophia said with a "pray-continue" gesture, "by all means, make your inquiries. Though I'm afraid the details of my time with the vicar last night will be sorely disappointing to you."

"Well, you cannot blame us for being curious," Ivy said, handing her a cup of steaming tea. "Lord Benedick is deliciously handsome and his manner last night when he tucked you into the carriage was quite solicitous."

A memory of that moment when he'd been close enough to kiss flashed into Sophia's mind, but she ignored it. "He is a kind man, who took it upon himself to help me. It's hardly surprising given his vocation. I daresay he'd have done the same if it had been Gemma or Serena who needed his assistance."

"I've never seen him look at Serena the way he looked

at you," her sister said dryly. "Though if you wish to pass it off as mere Christian kindness, then I suppose that's your right."

But Daphne looked disappointed. "Do you mean to tell me that nothing happened when you and the vicar were alone in the gallery?"

Thinking back to the conversation she and Ben had overheard, Sophia thought that Daphne's assessment wasn't entirely incorrect, but kept her own counsel on the latter. Instead she said, "Nothing like what you lot were hoping for. I must say I thought marriage would have both of you focused on your own affairs, but it would seem that it's turned you into hopeless romantics. Not every conversation is a prelude to a kiss, you know."

"They cannot help themselves," her sister said reaching for an almond tea cake. "It's like an illness they can't help but wish on everyone else."

Setting the silver teapot back down on the tray, Ivy then dropped a lump of sugar in her own tea and stirred it. "Just you wait, Gemma," she said with a knowing smile. "It will happen to you and when it does I will be the first to congratulate you."

"Then I hope you will live to see that day," Gemma replied. It would take more than teasing to convince her sister that love was something she should consider, Sophia knew. Another personality trait that could be laid at their parents' door. "Though I cannot think it will happen in either your lifetime or mine."

"Never say never, my dear Gemma," was Ivy's only response as she sipped her tea. "There was a time when I thought no man could possibly be secure enough in himself to want a wife who could match him in wits and sense. But then I met Quill."

To Sophia's surprise, it was Daphne who played the peacemaker. "We only want you both to be happy, Gemma," she said with a sweet smile. It was times like this that made friendship with the unconventional mathematician worthwhile. "I certainly never thought a man like Maitland of all people could bring me such joy. But here we are."

Seeing the mulish set to her sister's jaw, Sophia intervened before she could say something cutting. "And do not think we don't appreciate it." She gave her sister a speaking look and Gemma had the good grace to look sheepish. "Of course we do. Especially since we've seen your transformations for ourselves. But you must know we have to make our own ways. And sadly, there are no more of Lady Celeste's nephews coming to stay, so it might take a while."

Ivy colored a little. "I'm sorry, ladies. I just want your happiness, as Daphne says."

The marchioness could be a bit autocratic at times— not because of her title, but because she was used to knowing exactly what she wanted—but she meant well, and Sophia loved her, bossiness and all. Sophia's ankle gave a throb of pain then, and she winced, adjusting the cloth covered ice on it.

"Oh, dear," Ivy said, noticing Sophia's discomfort and setting down her cup and saucer. "We shouldn't have descended on you like this. You're obviously in pain."

A brisk knock at the door sounded before Sophia could respond.

"Only look who's come to look in on you, Sophia," said Lady Serena brightly, as she preceded Ben into the room.

The vicar looked a bit nonplussed to see all four of the Beauchamp Bluestockings assembled, but soon regained his aplomb.

He was dressed for the country, in a pair of fawn breeches that showed his muscular legs to perfection, and a cutaway coat that did nothing to hide the broadness of his shoulders. But it was the way his gaze zeroed in on her once he stepped into the room that made Sophia's breath catch.

"Good morning, ladies," he said, bowing. "I had hoped to see you up and walking, Miss Hastings, but I'm sorry to see that is not the case."

To Sophia's surprise, he proffered a small posy of pink roses and nasturtium to her. "I had my housekeeper choose these. I'm afraid I'm hopeless at such niceties. In town one only needs the services of good florist, you see."

Their hands brushed as she took the bouquet, and to cover her blush, she buried her nose in the blooms. "They're lovely, my lord. Thank you so much."

Ivy and Gemma exchanged a look, and soon they rose and none too gently pulled Daphne along to join them. "I've just recalled that we were planning to organize the library section on animal husbandry this morning," Ivy explained as she and Gemma dragged a protesting Daphne from the room.

"I'll send up the doctor when he arrives, Sophia," said Serena before she too decamped.

Left alone, with a half empty tea tray between them, Sophia and Ben stared at one another in disbelief.

Then burst out laughing.

"Oh, I am sorry," Miss Hastings, said as she wiped tears of mirth from her face. "I don't know what has got into them. It's as if they've never interacted with human beings before."

He was glad to see she'd kept her humor intact despite her injury and last night's disturbance. On his walk over to Beauchamp House, Ben had debated whether to share what he'd learned from Freddie last night with her. There was no need to drag her into the matter, especially if, as the conversation they'd overheard had indicated, the men involved were ruthless.

Now, settled across from her in a tastefully appointed sitting room, he welcomed the moment of levity. Faced with the sight of her draped ankle, propped on a tasseled pillow, and the obvious shadows beneath her blue eyes, he was reluctant to add to her worries. Though he knew he must do so before the visit was over.

"There's no harm done," he said, leaning back a little in a surprisingly comfortable armchair. "And they are clearly fond of you."

The easy manner between the ladies of Beauchamp House had been something that struck him when he first met them. It was not unlike the sort of bonds formed at school. And with the various upsets and disturbances they'd faced together over the past year—including attempts on two of the ladies' lives—those ties were more than skin deep. These friends genuinely cared about each other.

"Yes," she said with a rueful shake of her head. "I just wish they didn't all turn into Mrs. Bennet from *Pride and Prejudice* when a gentleman calls."

At the mention of Miss Austen's novel, he grinned. "So long as they don't cast me in the role of Mr. Collins. I am a vicar, but I hope that is where the resemblance ends."

This surprised a laugh from her. "I hardly think

Mr. Collins would be the recipient of longing gazes from nearly every female in three counties," she said tartly.

"Do not go on about that again," he chided, referring to their discussion the night before. "I'm of no more interest to the ladies of the village than the next man."

"If you say so," Miss Hastings replied, not convinced. "Though I suspect there is a surfeit of baked goods in the vicarage kitchens that would contradict you.

"Well, I do say so, Wallflower," Ben returned. "There is nothing unusual about the ladies of a village trying to feed their bachelor vicar. It's a time-honored tradition."

Her response to the endearment—warmth in her cheeks and a nervous nibble of her lower lip—sent a jolt of awareness through him. He might not be moved by the blandishments of the other women in the village, but putting this particular lady to the blush was dangerous to his own peace of mind.

"The tea is still warm," she said with false brightness. "Shall I pour you a cup?"

Taking the proffered distraction with gratitude, he agreed and watched as she drew the teapot toward her and began fussing with the silver.

"Have you learned anything more about the mysterious men we heard last night?" she asked, as she handed him a cup and saucer.

Something of his dilemma must have shown on his face, because Sophia gave a little gasp as she looked up. "You have. Who were they? Do you know who it is they mean to harm?"

If he revealed to her what Freddie had told him, it might just endanger her further. But the intelligent gleam in her eyes told him that keeping the information to himself would likely do nothing to dissuade her from searching for more news on her own. Which might be even more dangerous.

"I received a visit from my brother Freddie, that is, Lord Frederick Lisle, last evening after the ball," he began. Keeping his explanation as vague as possible, with no mention of the Home Office, or the possibility of a network of criminals involved in the business, told her that it was suspected a forger was working in this part of the country. "He thought he'd better warn me since the miscreant might be one of my parishioners."

"That seems an odd bit of information for a gentleman about town to acquire," Sophia said, a line appearing between her tawny brows.

"He has friends in the government," Ben said with a slight shrug. Nothing he said was false. He simply didn't go into the complex details or dangerous implications of the matter with her. She was injured, after all, and as a lady could hardly set out to capture the ruffians on her own. He would tell her the whole truth if the need arose. Now was not the best time, however. To Ben's relief, she seemed to accept his explanation at face value. "I suppose Little Seaford is as good a place as any for an art forger to work," Sophia said thoughtfully. "It takes only painting supplies and a store of sufficiently aged canvas."

"And there's no shortage of artists here," Ben added wryly. "The proximity of the artist's colony at Primrose Green certainly makes it a safe place to hide in plain sight."

Sophia looked thoughtful. "The man yesterday said that they wished to wait until their man had shown his work in the exhibition before ridding themselves of him. Perhaps I can ask the Primbles for a list of everyone who has submitted work for it."

Mr. and Mrs. August Primble were the owners of Primrose Green, a local manor house that had been in August Primble's family for generations. When he inherited and married, he and his wife made the unconventional decision to open the house and grounds to artists in need of lodging and support. Thus was born the artist's colony at Primrose Green. The setting so close to the sea gave the inhabitants ample fodder for their work, and the Primbles got to pretend they were as talented as the artists who lived with them. They were not, but Ben had found them to be sensible people despite their eccentricities.

They were also the organizers of the annual Exhibition to which Mr. Morgan had referred. It was open to anyone in the county who wished to exhibit their work, but the largest number of works by far came from Primrose Green.

"There might be a hundred names on that list." Ben couldn't keep the frustration from his voice.

But Sophia didn't seem worried. "I'd say closer to thirty at most. There are only twenty or so places at Primrose Green and there aren't that many of us in the county at large."

"They were definitely discussing a man, which narrows it a bit too."

Though success in the world of art was often bestowed upon males, it was also the case that any young lady with a rudimentary knowledge of watercolors was encouraged to enter the exhibition. Which meant the list of men entered might be even shorter, he was relieved to realize.

"How on earth did your brother manage to arrive on the very night we heard them planning a murder?" Sophia asked, shifting a little in her seat. Her position, reclining along the length of the sofa, made it necessary for her to twist her torso to face him.

"We surmised it must have been coincidence," he said, moving to perch on the arm of the sofa so she needn't contort herself to face him. At her expression of surprise, he shrugged. "You're already in pain from one injury," he explained. "I don't wish to cause a crick in your neck as well."

"Thank you," she said, with a grateful smile. "Now, what is our next move?"

"Your next move is to rest your ankle and do as Dr. Holmes says," he said firmly. At her look of outrage he raised a staying hand. "My brother is here for the next few days and we will look into the matter. I promise to keep you informed of any developments. But if you are to be present for the exhibition, and to show your own work, then you need time to heal."

Sophia scowled. "I detest that you are right," she said crossly.

"It does happen sometimes." He stood, and moved to take her bare hand in his gloved one. "I'll bring Freddie to meet you tomorrow. You'll like him. He's the charming brother."

Not waiting to hear her reply, he left, closing the door to the sitting room firmly behind him.

Chapter 7

To Sophia's great relief, Dr. Holmes pronounced that her ankle was not broken, only sprained, and after wrapping it tightly with strips of cotton, he advised her to give it rest, and prescribed a mild sedative for when the pain prevented her from sleeping.

If she had been worried that she would spend the next few days in isolation, however, she was disabused of that notion by the steady stream of callers that began not long after the physician had bid her good day.

"I was unable to rest a moment longer until I inquired after your injury, Miss Hastings," said Mr. Toby Walsh, his intricately patterned waistcoat causing Sophia's eyes to cross slightly. With a flourish, he proffered an over-large bouquet of crimson roses. Sophia accepted them with a smile of thanks, but couldn't help but glance at the smaller nosegay the vicar had brought her, which was now in a vase of water on the marble mantelpiece. There was no denying that the red roses were lovely, but they seemed overblown and loud in comparison to the pink and white flowers.

Handing the bouquet to her waiting maid, Sophia smiled with more warmth than she felt. "You are too

kind, Mr. Walsh, but as you can see, I am no more injured now than I was last evening. I pray you will set your
mind at ease."

A knock at the door heralded the arrival of another
visitor.

"Ah, Walsh. I might have known you'd be here."
Mr. Walter Ellis shot a narrow-eyed glare at his friend
before stepping forward to bow to Sophia. "Miss Hastings, how relieved I am to see that you've suffered no ill
effects from overtaxing your . . . ah . . . limb at the ball."

Instead of flowers, he proffered a small stack of books.
Sophia was surprised to see that it was the three volume
set of Frances Burney's *Evelina*.

"M'sister is quite fond of this one, and I recall how
dull it was to be laid up when I broke my leg," the young
man said sheepishly.

Touched by his thoughtfulness, Sophia gave him a
genuine smile. She already had her own dog-eared copy
of the novel, but his gesture made her rethink her earlier
assessment of the young man's character. Perhaps Mr.
Ellis wasn't quite as silly as his friend.

As if to add further proof to this realization, Mr.
Walsh spoke up, clearly jealous of the attention his friend's
gift had garnered him. "I daresay the library at Beauchamp House has plenty of novels in it, Ellis, old fellow.
It was stocked by a lady, after all. Personally, I don't care
for them. Far too much nonsense in them."

If he'd wanted to elevate himself, however, this was
entirely the wrong thing to say. But before Sophia could
give him a richly deserved set down, it was delivered by
Gemma, who had been quietly watching their interac-
tions from her chair near the window.

"I daresay you're one of those gentlemen who hides
his novel reading from his friends under the supposition

that it is unmanly," she said with a sad shake of her head. "But I've found that men of intellect and sense enjoy a bit of fictional escape every now and again. Perhaps you should ask Lord Kerr or the Duke of Maitland which authors they prefer. Unless, of course, you consider them unmanly in some way?"

Sophia hid a smile at the myriad of emotions flitting over young Mr. Walsh's face. He seemed unable to decide whether to take offense, or to thank her for her suggestion. Perhaps recognizing that they were outgunned, Mr. Ellis clapped his friend on the back. "Let us leave Miss Hastings to her rest, Walsh. I have a feeling we've outstayed our welcome."

Reluctantly, Mr. Walsh agreed and soon was accompanying the other man from the room, leaving Sophia alone with her sister.

"You were a bit hard on poor Walsh, weren't you?" Though Sophia knew her sister had never been one to suffer fools gladly, but nor was she one for delivering a strong rebuff to an unarmed opponent.

"Perhaps I was." Gemma smoothed the skirt of her deep green gown, as if needing something to do with her hands. "But I've had a surfeit of gentlemen pretending to some sort of divine gift of intellect that gives them the right to pass judgment on whatever we ladies choose to occupy our time with."

Blinking, Sophia tried to recall when she'd seen her sister so annoyed. It wasn't as if she was meek or mild. But in general Gemma was an even tempered and steady sort of lady, who wished to pursue her own studies in natural history and ignored most other distractions.

"Strong words," she said aloud. "Has someone in particular said something to push you over the edge?"

Suddenly restless, Gemma rose and moved to examine Sophia's bouquet on the mantle. "I have received a rejection today from the editor of the *Annals of Natural History*. For my article outlining the three fossils I've unearthed since we came to Beauchamp House. They are significant finds, I believe, and could do much toward explaining some of the history of this part of England. But he claimed that because I am a lady, and unaffiliated with any particular institution or legitimate scholar, my work cannot be verified or given the aegis of his publication."

Sophia was all too familiar with the bias against scholarship conducted by the so-called fairer sex within most of the scholarly world. But it did at times seem that the greatest misogyny lay with the sciences. "Who is this horrid fellow and what must he look like? I will sketch a caricature of him for you to use on your archery target." It was a process the sisters had practiced since girlhood—Sophia providing the exaggerated image of whomever had crossed them, and Gemma filling said image with arrow holes. Childish, perhaps, but infinitely satisfying.

Turning, Gemma faced her sister, her pretty countenance wreathed with irony. "I'm not quite sure what he looks like but he is no doubt thin as a rail with a giant wart on his nose."

Laughing despite her sister's upset, Sophia made a mental note to sketch the miscreant as a gift for her sister as soon as possible.

Still, it was clear that her sister's ire was not going to be diminished by a few calming words and a cathartic drawing.

"You might write this fellow a reply," she said reasonably. "Outlining all the reasons you think he is wrong, and perhaps suggesting that he learns to curb his prejudices when it comes to choosing articles for his publication."

"That's a brilliant idea," Gemma said, brightening.

"I'm not finished," said Sophia raising a hand. "Write the letter, seal it and write his direction on it. Then, burn it."

"Burn it? Why?"

"Because you don't wish to burn bridges. What if you need this fellow at some point in the future? Burn the irate letter then write another, more reasonable one. Post that one and see what his reply is."

Even the calmer letter would win Gemma no favors, Sophia knew, but one of the reasons Lady Celeste had chosen her sister to come live at Beauchamp House was her determination in the face of adversity from the scientific establishment: which meant male scholars. And Sophia herself had fought against similar unfairness from the Royal Academy, which was reluctant to show the paintings of ladies who didn't confine themselves to landscapes or portraits.

She was proud of her sister, and despite her concern over her possibly raising the ire of this editor, she knew that confronting him about his dismissal was necessary.

At least she hoped they would not.

"I know it's difficult to be turned down." Sophia watched as Gemma returned to her chair and began to drum her fingers on the arm. Placing a gentle hand over her sister's, stopping the motion, she continued, "You mustn't let such things get the better of you, my dear. You and I both know how intelligent and talented you are. The rejection of a single man and a single journal will not change that."

Gemma turned rueful eyes to her. "I know you are right," she sighed. "But I was so looking forward to seeing my findings in print. And I thought—perhaps foolishly—that this editor would turn out to be a fair-minded man . . ."

Gemma nodded and Sophia couldn't help but give her arm a comforting squeeze.

"Let's talk about something more pleasant," Gemma said with a determined effort at cheer. "Lord Benedick is certainly paying a lot of calls on you these days."

Sophia felt her ears redden. "That's hardly the case. He was merely checking in on me this morning. And the visit with Lord Frederick will be to introduce him to the household at large." That Lord Frederick's visit was also planned to give her more information about the possible art forger run amok in Little Seaford was something she couldn't reveal just yet. But she was confident that despite her fascination with Ben's person, his increased attentions sprang not from affection on his part, but from a desire to get to the bottom of the conversation they'd overheard.

"Whatever you say," Gemma said, not looking convinced. "But, I think I know what a gentleman with an interest looks like at this point—having seen both Lord Kerr and the Duke losing their hearts to Ivy and Daphne."

"Don't be absurd," Sophia chided. "We are friends. And he simply wished to check in on me."

"Hmph. I'm not sure I believe you, but I will let you have your little self-deceit." Rising, she gave her sister a brief hug. "Shall I see if Gladys will bring up a luncheon tray for you?"

Sophia's stomach gave an emphatic growl. "I suppose that's a yes," she said with a raised brow.

* * *

After his visit to Beauchamp House, Ben stopped in at a
local farmer's house to look in on that man's mother, who
was ill.

Giving comfort to the sick and looking after his
parishioners was an aspect of his work that he found
especially fulfilling. He'd always been interested in
people. And though one might think that growing up in a
ducal household would have turned him into a different
sort of man altogether, his father had instilled a sense of
responsibility and stewardship in all his sons. It had been
Ben who accompanied their mother on visits to the ten-
ant farms when he was a boy. He'd watched and learned
as she held the hands of the sick, asked after the health of
families, and counseled when asked for advice.

Neither of his parents were typical for their rank,
something he'd quickly learned once he went to school
and began socializing with others of their class. And he
was grateful for it. Their teaching had made it possible
for him to perform his duties as a man of the church
with ease. At least, the caring for his flock part. Church
politics was something altogether different, and an aspect
of his calling he avoided at all costs.

Having offered what comfort he could to both the
sick old woman, who was unlikely to survive the pleu-
risy in her lungs, and her son and his wife, Ben was in a
contemplative mood when he returned to the vicarage. It
was difficult these days to see families suffering from
the loss of their elders without putting his own parents
in their place. Though both the Duke and Duchess of
Pemberton were in excellent health, there was no denying they were getting older and the time would come in
the not too distant future when he'd have to say goodbye
to them.

But he was snapped out of his brown study by the troubled look on his manservant's face when he stepped inside. Taking off his hat and coat, he handed them to Jeffries, who took them as he spoke.

"My lord," the older man said, his bushy gray brows drawn together in concern, "You have a visitor. I put him in the front parlor, but I believe your brother happened upon him before I could introduce them."

Ben bit back a sigh. While a competent butler, and a dab hand with a cravat, Jeffries had a tendency to become overset at the oddest times. When important figures from the village paid calls, for example. He was well able to handle lords and ladies, but let the mayor call at the vicarage and Jeffries became skittish as a cat.

"I feel sure my brother will not embarrass the household, Jeffries," he said wryly as he pulled off his gloves. "Who's called?"

Recovering himself, the butler looked slightly abashed and said, "It's Mr. Peter Morgan, my lord. I told him you were away for the morning, but he insisted on waiting. He seemed quite agitated."

There was a slight censure in his tone, but Ben ignored it. Jeffries might be intimidated by the industrialist's bluster, but he wasn't.

His response to the butler was a noncommittal sound.

Curious to see what Freddie was up to, he followed the sound of conversation. And when he opened the door, it was to find his brother lounging with one booted foot on his knee in Ben's favorite chair near the fire. In contrast to Freddie's relaxed pose, Morgan was standing before the fireplace, his back ramrod straight, a scowl on his blunt features. Neither man's demeanor changed when Ben entered the room.

"Mr. Morgan," Ben said, shutting the door behind

him and stepping forward to shake the man's hand. "I am sorry to have kept you waiting. I hope my brother and my staff have made you comfortable."

The set of Morgan's jaw said that the opposite was true, but someone had instilled basic good manners into him, and he gave a short nod. "Yes, your brother has been welcoming." And that, apparently was all the time he wished to spend on pleasantries. "I wish to speak to you about a very important matter, Lord Benedick and I need to do so in private."

Ben exchanged a look with his brother, who gave a slight shrug and rose. "I'll just take myself off to the library, then. It was quite interesting to speak with you, Morgan. Quite interesting."

And giving a slight bow to the man, he slipped out of the room, shutting the door behind him.

With Freddie's departure, Morgan seemed to relax very slightly. Ben made a mental note to quiz his brother about what must have been a very odd conversation. Freddie could talk the hind legs off a goat, but he had a feeling that Morgan wasn't the sort to fall into easy conversation with a man he'd dismiss as a useless fribble based on his apparent lack of gravity. Of course, there was more to Freddie than met the eye, but Morgan wouldn't know that. And likely wouldn't care.

"Can I call for some refreshment, Mr. Morgan?" Ben asked once they were alone. "Tea, or perhaps something stronger? I believe I've got a bottle of brandy in the sideboard."

But Morgan shook his head. "What you can do for me, Reverend Lord Benedick, is to use your influence to ensure that the upcoming art exhibition in our village is safe from the polluting influence of a Miss Sophia Hastings' work."

Chapter 8

Ben rocked back on his heels at the other man's mention of Sophia.

"I'm not sure what you mean, sir," he said with a mildness he didn't feel.

"I have been assured by someone very close to her that Miss Sophia Hastings plans to place three highly improper paintings in the exhibition," Morgan said with a scowl. "One, in fact, depicting a common whore, and another showing a child on the brink of death. I do not know the subject matter of the third one, but I have no doubt it will be equally repellent."

The vicar could see that Morgan was not the sort to listen with any seriousness to an explanation of art and the role it played in pushing for social change. Or, for that matter, to discuss the fact that some of the most explicit and disturbing paintings he'd ever seen were religious in nature. This was a man who merely needed to hear a few words of describing the painting's content to determine its unwholesomeness.

That the artist in question was Sophia Hastings, whose very presence in a household of lady scholars was questioned by some in the village, was not lost on him either.

Still, as the minister to the whole of Little Seaford, he
had to do what he could to see things from every point
of view—even those that made him itch to abandon his
clerical collar and challenge the holder of said opinion
to a fist fight.

"I'm not sure what you wish me to do about the paintings to which you refer, Morgan."

"You must use your office as the spiritual leader of this
village to keep that woman from exposing not only my
wife but all the gentle ladies of the district to such filth.
The innocence of our wives and daughters must be protected at all costs." Stifling his instinct to plant the other
man a facer, Ben pretended puzzlement. "I'm not sure I
see what the problem with Miss Hasting's work is. Is
the fallen woman depicted in the nude?"

Morgan scowled. "Not that I've heard," he conceded,
"but it needs only the implication that the woman in the
painting makes her living on her back. I want no daughter
of mine looking at such a person. Even on canvas."

"But surely you've read about Mary Magdalene in the
gospel, Mr. Morgan. If our Savior can bring a woman
who once plied that trade into his flock, then I don't see
the harm of showing another such lost soul in art. Knowing Miss Hastings, I have little doubt that the painting
will be quite tasteful, and will likely carry a moral message. She might be a bit unconventional, as are all the
ladies at Beauchamp House, but she is hardly a purveyor
of indecency."

"Jesus also consorted with lepers, my lord," said Morgan tightly, "but that doesn't mean I wish my family to
do so. It is my job as their protector to keep such ugly
facts of life out of their purview. And as a leader in the
village of Little Seaford, I extend that protection to all
the innocent ladies and children of the town.

"As for Miss Hastings, my lord," he continued, "I find it difficult to believe a woman who looks like she does is unfamiliar with the sort of scenes she shows in her art. Her father is barely a gentleman, I think. She would do well to preserve what reputation she has instead of flaunting the proprieties as she does. I cannot think either she or her sister will escape their time in that very unconventional household without ruining themselves."

Vowing silently to ask Kerr or Maitland for a bout of fisticuffs as soon as he extricated himself from this interview, Ben clenched his jaw against a string of profanity.

Still, he wasn't required by his vows to allow men like Morgan to speak ill of ladies, no matter how unconventional their circumstances might be.

"I should be more careful about what I said about the very dear friend of both the Duchess of Maitland and the Marchioness of Kerr, sir. You may have your opinions about the suitability of the Misses Hastings, but I can assure you that they are not without friends. And I believe any attempt on your part to slander them with such musings in public would be met with a very sharp rebuke from both the houses of Maitland and Kerr. Not to mention, that I myself count the Hastings sisters as friends, and have never seen a hint of the character flaws you suggest."

As he warmed to his subject, he felt his temper rise. Who was this uncouth lout to cast aspersions on Sophia's reputation solely because she'd been gifted by God with a beautiful face and a curvy figure? Was Morgan's own wife—whose looks, to be honest, paled in comparison—to be considered virtuous because she was plain? Good character wasn't determined by one's physical beauty or lack thereof.

"I also cannot see how you are able to determine the morality or immorality of Miss Sophia's paintings without having laid eyes upon them yourself." He could see that Morgan wished to respond but wouldn't let him get in a word. Not yet. "I understand you may not be all that familiar with art, sir. However—"

There Morgan cut him off. "I am actually quite familiar with art, Lord Benedick," he said with a sniff. "I have the pleasure of acting as the patron of a very talented young man whose work is what art should be—uplifting, moral, beautiful and entirely appropriate in mixed company. Mr. Thomas Ryder is everything that Miss Sophia Hastings is not. And I intend to see to it that his work is given a place of prominence in the exhibition."

Ah, Ben thought. So Morgan was worried that Sophia's paintings would eclipse those of his protégé's. It was quite possible that the man was indeed as worried about protecting the fragile sensibilities of Little Seaford's ladies as well, but it was far more likely that he was trying to eliminate competition from Sophia. That he had suggested the Hastings sisters were no better than they should be in order to elevate his favorite was despicable, however.

"And who is this Thomas Ryder you've taken under your wing?" he asked aloud, unable to keep a hint of skepticism from his tone. "A local fellow?"

The exhibition was intended to be a showcase for the artwork of local painters and the grand prize—an exhibition in a very influential London Gallery, which had been secured by the head of the artist's colony at Primrose Green—had the potential to bring the winner to national prominence.

"He is a young man I have brought with me from

Yorkshire," Morgan said grudgingly, as if he knew exactly what Ben was thinking about the exhibition's intent. "But as he resides with my family now, he is a local. And since Miss Hastings is only a latecomer to Beauchamp House, I cannot think that you would consider the matter of length of residence to be a problem."

He had a point, Ben acknowledged, with a nod of his head. Still, there was something havey-cavey about this business. Deciding he'd had enough of Morgan's bluster, Ben gave him a friendly but cool smile. "As you may have guessed, I cannot support you in this matter. I would encourage you to wait until Miss Hastings' work is unveiled before casting aspersions on it, but I can see that advice would fall on deaf ears. I see nothing about the subject matter in general that would endanger the souls of my congregation, and in fact, I can only think that seeing how the less fortunate among us live would do a bit of good."

He offered his hand in a gesture of goodwill, but was not surprised when Morgan ignored it and stomped to the door. Wrenching it open, his large frame filling the doorway, he turned to glare at Ben. "You'll regret this, vicar," he said with a scowl. "I am an influential man in these parts. And I have friends in the church. When the Archbishop of Canterbury hears about this, you will find yourself in a much less convivial post."

Since the archbishop was his mother's first cousin, Ben had no worries on that score. Whatever influence Morgan thought he had, it was far less than that the Lisles wielded. He might dislike the politics of his position, but that didn't mean Ben was unwilling to use them when necessary.

Especially when it was in support of his innocent friends who were being targeted by a bully.

"I hope I'll see you Sunday, Mr. Morgan," he said to the man's retreating back, unable to stop himself.

When the front door closed behind him, Ben heard Freddie come downstairs and into the parlor.

"What. An. Ass." His brother said in his wry way.

Though Ben didn't disagree, he wasn't quite so comfortable dismissing the man altogether. He'd clearly got it into his head to ruin Sophia's reputation. And that was something Ben wasn't going to stand for. Not because he was attracted to her, he told himself, but because what Morgan was doing was both unfair and wrong.

"I very much wish that Peter Morgan was one of the men you overheard at his ball," Freddie said emphatically. "It would be quite satisfying to see him in manacles being hauled off to jail."

Ben didn't disagree. It was perhaps unchristian of him to wish the other man ill, but he was human. And his sense of justice demanded that Morgan see some sort of ramifications for his unfairness toward Sophia.

"I just can't be sure," he said aloud. But silently, he agreed. It would be eminently enjoyable to see Morgan get his comeuppance. Not Christian, perhaps, but every man had his trials.

Even vicars.

By the afternoon, thanks to Dr. Holmes' tight wrapping of the joint, Sophia's ankle was feeling improved enough to make her chafe at the restrictions of her injury. The physician's manipulation of the joint had shown it to be only sprained, not broken, and he'd assured her that it would be much more the thing in a week or so. For the pain, he'd suggested laudanum, but Sophia disliked how it made her feel, so as an alternative he recommended willow bark tea. And with the assurance that he'd look in on her again in a few days, he left her to take a much needed nap.

When she woke several hours later, she felt better, and the swelling in her ankle had abated considerably.

She tried to keep herself occupied with a book, but soon the dullness of the sickroom got the better of her.

A short time later—having endured the indignity of being carried bodily up to the third floor by a footman—Sophia found herself settled comfortably on the settee in her attic studio.

Upon her arrival at Beauchamp House, after paying a visit to the magnificent library with its gilt trimmed shelves and intricately patterned recessed ceiling, her next priority had been to see the studio space Lady Celeste had spoken of in her letter. Taking up what might have originally been intended as a nursery, the open room ran the width of the house and its wall of windows overlooked the manicured gardens, the rolling green beyond, and finally the cliffs and sea beyond that.

Sophia had yet to enter the room without a sharp intake of breath at the sight. In the daytime, the view of the countryside leading to the sea could be bright with sun and blue skies, or more often, gray with roiling clouds and hints of rains to come. At night, especially when the moon was visible, the view was just as compelling.

But it was the natural light that streamed through those windows into the chamber that made it special. As any artist would surely agree, light was a chief consideration for anyone who put brush to canvas. And whoever had designed this room—no doubt Lady Celeste—had known that better than most.

Without the wall of windows, the shape of the chamber would have put Sophia in mind of a barn. Especially with the peaked roof. But the skylights in that roof, coupled with the plethora of windows, not to mention the smell of turpentine and oil, marked it as exactly what it was. A magnificently appointed artist's studio.

And it was all hers.

At least for the next six months.

She and the other heiresses hadn't discussed what would happen if all four of them managed to remain in Beauchamp House for the full year stipulated in Lady Celeste's will, and therefore inherited equal shares in the house. Ivy and Daphne had remained in spite of their marriages to titled men who had multiple houses of their own. But both Kerr and Maitland had been nephews of Lady Celeste, so therefore had sentimental attachment to the house itself. There was little chance at this point that Beauchamp House would become the sole property of any of them.

The studio, however, Sophia secretly thought of as her own.

With its multiple easels and ingeniously devised rolling walls that could be hung with works in progress and used to form smaller rooms within the large one, the studio was more perfect that she could have ever imagined for herself. And stocked as it was with canvas and supplies and everything she could possibly need, it was as close to heaven as she would get on this earth.

Now, however, thanks to her ankle, she was unable to put the room to its proper use. At least not for painting. She had instructed the footman to move one of the rolling walls—hung with her three paintings for the exhibition—to a spot where she could sit back and examine them as a critic might.

The first, which she'd titled "Fallen" was of a scene outside the entrance to a theatre. In the foreground, black carriages disgorged their wealthy occupants who paused in mid-laugh, mid-step, amid the chatter of the *haute ton* seeing and being seen, entirely at home in their world—its confines as real as the carriage interior they'd just stepped out of, if invisible. Lamps hung on either side of the wide doorway, paling in comparison to the almost blinding light of the entryway. And just to the right of the steps leading into the theatre, in a small recess between the stair rail and the iron gate of the next building, lay the crumpled figure of a woman. Her shiny gown, its bodice too low for propriety, was rucked up a little to show her calf. And thrown out to her side, her hand was open, relaxed. In the palm rested a shining gold guinea. Sophia had purposely left the woman's face in the shadows, because women like that are so often unseen by the type of people who are blithely walking past. It was perhaps a bit too literal a symbol, but she thought it worked. At least she hoped it did.

Her stomach clenched at the idea of unveiling it for the residents of Little Seaford to judge. In the time since she'd come to the seaside village, she'd come to, if not love the residents, at the very least respect them. They might not be quite comfortable welcoming her or the other bluestockings into their bosom, but neither did they hold the heiresses in contempt, in part because despite her eccentricities, Lady Celeste had been a favorite among them.

This painting, Sophia knew without consulting them, would not be something they immediately understood or appreciated. It was, she feared, a bit ahead of its time. And would cause a bit of a stir among her neighbors. But it was the other percentage of Little Seaford's inhabitants—the artists at Primrose Green, the local gentry, and the educated, somewhat cosmopolitan few—she hoped to speak to. That contingency might not like the painting, but they'd appreciate its technique, and might even agree with its message. Hopefully, it was these visitors to the exhibition who would also serve as judges.

The thought of the exhibition reminded her of the overhead conversation and once again she felt a pressing need to find out whose life was in danger. And to warn him. Even if the man was a forger, he didn't deserve to die for it.

She cursed her injured ankle again and rested her head against the back of the settee with a sigh.

Which is when she heard the knock on the door of the studio.

"I hope you don't mind the disturbance, dearest," Gemma said as she stepped into the room, followed by Ben and a man who could only be his brother Freddie. The two men weren't enough alike to be twins—Ben's hair was slightly darker, and curlier, and his build was a bit less lean—but they had that general similarity that couldn't be pinpointed but marked them as having emerged from the same set of parents. "Lord Benedick and his brother, Lord Frederick Lisle. They said it was a bit urgent."

Sophia was surprised to receive a second call from the vicar in the same day, naturally, but her sister's mention of necessity gave her pause.

"What is it, my lord?" she asked, attempting to sit up straighter. "Has something happened?"

Sophia didn't miss the hesitation before Ben said, "Well, not precisely . . . that is to say . . ."

"It's no worry," she assured him with a smile. "My sister told me some of what you overheard at the ball last evening. But I'm off to work for a bit now. I'll leave you to it." To Sophia she said pointedly, "Do not overtire your injury. You may have bullied the footmen to carry you up here, but they can just as easily be instructed to take you back to your bedchamber." And with that admonition, she left them. Leaving the door of the attic rooms ajar for propriety's sake.

"You told your sister about what we overheard?" Ben asked with a slight frown.

"I was in pain and needed some distraction," Sophia told him baldly. "And Gemma is trustworthy. She won't tell anyone. Not unless I tell her she may."

"Don't be a stickler, Ben," said Lord Frederick, stepping around his brother to take Sophia's hand in his and kiss it. "I'm the handsome one, Miss Sophia," he said with a wicked grin. "I regret, however, that I'm taken, so you should dampen any pretensions you have toward my very handsome person."

"If Leonora heard you say that she'd have your guts for garters," Ben said wryly. "And stop flirting. It's quite true that you are taken and you should stop raising expectations."

"If I may be so bold as to speak," Sophia cut in, "I am in no danger of succumbing to your charms, Lord Frederick, powerful as they are. Though I do thank you for exerting yourself on my behalf."

With an unrepentant grin, Freddie bowed again. "She's got spirit," he said to his brother. "I like that." To Sophia he said, "I do apologize, my dear. Old habits die hard, I'm afraid, and I find it impossible not to flirt, especially when it offers such a rare opportunity to tweak my brother's nose."

Sophia shook her head a little, dazzled despite herself. Then, having collected herself, she said, with what she hoped was credible sobriety, "Perhaps you should both bring a chair over and explain what it is that has you here in such haste. Especially when I thought we'd agreed to see each other tomorrow, Lord Benedick."

Exchanging a look she could not read, the brothers retrieved chintz-covered wingback chairs from where they sat on either side of a trestle table, and moved them to sit facing Sophia's settee.

"Well?" she prompted when they'd settled. "What is it?"

Ben's mouth tightened. "Someone has taken it into his head to challenge your entries in the exhibition. He claims they're obscene. And he asked me, as the vicar of the parish, to support him in it."

Chapter 9

"I suppose it's Mr. Morgan who finds my work so objectionable?" Sophia asked, her blue eyes narrowed with annoyance.

Ben had only been mildly surprised to learn that she'd abandoned her sitting room for the art studio. It was impossible to imagine her sitting quietly while she waited for her ankle to heal.

The room itself was impressive. Large enough to allow for paintings of all sizes, and with a view that could inspire even the most novice of artists to capture it. Lady Celeste Beauchamp had been an accomplished woman, with talents ranging from classics to mathematics. But this room made it clear that she had as much love for art and painting as she did for the others. This was a shrine to color and light and had been carefully crafted as the perfect space for creation.

Now, settled across from where Sophia reclined on the settee, he was relieved to see that she appeared better rested than she had that morning. Though the news of Morgan had put a crease between her tawny brows.

"It is, indeed, Morgan who has come forward asking that your paintings not be shown in the Exhibition," he responded. "He hasn't even seen them, but apparently the description of their content was enough to convince him that they are inappropriate for a public event that will include mixed company."

"He must have seen the title and description that I turned in to the exhibition committee,' Sophia said, her rosy lips pursed with anger. "Because no one has seen them but the members of this household and the servants. And after the difficulty we had with disloyal footmen in the past, Kerr and Maitland have made quite sure that our men now are corruption proof."

"Who might have shown him your submission forms?" Freddie asked, serious now that they were discussing Morgan. "Is there someone on the committee who is particularly friendly with him? Or who might have alerted him to the content of your work?"

Ben watched as she thought about the question. Her rose colored gown showed her creamy complexion to advantage, and he couldn't help but appreciate the way the bodice—which was all that was respectable—framed her bosom. When he looked up, Freddie caught his eye and gave him a wink. Caught out, he gave himself a mental shake and turned his attention back to Sophia's face.

"There are any number of people on the committee who might have alerted him," she said grimly. "He's done a good job of ingratiating himself with many of the village leaders. Times have been difficult for the farming families since the bad harvests a couple of years ago. And that in turn has affected business in the village shops. Morgan has been quite good at using that discontent to his advantage, playing the benevolent industrialist, making contributions to local groups that were in need of funds. Offering jobs at his estate. People are grateful to him. And willing to overlook some of his more questionable pronouncements."

"Such as crying foul over artwork that just happens to call into question the morality of his own wealth?" Ben asked.

"Precisely," Sophia said with a nod. "I knew, of course, that the factory worker painting would draw his ire. His own textile mill in Yorkshire is responsible for any number of child workers being killed in the machinery, or dying more slowly from cotton lung. He feels guilty, and I want him to."

"May we see them?" Ben asked, suddenly needing to see the works that Morgan found so obscene.

"Of course." Sophie gestured to the area behind them.

Turning, Ben saw for the first time that what he'd thought was a partition, was actually a rolling wall of sorts. And it was hung with three paintings. He'd been so focused on Sophia when they entered the room he'd been blind to the details of what hung on the walls.

He and Freddie rose so that they could look fully at the works.

And he was nearly overwhelmed by them.

If you didn't look closely, it would be possible to miss the crumpled prostitute in the first painting. The light and animation of the theatre entrance was so engrossing. And yet, it gave pathos to the fallen, forgotten woman whose death was of no concern to the rich and powerful who passed only a few feet away. It was dark, and engrossing, and perhaps one of the most provocative works of art he'd ever seen.

Beneath it was a different tableau—it had the same effusive use of light as the other had—that depicted a child lying lifeless on a bed, his mother weeping at the bedside. In a small vase on a bedside table was a cotton blossom.

Impossible to get in England, of course, but it was symbolic here. A nod to the cotton mill that had taken the boy's life. On the floor lay an advertisement for child workers at just such a mill. It was nameless, but Ben could well imagine Morgan seeing his own factory in the image.

"You have real talent, my dear," said Freddie at last, turning to face Sophia. "I admit to having a certain degree of skepticism when I heard you were a painter. There are so many who fancy themselves artists simply because they're able to pick up a brush and daub on a few spots of color. But these are . . ." he seemed, to Ben's amusement, at a loss for words. Freddie Lisle was very rarely unable to find something to say.

"They're powerful," Ben said moving to take Sophia's hand. He found himself needing to convey his appreciation with touch. Which was odd, but the artwork had engendered strong emotions in him. Despair for the people depicted, anger at those who had put them in such straits, and oddly, thanks to the skill and beauty of the art itself, hope. "I, too, I must admit, was not expecting such dramatic work from you."

At Sophia's frown, he raised a staying hand. "Not because I thought your paintings would be boring. It's just that your personality is so . . ."

He searched for a word—well aware that he was in the same position his brother had been in. And to his disappointment, Sophia made no move to supply one.

"You're so effervescent," he finally settled on. "You're funny and frank and you have such a practical demeanor. I suppose I didn't imagine you would have such bold and challenging things to say in your art."

Sophia gave his hand a squeeze. "I think that's the most insightful thing anyone has ever said to me about my work."

Reluctantly he let her go and moved back to sit in his chair facing her. If Freddie weren't there, he'd have been sorely tempted to pull her into his lap and hold her. Which was utter madness. But it seemed that madness was becoming his default emotion in her company.

"I am rather prosaic about most things," she continued, staring down at her hands. "It comes of having impractical parents, I think. Gemma and I had to fend for ourselves when it came to the practicalities. But that doesn't mean I am without feeling." She looked up and met Ben's eyes. He could see that she was sincere and a bit defensive. "I feel things very strongly. But it's not always convenient to dwell on emotions when you're concerned about making sure cook will have dinner ready, or the laundry maid won't ruin your best gown. Beauchamp House had allowed me the luxury, for the first time in my life, of letting my emotions flow onto the canvas. I can say without exaggeration that this is my best work. And it was done here, in this very room."

Ben wanted to question her further about her life with her parents. Where had they been while she was seeing to the running of the household? As far as he knew they were both still living. So, why had she been burdened with such chores? But he could see it wasn't the time for that discussion. Instead, reluctantly, he turned the subject back to Morgan.

"How can we ensure that Morgan doesn't get his way?" he asked. "These paintings deserve to be seen. They deserve to hang in the exhibition along with the other locals' art. You are just as much a resident of this village as they are. And I would venture to guess that no one else's work will be as powerful or carry as necessary a moral message."

"We'll need to speak to the committee," Sophia said

with a martial glint in her eye. "And I know just where we should begin."

"Not to dampen the fight to get your paintings seen, Miss Hastings," Freddie said, "but there is also the matter of the forgery ring, and its implications for the nation's safety, operating out of Little Seaford. I believe my brother told you we think the conversation you overheard at the Morgan Ball could be related?"

Ben bit back a curse as he saw Sophia's expression turn from excitement to annoyance. "We discussed the possibility of a forger, of course, but not a forgery ring. And certainly nothing about it affecting England's security. I hope this isn't another of your attempts to protect me, Vicar, for I will tell you here and now, that I will be quite put out with you if that is the case."

For a man who'd been seconded by the Home Office, Ben thought darkly, his brother had an extraordinary skill for spilling secrets.

"I can assure you, Miss Hastings," he said aloud, "I intended to tell you about the full extent of the plot and its interest to the Home Office just as soon as I was able. I only learned of it myself last evening when my brother showed up unannounced on my doorstep."

All of which was the truth. However, he chose not to tell her that he'd planned to keep the news from her until she was recovered from her injury, and therefore less likely to risk her health through overexertion. If it was a sin, it was by omission. And surely keeping her from harm would be looked upon as a virtue by anyone other than the lady he was attempting to protect.

He had the distinct feeling that Sophia was not convinced, and yet, she didn't argue. With a raised brow, she turned to his brother and said, "I suppose I'd best hear the whole tale, then."

But Ben didn't want her to know about something that might put her in danger. "Perhaps when you're more recovered, Miss Hastings," he said with a speaking look at his brother.

"Lord Benedick, you begin to annoy me," she said with a tilt of her head, her blue eyes lit with a spark of pique. "My brain has not been injured. Only my ankle, which the last I checked, is incapable of reason. I should hate to think you are one of those tiresome males who believes us to be the weaker sex, who cannot endure more than two thoughts in our heads at a time."

The accusation stung. Especially since he'd only just finished telling her in plain terms what Morgan thought of her paintings. "Miss Hastings," he said, feeing an unaccustomed wash of anger, "I thought we understood one another better than that. Of course I don't see you— or any woman—as unintelligent merely because of your sex. I merely wished to ensure that you do not come into danger by knowing more than you should about matters that are known to only a handful of people. My brother and myself included."

Sophia opened her mouth to respond, but Freddie spoke up, holding up a staying hand to stop them both from speaking. "If I may interrupt, Miss Hastings, being married, myself, to a headstrong, intelligent lady, I do understand your annoyance with my brother. But having known him for many more years than you have, I can attest to the fact that he is the least likely man of my acquaintance to dismiss a lady's mind as inferior. He is, however, quite concerned with the safety of everyone who falls within the scope of what he sees as his responsibility."

He wasn't wrong, Ben reflected, but it was damned uncomfortable to be summed up so easily.

"I can assure you that he knew nothing about the government's interest in the forgery ring until I told him not long after my arrival last evening," Freddie continued. "I cannot say whether he intended to tell you before my clumsy revelation, but my guess is that he would have told you eventually. Just hadn't decided when to do so."

Ben met Sophia's eyes, which had softened at his brother's words.

Looking a bit sheepish, she said, "I suppose I should apologize, Lord Benedick. Perhaps I am more snappish than usual thanks to a lack of sleep."

"Think nothing of it, my dear," he told her with a smile. Then, unable to let the moment pass without owning up to his own wrongdoing, he admitted, "I might have been waiting to tell you about the Home Office later, as Freddie said. But not because I think you to be inferior. Simply because I thought Morgan's threats against your paintings were enough to bring to you while you were under the weather."

Sophia sighed. "I suppose that's not entirely a bad idea. As much as it pains me to admit it."

Quickly, Freddie gave her a summary of what the Home Office knew about the criminal activity they suspected was centered in Little Seaford.

"I had no notion," she said when he was finished. "And you really work for the Home Office?"

Ben gave a soft cough at his brother's momentary pique at the skeptical tone in her voice. Then, his good nature overcoming his wounded pride, Freddie gave an elegant shrug. "They are, at the moment, short of investigators. And my friend who works with them recalled that Ben had been living here, so thought he might be drafted into service."

"Which I am, of course happy to do," Ben said with a

shrug. "I am in a position to know most of the families in the area."

He gave Sophia a mischievous look, "And perhaps a friendship with one of Little Seaford's foremost artists can help me understand more about painting and the art world."

She shook her head. "I might have known you'd find a way to charm your way back into my good graces."

"My dear Miss Hastings," Freddie said, raising his quizzing glass, "he is a Lisle. Of course he is charming."

She didn't comment, but said, "I do believe I know just the people we need to ask about both Mr. Morgan's objections and who might be involved in any sort of art forgery in the area."

"Don't keep us in suspense." Ben thought perhaps Sophia was enjoying the prospect of a fight. Not the need for it, certainly, but she wasn't someone who backed down from a challenge. And she now had several.

"Of course you already know them, Lord Benedick." Sophia said with a grin. "But I believe your brother will enjoy making the acquaintance of the Primbles."

They were just the sort of people Freddie would find fascinating.

"Freddie, old son," he said, clapping his brother on the shoulder. "I believe you're in for a rare treat. And Miss Hastings is perfectly correct. The Primbles, whose home is an artist's colony of sorts, will be able to ensure Morgan doesn't get his way, as well as give us some idea of who among the local artists might be involved in the forgery ring."

Freddie's brows rose with interest. "Then lead the way to these fonts of artistic wisdom."

Before Ben could remind him of Sophia's infirmity, she spoke up.

"Tomorrow," Sophia promised with a gesture to her ankle. "I'm afraid today I'm still not up to a carriage ride. And if the two of you try to go visit our resident eccentric artists without me I will never forgive you."

Ben knew from her tone that she was serious. "I wouldn't dream of it, Miss Hastings. Though I've met the Primbles in my capacity as vicar, we will need your artistic credentials to lead the way. I don't know a Rembrandt from a Rubens."

"We would never be so ungentlemanly as to leave you behind, Miss Hastings," Freddie said with a hand over his heart. "No matter how much my brother urges me to do otherwise, I will not allow him to abandon you."

To Ben's amusement, Sophia only pursed her lips a little at Freddie's foolishness before turning to speak to him. "I trust you, Lord Benedick," she said. And it was hard not to read more than was likely intended by the words.

"I shall see you tomorrow, gentlemen," she continued with a firm nod. "You may pick me up at ten in the morning. And I promise not to make you wait overlong for me to find just the right hat."

"You didn't tell me she was considerate as well as a lovely, brother," Freddie said in a stage whisper.

Ben took his brother's elbow to his ribs with good humor, though he didn't miss that Sophia's color rose at the bit of flattery.

He'd have liked to have a few moments alone with her to assure himself that she was indeed improving, but there were lines of fatigue around her eyes that told him she was in more pain that she professed.

"Get some rest," he said aloud, though his tone was gentler than his words. "We'll see you tomorrow and determine whether you are ready for a jostling drive then."

Before she could argue, he and Freddie bowed and took their leave.

Later that evening, Sophia was reading in bed when, to her surprise, Lady Serena came to her.

"You seem to be feeling better," she said with a gesture to Sophia's injured ankle as she took a seat in the chair beside the bed. "I take it Dr. Holmes' treatment has helped?"

Setting her book aside, the first volume of *Pride and Prejudice,* which she'd sought out after her discussion of it with Ben that morning, Sophia nodded. "And rest," she admitted sheepishly. "I am ready to admit that my decision to attend the ball last evening was not my finest decision."

Serena's blue eyes, so very like her brother the duke's, lit with mischief. "Oh how I could use that information to my advantage. An admission of wrongdoing from one of the Hastings sisters!" She clasped her hand to her chest in mock astonishment.

"I am hardly the only lady in this household with a reluctance to admit fault," Sophia said with a sniff. "And besides, I seem to recall you were not so eager to call for the physician when you had a cough last month."

To her credit, Serena lifted her hands in surrender. "You are right. I am just as bad as any of you heiresses."

Once their shared laughter had diminished, however, she got to the point of her visit. "Dearest, while you are here at Beauchamp House, I am not only your friend, but also your chaperone. And as such, am here to serve as your guardian in the absence of your parents."

Having some notion of where this conversation was headed, Sophia shifted uncomfortably. Though she and Gemma had never been outright disobedient to their parents back in Manchester, nor had they been particularly slavish to their wishes. For one thing, doing precisely what their mother wished them to do would have meant spending days on end in a darkened room with a cloth soaked in lavender water on their brows. For another, Aunt Dahlia, who had a far more outspoken persona than either her brother or sister-in-law, had taken her nieces under her wing almost as soon as she came to live in the Hastings household.

Sophia could hardly wave away the older lady's concerns by telling her that she needn't worry since Mr. and Mrs. Hastings were indifferent parents at best and neglectful at worst. She could only imagine poor Serena's response to that sort of confession.

In truth, her parents weren't that bad. Mama and Papa simply delegated the day-to-day care of their daughters to Mr. Hastings' sister Dahlia, who'd come to live with them. Mr. Hastings was far too busy with his work as a solicitor, and Mrs. Hastings was so often taken ill that she couldn't accompany her daughters on social or educational outings.

Still, Sophia understood what Serena was getting around to. And the subject wasn't one she was particularly eager to discuss.

Before she could respond, however, Serena pressed on. "It cannot be a surprise to you that I should come to you about this early on. Especially given the . . . precipitate manner in which both Ivy and Daphne managed to find themselves wed. That my own cousin and brother were the gentlemen who compromised them is not precisely something I am proud of. In fact, I daresay if there were a governing body of chaperonage, I should have already found myself summarily dismissed long ago."

Despite herself, Sophia giggled. At Serena's scowl,

she held up a protesting hand. "You must admit, Serena, that it's amusing. And I hardly think anyone who cares about such things places the blame at your feet. Special licenses are quite common among the peerage, are they not? And besides that, both Ivy and Daphne are known to be unconventional. It can hardly be a surprise to either the village of Little Seaford on the *beau monde* that their marriages were secured in hasty fashion."

But Serena was not to mollified. "You might find it amusing, my dear, but it is deadly serious to me. I am responsible for the four of you. And I've done a terrible job of watching over Ivy and Daphne. I do not mean to make the same mistakes with you and Gemma."

Sophia didn't pretend not to know from which gentleman in particular Serena was supposed to protect her. "You are leaping to conclusions about the vicar and me that are far too premature. I enjoy Lord Benedick's company, it's true. But I am hardly the sort to make a suitable vicar's wife. I'm not even sure I believe in all the teachings of the Church of England. And aside from that I'd be provoked into jealousy every time one of his flock batted an eyelash at him."

That she did harbor an attraction for him despite her sensible objections to any sort of match between them was something Sophia would simply need to control. Once their shared investigation into the forgery ring was over, she would simply go back to her painting and leave him to be snapped up by some wholesome lady more suited to becoming a clergyman's helpmeet.

Serena, however, didn't appear to believe Sophia's protestations. "You might claim otherwise, but I've seen you together. He's smitten with you, or at the very least, taken. It would only take the slightest bit of encouragement on your part to have him eating out of your hand."

"You make me sound like some sort of biblical tempt-ress, Serena," she said with a frown. "I've hardly got the sort of stunning beauty that makes men of God aban-don their principles and sin with abandon."

To her surprise, Serena shook her head. "You really don't know, do you?"

"Know what?" Sophia asked, plucking nervously at the bedclothes. She was growing uncomfortable with all of this talk of attraction and temptation.

Wordlessly, Lady Serena took her hand. "My dear girl, you are beautiful. I know any number of ladies in London who would sell their teeth to have a figure like yours. Not to mention your passion for your work only adds to your charm. Together, these traits are almost ir-resistible. I'm not surprised Lord Benedick finds you fascinating. My only shock is that we don't have more than a few local gentlemen paying calls on you weekly."

Sophia felt her face heat. "You needn't exaggerate, Serena. I know I'm far too short and . . . round . . . to be fashionable. And you and I both know that the gentlemen who call here are not just for me. I have a good mind that Mr. Tewksbury comes only to see you, in fact."

At that, Serena's cheeks turned red. "I will admit Tewksbury might not be here for you, but the rest are. Gemma never makes an appearance and Daphne and Ivy are married. And while your figure might not be in fashion at the moment, you are most definitely the sort that most gentlemen prefer."

It wasn't hard to guess that in this case, Serena was very likely speaking of her belated husband and his preferences. She was tall and willowy—like Lady Ce-leste, she'd once told them. And though she was quite pretty, she would never be called buxom. Though the heiresses didn't know the entire story, it was known among them that Lord Fanning had not been good to her and that Serena still bore some of the emotional scars of his ill treatment of her.

She gave her chaperone's hand a squeeze where she still held it. "I thank you, Lady Serena," she said with a soft smile. "I still don't quite believe you, but I'm grateful for the compliment. And while I beg leave to disagree with you that any gentleman would find himself overcome with lustful thoughts over my person, I will endeavor to rein in my charm when in the company of our handsome local vicar."

Serena sighed. "I don't mean for you to hide your light under a bushel. And by all means if you wish to allow Lord Benedick to court you, I will not object. Just please try for a bit more discretion than Ivy and Daphne managed. That's all."

That made Sophia laugh. "Since it will not be at all necessary, I have no qualms about making that promise. I will even make you a small wager. If, by chance, I am forced to marry by special license, I shall gift you with whichever of my paintings you wish. Even one of those I've promised elsewhere."

Serena's eyes narrowed. "And what shall I do for you if I lose?"

"You will accompany Ivy, Daphne, Gemma and me to London on a shopping trip," Sophia said without blinking. "I should like to see you devote a bit of time to yourself for a change. You spend so much of your daily life tending to Jem and looking after us. You deserve a bit of fun."

Serena's young son, Jem, was a favorite with the heiresses and his older cousins, but Sophia knew well enough what a handful he could be. And though the widow would deny it, she gave far more to others than she received.

For the barest moment, Serena's eyes lit with excitement at the prospect of a holiday. Then, as if reality had intruded upon her like a wet blanket, she grew serious again. "It's a nice thought, but really I have far too much to do here, and Jem . . ."

"Jem will be perfectly content to remain here with his favorite uncle and cousin." Sophia countered. "And I know the others would like the opportunity to do something for you after all your kindnesses to us."

"Gemma won't like it," Serena said stubbornly. "Nor will Daphne. They both detest shopping."

"Well, we will find some other activity to entertain them while we're in London," Sophia said with a shrug, hiding her triumph at the note of concession in Serena's voice despite her argument. "So, I will simply have to keep myself from marrying by special license in the next month or so. I don't believe I've ever won a wager so handily."

With a shake of her head, Serena rose. "Don't count your winnings yet, old thing," she said in a tolerable impression of her brother, the Duke of Maitland. In her normal voice, she added, "I don't know what it is about this house, but it is clearly endowed with some sort of magnetic properties that lead sensible young ladies into mischief. And I intend to protect both you and your sister from following Ivy and Daphne down that selfsame path."

When she was gone, Sophia chuckled merrily to herself. "Magnetic properties, indeed." She wished her ankle weren't throbbing or she'd have searched out the others to tell them.

Picking up her book again, she began to read. But in the back of her mind, she was already planning which shops she'd take Serena to on their trip to London.

Chapter 10

To Sophia's relief she slept the night through, and the next morning she was able to put weight on her ankle without the blinding pain of the day before. There was still some discomfort, however, but she was able to have breakfast with the rest of the household without needing to be transported there by one of the footmen.

She did allow Greaves, who was replenishing the tea and coffee service at table, to bring her a plate of toast and eggs. It was customary for residents of the house to serve themselves at breakfast, but she was a favorite with the butler, and he made sure she was settled.

"Thank you, Mr. Greaves," she told him with a smile. "You're too good to me."

The older man, so proper most of the time, gave one of his rare smiles. "Of course, Miss Hastings."

Then he hurried from the room.

"If I hadn't seen it, I wouldn't have believed it," Lord Kerr said with a grin from his place beside Ivy. "You've wrapped poor Greaves 'round your finger. I can't be sure but I think he was blushing."

"Hush, Quill," Ivy chided. "Sophia is just being herself.

She cannot help it if the majority of the male population succumbs to her pretty face."

"You're hardly an antidote," Sophia told her friend with a laugh. "In fact, I'd say as a whole we're not a bad looking group."

"Intermarriage within the aristocracy leads to exaggerated features on most of the offspring in the *ton*," Daphne said as she spread marmalade on her toast. "Statistically, Kerr, Maitland, Serena and myself should be frightful looking. Fortunately, we've all managed to turn out rather attractively. It's a wonder, really."

"I, for one, am relieved to have escaped the overlarge ears and weak chin of my fellow aristocrats," said her husband, the Duke of Maitland, raising his teacup with a flourish. "Else Daphne might never have set her cap at me.

"I did no such thing," his wife responded without rancor. "I simply noted that you were a handsome man and acted accordingly."

"Yes," Gemma intervened before Daphne could expound on the subject, "and we all know the outcome."

"We do, indeed," Ivy agreed with a grin. "Now, speaking of good-looking aristocrats, I couldn't help but notice that our vicar paid not one but two calls on our Sophia yesterday. I know he takes his duties as minister seriously, but that seems a bit overly conscientious to me. What say, you, Sophia? Has our vicar fallen prey to your winsome ways?"

This sort of teasing was *de riguer* for their group, so Sophia didn't take offense at her friend's words. Though she had hoped that no one would notice Ben's second appearance at Beauchamp House yesterday.

Even so, she had to tell them about Morgan's threat to have her paintings taken out of the exhibition at some point.

Quickly she told them the reasons for Ben and Lord Frederick's visit, including the presence in the village of an art forger.

When she'd finished, her friends were gratifyingly angered on her behalf.

"I wish we'd declined the invitation to that man's ball," Ivy said fiercely. "He has rubbed me the wrong way since he first arrived in Little Seaford, and now I am convinced he's the worst sort of hypocrite. His kind always has a fancy woman in town while he condemns the rest of the world for their perfidy."

"What can we do?" Daphne asked, cutting to the heart of the matter. "Shall the duke and I pay a call on him and let him know he's crossed a line? I have no fears about playing the outraged duchess for a good cause. Just say the word."

"Alternatively," Kerr said thoughtfully, "Maitland and I could go alone. Talk to him man to man. His type enjoys bullying women, but rarely stands up to other men. Indeed, it would be quite pleasant, I think, to put the man in his place. He's swept into the village as if he owned it and seems to think everyone else should accept his leadership. Last I heard, the village has a competent mayor in Mr. Givens."

But the idea of any of them approaching Morgan and possibly riling him further made Sophia nervous.

Morgan, like most men of his station, found it galling enough that he'd worked—or rather, his factory workers had—for his every penny when aristocrats simply inherited their wealth through the good fortune of birth. Maitland and Kerr were not as snobbish as some others of their class, but they did possess that certain bred-in-the-bone sense of authority that Sophia sensed would anger Morgan. He was both jealous of them and resentful.

"I do appreciate your championship," she told the cousins. "Indeed, I am grateful for all of you. So much. But I believe this is a matter that requires an appeal to a higher authority."

Gemma blinked. "Lord Benedick is going to pray for you?"

Sophia laughed. "I imagine he will, as vicar, but I was talking about someone else. A higher artistic authority. The chairman of the Little Seaford Art Exhibition, Mr. Primble."

"Oh, excellent," Maitland said with a grin. "For all of his eccentricities, Primble isn't a man to stand for interference in his art business. I once saw him deliver a withering set down to Mrs. Northman, the Squire's wife, when she attempted to give one of the artists in the Primrose Green colony some suggestions for how he should frame his painting. I don't think a Beau Brummell at the height of his influence could have been more cutting."

"I hope it won't come to that," Sophia said with a slight shudder. Mr. Primble could indeed be sharp, and that might be just as counterproductive with Morgan as being approached by Maitland and Kerr would be. "Instead, I believe Lord Benedick and I will be able to persuade Mr. Primble to simply ignore Morgan's request. He is, after all, the chairman of the exhibition committee. And he has an appreciation for art that challenges."

Just then Mr. Greaves returned with the news that Ben and his brother Lord Frederick Lisle had called. "I have put them in the drawing room, Miss Hastings. I took the liberty of sending your maid for your hat and cloak."

Ignoring the grins of the rest of the table, Sophia

thanked him, and when the butler was gone, stood with the help of her walking stick. "Now, if I've amused you enough this morning, I'll just be off to pay a call at Primrose Green."

"Good luck," said Ivy as Sophia made her way to the door. "And be sure to bring Lord Benedick and his brother for luncheon. I have a feeling this visit will leave you needing sustenance."

Chapter 11

The following morning, Ben and Freddie waited in the drawing room for Sophia or word that she was not well enough to accompany them to call on the Primbles.

Ben had suspected she was a bit overconfident about the degree to which her twisted ankle would have healed by this morning, but he hadn't been able to say no when she all but begged them not to leave her behind. And he hadn't been lying when he said that he and Freddie would need her artistic expertise to communicate with any sort of sense at the artists' house. If she was unable to accompany them, they'd simply have to put the visit off until she was recovered enough.

While the brothers waited, they wandered the well-appointed chamber, examining the various objects d'art and paintings Lady Celeste had used to adorn the room. The walls were hung with blue fabric and the inset ceiling was decorated with plaster reliefs in an ivy pattern. But it was the smaller items that lined the mantle and the recesses in the walls that caught the eye.

The shepherdess figurines of the ordinary drawing room were far too tame for late Lady Celeste.

The mantle, for instance, was lined with several figures that seemed in the style of the Elgin Marbles. Upon closer inspection, however, Ben realized that they were all different depictions of the god Priapus—at least that's what he assumed given the outsized proportions of the genitalia of the statues in comparison to the rest of their bodies.

On the other side of the room, Freddie must have encountered something similarly shocking because his usually unflappable brother gave a short laugh, which turned into a coughing fit when Sophia entered the room.

"Oh dear, Lord Frederick," she said with a frown, "I'll just call for some water for you."

She was almost to the bell pull when Freddie recovered himself. "Not at all, Miss Hastings. I'm well, I assure you."

And to Ben's relief, Sophia was also looking much improved.

Though she still limped a bit, her eyes had lost the shadows beneath them, and her cheeks glowed with renewed energy.

"Good morning, Miss Hastings," he said to her, offering a bow. "I hope your appearance means you will be able to accompany us to visit the Primbles."

Sophia glanced at the mantle behind him, and seemed to hide a smile before responding. "Yes, you're quite correct. My injury is almost healed. And thanks to Lady Celeste's walking stick, I shall be able to come along with you. Shall we be off?"

Offering her his arm, Ben escorted her from the room, feeling his brother's amused gaze on his back as they walked. He was always pleased to see his siblings, but he'd be damned glad when Freddie went back home. It was difficult enough to maintain his calm demeanor in the face of Miss Hastings' beauty, but he felt like a damned schoolboy under the watchful eye of his younger brother.

When they reached the entryway, where Greaves was ready with Sophia's pelisse and hat, Freddie took his own hat and bowed to Sophia. "I'll be riding Ben's gelding to Primrose Green. He's got my curricle for the two of you, in deference to your injury."

With a wink in Ben's direction, he exited and hurried down the front portico of the house.

Sophia and Ben followed at a more sedate pace, and when they reached the curricle, he lifted her by the waist into the vehicle. It took no more than a few seconds, but the brush of her warm body against his coupled with her sweet rose scent had him a little light headed.

By the time he'd climbed up beside her and taken the reins from the groom, he'd regained his composure.

They were silent as he steered the light carriage over the gravel drive and toward the road leading to Primrose Green, which was on the other side of the village from Beauchamp House.

"Your brother seems nice," Sophia said, which almost made him laugh. Polite chitchat was not what he expected from Miss Sophia Hastings.

Even so, he responded easily. "He's a good man. Pesky as younger brothers often are, but since he's married and become a father, he's much more himself, I think. Freddie was always a bit wild. Certainly the most prone to get into scrapes of the Lisle brothers. But Leonora has had a calming influence on him."

"Marriage has that effect on some men," Sophia said with a nod. "Though his wife is Leonora Craven Lisle, is she not? Certainly not the sort of staid society wife one would think of as a steady hand."

Freddie's wife, Leonora, was a celebrated poet and

had been rather famous in her own right long before she married Freddie. "I thought the same thing before I met her," Ben said with a shake of his head. "But it turned out that far from being the sort of flighty, head-in-the-clouds poet one might expect, Leonora is rather comfortingly sane."

He turned to glance at Sophia, where she sat beside him with one hand holding her hat in place thanks to a burst of wind. "She's not unlike you, to be honest. She has that same sort of practicality mixed with idealism. I think you'd like each other if you were ever to meet."

From the corner of his eye he could see that she'd colored a little. "Thank you. It's a high compliment to be compared to someone of her stature."

"I only tell the truth," he said with false seriousness. "I'm a vicar, you know. It's in the vicar handbook."

"The Ten Commandments, you mean?" she asked with a raised brow.

"That would be one of them, yes," he conceded with a sniff.

"Far be it from me to question you about church business, vicar." Her tone was solemn, but there was a twinkle in her eye.

"See that you do not, Miss Hastings," he returned. "See that you do not."

After a brief, companionable silence, he said what he'd been thinking since she first walked out with the cane. "You seem to be feeling better."

"Yes, thank goodness," she agreed, the relief evident in her voice. "I was afraid it would be worse today and keep me from accompanying you. And I really do think you'll need me to translate for you with Mr. Primble."

"Come now," Ben said. "I've met the man, and we had no trouble understanding one another."

"It's not that communication is the issue," she said with a shrug. "It's more that I will need to plead my case with him. Artist to artist."

"But I thought Primble wasn't much of an artist himself."

"Oh, he's not," Sophia assured him. "He's dreadful. But he fancies himself one, and that is all that's needed for him to take up my cause. An attack against one of us is an attack against all in his eyes. It's one of the reasons he turned Primrose Green into a colony. He wanted somewhere that artists could be together, in the spirit of community. Us against the world."

"It sounds rather intoxicating," Ben said, seeing when he glanced at her that she looked a bit like a champion. "Why aren't you at Primrose Green?"

Sophia gave a snort of laughter next to him. "Because while I appreciate the ideals that the Primbles promote, I do not trust them to protect my reputation. And, scandalous as Beauchamp House can be to some, Primrose Green is far more dangerous. There's a reason there's only one lady artist in that house and she's over fifty. The male artists who reside there are, not to put too fine a point on it, rogues every one of them."

Ben had known that the Primbles' household, filled as it was with various unrelated artists, was odd, but the trouble Sophia mentioned hadn't occurred to him. Suddenly he was quite glad she hadn't chosen to join the artist's colony.

"Sounds like you made the right decision, Wallflower," he said with quiet vehemence. He made a mental note to make sure she stayed in his view while they were at the colony.

"Oh, not that ridiculous nickname," she said with an

impatient noise. "I'm the least wallflowerish person you've ever met, I'd wager."

"I wouldn't say that," he responded, not looking her way, but feeling her gaze on him. "I suspect you fancy yourself a sociable, chatty sort. And you are, to a point. But there's also a bit that you hold in reserve, Miss Hastings. As with the emotions you show only in your art, I think there's another side of your personality. A shyer side. That you tamp down when you're in company."

"You've thought a great deal about this, haven't you?" she asked wryly, though when he turned to look at her, there was hectic color in her cheeks. He must have hit a nerve. "Well, perhaps I am more complex than I let on to social acquaintances. But I don't think you're as cheerful and sunny as you pretend to be when you're playing the role of vicar."

Her shrewd analysis took him off-guard a bit. He was, as a general rule, an easy-going man, but there were times when even he didn't feel as chipper and pleasant as his position required of him. But he'd learned long ago that not unlike Descartes, with his admonishment to kneel down and pray in order to become a believer, it took only a concerted effort to project good humor for it to eventually convert itself into the real thing.

"I'm no more a simple character than you are, Miss Hastings," he agreed. "I may even have hidden depth. But that's for you to learn at a later time. For it would appear we're on the drive leading to Primrose Green."

He watched as Sophia turned and noted that they were indeed on the straight drive leading up to the red brick manor house that was covered in ivy.

"So we are," she said with a brisk nod. "I think I see your brother just ahead of us."

And sure enough, Freddie, riding Ben's gelding Gabriel, was almost at the end of the drive.

"So you do, Sophia," he said. It was a little heady how good her name felt on his tongue. And with that thought he tamped down his attraction for his companion and focused on the meeting ahead of them.

Sophia soon found herself, along with the Lisle brothers, following the Primbles' rather slovenly butler down a narrow hallway toward a pair of French doors.

As they walked, Sophia with one hand on her walking stick and the other resting on Ben's arm, she couldn't help but notice that every available inch of wall was covered with paintings. It hadn't occurred to her that the artistic output of a household with multiple artists in it would of necessity need space in which to hang their works. Did the colony have so little luck selling their pieces, she wondered?

She'd only ever been in the drawing room of Primrose Green on social occasions. And then it had only been a couple of times. The general aesthetic of the Primbles seemed to be "more is better." Not unlike this hallway with its abundance of paintings, from landscapes to portraits to classical scenes, the drawing room was a showcase of other sorts of *bric a brac*. From figurines, to tapestries, to mirrors.

"It's a veritable museum's worth of not very good art," Freddie said in a low voice that only Sophia and Ben could hear.

Before they could reply, they reached the doors, which opened directly onto a wide sweep of green lawn. Sophia had forgotten that Primrose Green boasted one of Capability Brown's gardens. Rather than remaking it in the current style, the Primbles had maintained the ar-

tificial lake, faux antique Greek urns and follies along
the lake's edge and the tangles of trees and shrubbery beyond. On the expanse of green just near the house,
were the Primbles and several of their residents, set up
with easels and palettes as they tried to capture the landscape around them on canvas.

In the distance, Sophia could also see a man busy at
another easel while several people in what looked to be
Greek attire posed against the columns of the largest of
the follies.

The butler announced their arrival, and after some
initial pleasantries, the Primbles were ushering them
back inside to a library that was, thankfully, filled only
with books.

"My dear Miss Hastings," said Evelyn Primble once
she'd seen Sophia's ankle properly elevated on a leather
sofa, "you must take better care. It is the height of foolishness for an artist as talented as you to risk permanent
bodily harm. You need your physical strength to do your
work justice."

The lady of the house was, by appearances, exactly
what one would imagine when attempting to conjure the
dictionary definition of a lady artist. Attired in a brightly
colored patterned tunic, with a belt cinching the waist
and a rather unwieldy turban covering her hair, Mrs.
Primble gestured broadly with her hands when she spoke,
and was, in general, the sort of woman who took up a
great deal of metaphorical space in a room.

Her husband, by contrast, looked like a prosperous
businessman, a banker perhaps, or a lawyer. His clothes,
while following the customary country uniform of
breeches and frock coat, were drab in comparison to his
wife's. But he was a pleasant enough fellow, if a bit dull
in the shadow of his butterfly of a wife.

Mrs. Primble now turned to Ben with a scowl. "What on earth do you mean, Vicar, escorting this young lady out and about with such an injury? I thought you had more sense than this. She is a treasure, and we need her in top form for the exhibition."

"Now, mother," Mr. Primble chided "Miss Hastings is perfectly able to make her own decisions. It's not the vicar's fault . . ."

Exchanging an amused look with Ben, Sophia interrupted before the Primbles could continue their treatise on her well-being. "Actually, Mrs. Primble, the exhibition is precisely why we've come. That, and—" she gestured to Freddie who'd been watching the whole exchange with the enthusiasm of a small boy at Astley's Amphitheatre for the first time, "—something a bit more complicated that Lord Frederick has brought to our attention."

The husband and wife paused in their chatter and also exchanged a speaking look. Though Sophia had no notion of what it could mean.

"Then this calls for something stronger than the tea I've sent for," Mrs. Primble said. "I know it's not even time for luncheon yet, but I get the sense that this is serious business."

"I'll wait for the tea, thank you, Primble," said Ben to their host, who had produced a bottle of brandy from the sideboard.

"I will too," Sophia said with an apologetic smile. "I could do with a strong cup."

"Suit yourselves," Mrs. Primble said with a shrug as she handed a glass to Freddie. "Now, what's this business you've brought to us?"

Quickly, Ben outlined Peter Morgan's objections to Sophia's paintings being displayed as part of the exhibition. As he spoke, Mrs. Primble in particular became more and more incensed. By the time he'd finished with Morgan's threat to have him removed from the parish, both Primbles were nearly trembling with outrage.

"How *dare* that here-and-thererian, who has only himself arrived in this county within the last year or so, imply that Miss Hastings is not resident enough to show her paintings!" Mrs. Primble hissed. "That trumped-up figure of an artist he had under his wing is no more a painter than I am a blacksmith! His work is derivative at best, and near-forgery at worst."

"Miss Hastings," Primble assured her with a determined look, "you may rest assured that so long as Mrs. Primble and myself retain our positions on the exhibition committee, your work will have a place in our show. Not only is it thought-provoking and unlike anything else to be exhibited, but the fact that Lady Celeste Beauchamp herself chose you from the dozens of other female artists of a similar caliber gives you a stamp of approval that outshines any quibble that Peter Morgan might have. The man's a Philistine, and doesn't know good art from a machine in one of his blasted factories."

"While your support is reassuring," Sophia told them sincerely, "I cannot help but fear that he will find a way to turn the other committee members against me. The amount of largess he's pumped into local coffers speaks quite loudly. Especially during a time of diminished prosperity."

But Mrs. Primble seemed to have no worries. "You let us handle the matter, Miss Hastings. He might have money to flash about, but we are not without influence in the village. I will see to it that your art is displayed in a place of prominence, where it can do its work of stirring emotions."

Despite her reservations, Sophia felt a sense of relief at the Primbles' promises. They did hold a great deal of sway with the townsfolk, who held the artist's colony to be an eccentric attraction that made their village more interesting to tourists, whose custom had become important while the crops were failing.

"Now," Mrs. Primble said, as if they'd put the matter to rest, "what was this other business you wished to see us about?"

Rather than outline the entirety of what the Home Office believed about the forgery ring, Freddie told them only that a forger was suspected to be in the area and that the authorities were searching for him.

It would have been easy to assume that because of their eccentricity, the Primbles were foolish. But the shrewd look that came into Mrs. Primble's eyes as Freddie spoke told Sophia that she, at least, was up to every rig.

"And you think we might know who this forger is because we have an abundance of artists in our own household." It was a statement, not a question. And Sophia was pleased that Freddie didn't try to fob her off with a half truth.

"It is not unreasonable to think that the house in the area that shelters the most painters might be the first place to search for our culprit," he said with a nod. "I don't wish for you to betray a trust, of course. But as artists yourselves, you know that works that falsely purport to be the valuable creations of the world's finest craftsmen devalues everything in the market. You cannot wish your own works, or those of your residents, to lose value because of this charlatan."

Primble moved to slip a hand around his wife's waist, as if to give her support while she took in the news.

"There is someone, Lord Frederick," he said, his jaw tight with emotion. "Someone who once was a resident here, but has since gone on to enjoy the auspices of another patron. His work, while technically strong, never had enough originality to set it apart from that of anyone else's. There was no spark. No *je ne sais quoi*. When he was approached by Peter Morgan with an offer of patronage, he leapt at the chance. And he has, since moving into Morgan's household, found some degree of success. Though I wouldn't say his work is any better than it was before. It does help to have the backing of a man with a great many friends who have the funds but not the taste to furnish their mansions with art."

"You're speaking of Thomas Ryder, then?" Ben asked, his eyes sharp with interest. "I didn't realize he'd once been a resident at Primrose Green."

"Not for terribly long," Mrs. Primble assured him. "He didn't get along with the others, for one thing. A house like this, where many temperaments must live in harmony, isn't the best place for someone who is unwilling to cooperate with his peers. He often chose the best models and locations for his works without any concern for anyone else who might have previously made arrangements to use them. He had a rather mercenary approach to art itself, seeing it as a means to an end, rather than something to be created from one's soul. He didn't fit in here, and to be honest, when he left to go to Morgan's we were all relieved."

Chapter 12

Sophia had never met Ryder, though she'd been aware that Morgan had taken a painter under his wing. He'd been there the night of the ball, though he'd given her a wide berth because of her injury. He had danced every set and seemed interested only in those young ladies who had the boon of a large dowry to illuminate their charms. It sounded as if he painted with the same venial intent as he sought a wife.

"And you think he's good enough to reproduce the works of the Old Masters?" Freddie asked, rising from his chair, restless now they'd learned of a suspect.

"Absolutely," said Primble with a nod. "He might not be very creative when it comes to choosing his own subjects, but his brushwork is outstanding. And he often made it a point to teach himself the techniques of great artists in an attempt to improve his own work. He's one of those poor creatures whose paintings are flawless, but unfortunately don't depict anything particularly new or interesting."

Sophia was gaining a new respect for the Primbles' knowledge of art and painting. Like most people, she'd assumed that they surrounded themselves with artists because they lacked talent themselves. But the ability to differentiate between mediocre and excellent work was a talent in and of itself. Perhaps there was a reason for the hallway of not very good paintings. Something besides simply displaying the works of their students in a place of prominence.

Having elicited the information they'd come for, Ben also rose, and moved to stand beside Sophia's settee, holding her walking stick for her.

"I cannot thank you enough for your help, Mr. Primble." He shook the man's hand. Then, turning to their hostess, he bowed over her hand. "Mrs. Primble, you have saved us a great deal of trouble with your candor."

"I'll add my thanks, as well," Sophia said as she rose from the settee on her own power, but with Ben quickly offering a supporting arm. Really, she was much improved and didn't need quite this much assistance. But she couldn't help but admit it was no hardship to feel his strong arm beneath her fingertips.

"You are welcome, my dears." Mrs. Primble beamed at them. "I detest it when a man attempts to silence a lady. Especially when he uses ridiculous charges of impropriety and obscenity to do it. I would venture to guess that a great deal of what men like that consider obscene are simply things that bother their conscience. If he gives you another bit of trouble you must come to me, Miss Hastings."

"What will happen to Ryder?" asked Primble once they'd reached the entryway of the house. "If it is him, I mean? It's entirely possible that there's someone else in the area with a gift for copying. It's not an unusual way for artists to learn. And the odds of him being the only one in the area to use it are slim."

"I don't know at this time," Freddie responded. "But

I must ask you to keep this conversation to yourselves. We do not wish Mr. Ryder or Morgan to learn that he's a suspect now. If we are to catch him, we need him to remain unaware of our interest."

"Of course," Mrs. Primble assured him as he kissed her hand. "We will be silent as the grave. But you must let us know what happens, Miss Hastings. I expect a full report once the business is over."

Since Sophia had no notion of when that would be, she made the promise easily. If she was, for some reason, gone from Beauchamp House by the time the business with the forger was resolved, then Mrs. Primble would simply have to understand.

Once they were outside, and Freddie's horse and the curricle had been brought around, the brothers made arrangements to meet back of the vicarage once Ben had returned Sophia to Beauchamp House.

"Miss Hastings," said Freddie with a crooked grin. "I leave for London this afternoon, so I shan't see you again this visit. But I wish to say how pleased I am to have made your acquaintance. I feel sure we'll see one another again, but in the meantime I hope you'll take care of yourself."

He bowed low over her hand and kissed it.

There was no denying that Lord Frederick Lisle was a charmer. And that he was as handsome a man as she'd ever seen. But Sophia found she much preferred the understated wit and easy-going nature of Ben. Even so, she was pleased to have met the sauciest Lisle brother.

"You take care yourself, my lord," she said with a grin. "And please tell your wife she has several admirers in the village of Little Seaford."

He nodded, and once he was in the saddle, gave a tip of his hat and was off.

Ben grasped Sophia by the waist and lifted her into the curricle. Had she imagined the spark when their eyes met? She resisted the urge to press her hand to her chest. By the time Ben was up on the seat beside her, she'd managed to regain her composure.

Once they were settled, he gave the horses a signal to move and they were off.

"You'll miss him when he's gone, I think," Sophia said into the sound of the horses' hooves on the gravel lined drive.

"Of course," Ben said with a shrug. "He's family. He might drive me mad at times, but he's my brother."

"I know too well how that feels," Sophia laughed. "It's a good thing Gemma and I spend so much time devoted to our own pursuits. For if we had to spend our days in one another's pockets, I very much fear one of us would end up with severe bodily harm."

They spent the rest of the drive back to Beauchamp House in a discussion of the various merits and drawbacks of siblings.

When they reached the circular drive before the tidy manor house, Sophia was surprised to see an unfamiliar gig being led to the stables.

"A visitor?" Ben asked as he noticed her frown.

"It would seem so," she replied, trying to recall if anyone had mentioned expecting callers today.

He made quick work of lifting her from the curricle, and insisted on escorting her into the house, though Sophia was quite certain she could make it on her own.

"I took Mrs. Primble's admonishment quite seriously," he told her with a grin. "It's not every day I'm raked over the coals for risking a young lady's health. Not many people will dare question a vicar's behavior. Unless he behaves very, very badly."

At the twinkle in his eye, Sophia found herself imagining just the sort of situation in which Ben might do so. Perhaps Freddie wasn't the only charming Lisle brother, she reflected.

Just then, as she handed her hat and gloves to a waiting Greaves, she heard raised voices from the front parlor just off the entry hall.

"Who's visiting, Greaves?" she asked the butler, who looked none too pleased at the din in the next room.

"A gentleman came to see Miss Gemma," he said with a moue of distaste. "Only he didn't ask for Miss Gemma Hastings, but G.E. Hastings."

Not waiting for further explanation, Sophia moved toward the parlor, followed closely by Ben. Greaves gave a sharp knock on the door before opening it on a tableau of a man and woman in combative stance.

Her sister, her arms akimbo, was scowling as if she'd like to toss the gentleman out on his ear.

While the gentleman, in travel-worn garments, and sporting a head of familiar-looking light brown curls, looked equally put out.

Behind her, she heard Ben give a groan. "Cam, what the devil are you doing here?"

Ben wasn't sure who he'd expected to find exchanging heated words with Gemma Hastings, but it certainly wasn't his brother Cameron.

But, rather than admit that, yes, it was unusual for him to be in Beauchamp House, let alone Little Seaford in general, Cam did what he always did and turned the question around. "I might ask you the same thing, Ben. Are you acquainted with this . . . this . . ." he gestured to Gemma with a rare bout of speechlessness then found the word he was looking for, ". . . harpy?"

Beside him, Ben felt Sophia stiffen, while Gemma made a noise that was something between a snort and a howl. "You, sirrah, are a boor and a scoundrel and I will thank you to take yourself out of this house at once!"

"How do you know this man?" Sophia asked both Gemma and Ben.

When it appeared that Gemma wasn't ready to speak, Ben did so. "This rapscallion, who has clearly lost every bit of the social graces drilled into us at our mother's knee, is my brother, Lord Cameron Lisle."

Having calmed down a bit, Cameron had the good grace to look sheepish at Ben's reminder of social niceties. Bowing prettily, he said to Sophia with a grin that was not unlike Freddie's, "At your service, ma'am."

"This is Miss Sophia Hastings," Ben said tersely. "Miss Gemma Hastings' sister."

Cameron's light blue eyes glanced from one sister to the other, then back again. Finally able to see the resemblance.

"Ah," he said, infusing the syllable with a great deal of feeling.

Pulling away from Ben, Sophia limped over to her sister, brandishing her walking stick with a bit more force than he thought entirely necessary. Still, heeding the warning, Cameron stepped away from the sisters to stand near the window where he could see the room at large. He'd once told Ben it was a trick he'd picked up in his travels, to ensure that he could never be taken by surprise. Clearly he was more unnerved by the Hastings sisters than he was letting on.

"What made you think it was acceptable for you to upbraid my sister in her own home, my lord?" Displeasure dripped from her every word. Ben had never seen

Sophia in protective mode, but he had a feeling that, if necessary, she'd toss his brother bodily from the room.

It was quite exhilarating.

He was prepared to back up her question with one of his own if Cam proved recalcitrant, but to his secret amusement, his brother's ears reddened under Sophia's gimlet gaze and he looked as if his cravat had suddenly tightened itself.

"I . . . ah . . . it was badly done of me, Miss Hastings," he said, flags of red in his cheeks. "I'm afraid I lost my temper and . . ."

He was interrupted by a lusty sigh from Gemma, who was also looking sheepish. "It wasn't entirely his fault, Sophia. When I found out who he was I couldn't contain my indignation and I'm afraid I let my temper get the best of me."

Sophia's reddish brows lowered. "Well, I wish you would inform us just who Lord Cameron is besides Lord Benedick's brother, for I must confess, I find myself quite at a loss."

Then, as if she could no longer stand to be on her feet, she moved to collapse into an overstuffed chair near the fireplace. When neither Gemma nor Cam spoke up, she said, "Well?"

Ben went to stand beside Sophia's chair and watched as his brother and Gemma exchanged a series of looks that clearly were full of import. But it was in a language he had no idea how to translate. Finally, Gemma walked over to the chair beside Sophia's and sat.

"You recall I told you about the article I submitted to the *Annals of Natural History*, the one that was rejected?" Gemma addressed her sister without looking at either of the men in the room.

"Oh," Sophia said, almost without thinking. Then,

understanding dawned and she said again, with a wide-eyed look toward her sister, "Oooooh!"

Next she turned her narrowed eyes on Cam, and unless Ben was very much mistaken, his brother had made an enemy of both Hastings sisters at this point. If looks could kill, Cam would, at the very least, be mortally wounded.

"So, this is the narrow minded cloth-head who refused to publish your findings?" she asked Gemma, aghast.

"I say," Cameron objected. Though whether it was to being called narrow minded or a cloth-head, Ben couldn't tell. "I gave it the same sort of evaluation as I give every submission. It was interesting, but not particularly groundbreaking."

"Oh, I'm sure you gave it the same sort of evaluation as you give every article *written by a female* that crosses your desk," Gemma said hotly, crossing her arms over her chest. "I wouldn't be surprised if you read only the first three paragraphs before tossing it aside."

Before they could embark on another round of arguments over the paper, Ben broke in with the question that had been plaguing him. "We know now what set you at loggerheads, but why are you here, Cameron? In this house. Arguing with Gemma in person? Could this not have simply been settled by mail?"

At that, Gemma turned bright red.

Sophia turned to stare at her sister. "Gemma, what did you do?"

"You recall you told me I should write a letter to the editor who rejected me?" Gemma asked, looking as if she would rather be anywhere but in this room.

"Two letters," Sophia said. "Yes. One saying how you really felt, and the other more calm and thoughtful."

Gemma nodded and Ben saw dawning horror on Sophia's face. "You sent him the angry one?!"

"I got them mixed up!" Gemma said heatedly. "This is what comes of listening to your advice about writing two letters! Any other sane person would write one angry letter, tear it up and then think about something else."

"I was trying to help you make a case for yourself," Sophia said, hectic color in her cheeks. "When ladies are attempting to enter fields that are traditionally male, it sometimes takes a bit of persuasion to convince the male establishment to accept them."

"If my findings weren't enough to make him accept me," Gemma said tightly, "then maybe it's not a field I want to be a part of."

Not liking the sight of the two sisters, usually so supportive of one another, at odds, Ben asked tentatively, "Surely this letter can't have been all that upsetting, Cameron. You've been to the ends of the earth, for heaven's sake. You've been insulted by people all over the world."

His brother raised a brow. "You make me sound like the most delightful fellow, Ben. But, to correct you, yes this letter was all that upsetting. Miss Hastings called into question everything from my virility to my intelligence to my ability to sit a horse. I came here because she signed it with her initials only so I thought she was a man. I came to challenge this G.E. Hastings."

Ben's eyes widened. "What?"

Sophia turned to her sister. "I thought you said he knew you were a lady when he rejected your paper."

Gemma shrugged. "I send out papers under both my real name and with only my initials. I assumed this one was under my real name because it was a rejection."

"Gemma." The censure in Sophia's voice couldn't

have been more shame-inducing if she's been a fifty-year-old governess. "You called this poor man all manner of names without cause."

"I'm not an imbecile." Gemma said the words grudgingly. Then, to Cameron, she said, "It was badly done of me. I should have checked to see if you knew I was a lady or not. I realize now that my letter didn't really state my reasons that the paper should be published, but was rather a series of insults and epithets loosely strung together."

"How did he even receive it?" Sophia asked. "You only told me about the letter yesterday. It hasn't had enough time to reach Oxford. Or Cambridge. Or wherever it is Lord Cameron resides."

At that Cameron looked a bit rueful. "I've actually been in Lyme these past few months. That was the direction I gave on my letter to G.E. Hastings."

"Mrs. Tompkins said she'd have her son deliver it since he had plans to go to Lyme this morning," Gemma agreed stiffly.

Ben turned to his brother in astonishment. "You've been living just down the coast for months and never once came to see me?"

"I'm here now," Cameron said with a shrug. "Besides, you know how village life gets under my skin. I know hardly anyone in Lyme aside from the people I employ to help me search for fossils. If I came here you'd have me introduced to the entire village within a few days and I'd have no peace."

Despite his annoyance at his brother's avoidance of him, Ben couldn't help but admit that he had a good point. It was a vicar's job, in part, to know his parish. And he would very likely have had Cameron meeting and greeting the whole of the village if given the chance.

He also had to admit that he would have done so in part to take some of the pressure off himself from the local matchmaking mamas.

"Fine," he said with a shake of his head.

"So, you came here to confront G.E. Hastings?" Sophia asked, a glint of amusement in her eyes now. It was, after one got past the initial alarm of the scene they'd walked in on, an amusing scenario.

"Yes," said Cameron with a grin. "And not only was G.E. a lady, but she's got a sharper tongue than a Billingsgate fishwife."

"Gemma." Sophia's sigh this time was exasperated.

"I was angry, Soph," her sister responded. "You know how I get when I'm angry."

Seeing that the worst of the storm had passed, Ben turned to Sophia. "Perhaps some tea?"

With a sigh that was half exhaustion half amusement, she gestured to the bell pull. "By all means."

Chapter 13

The Lisle brothers did not stay for luncheon, given that Lord Cameron and Gemma were still at odds, their tacit agreement to stop shouting notwithstanding.

Unfortunately for Sophia, this meant that much of the discussion amongst the Beauchamp heiresses—Kerr and Maitland having left that morning for London to take care of business matters—was of the sudden abundance of Lisles in their small part of the county. Not that she was an authority on the subject. It was just that her friends seemed to see her as some sort of window into the minds of the Lisles.

"I suppose it's not that unusual for the vicar's brothers to visit him," Ivy said as she picked up her soup spoon. "It's just the appearance of two of them separately at around the same time. Don't you agree, Sophia? What does Benedick say?"

"I am hardly the man's confidante," Sophia said with frown. "We are working together on the matter of a possible forger, and he was kind enough to take my side against Mr. Morgan, but it's not as if we have spent hours together discussing our feelings."

"You must have talked about something on the drive

to and from Primrose Green this morning," Daphne said, tilting her blond head in that questioning way she had. Normally Sophia found it endearing, but today it had the opposite effect.

"You seemed quite friendly when you burst in on Lord Cameron and me," Gemma offered with a shrug.

She wasn't sure why, but Sophia felt cornered, and she didn't care for it at all.

"I wasn't expecting the Spanish Inquisition," she said tartly. "Would you like to go get the thumbscrews, Daphne? I'll wait."

Ivy bit back a laugh. "My goodness, it would appear that someone is sensitive over the subject of our handsome vicar."

"I am nothing of the sort," Sophia said crossly. "I simply do not enjoy being interrogated by my friends. And my sister. We didn't quiz you when you were suddenly going off with Lord Kerr on various errands alone."

"But that implies that your errands with the vicar are of a similar nature," Daphne said triumphantly. At Sophia's scowl, she added with a shrug, "It's logic. You cannot argue with logic, Sophia."

"Can we not just enjoy our meal without discussing the vicar, or his brothers, or your sudden baseless speculations about the nature of my friendship with him?" It was odd even to Sophia that she was so overset by their teasing. She only knew that whatever it was she had with Ben was new enough to be fragile and might not stand up to the harsh light of day. And aside from that, she had other things to worry about. Ensuring that the most important work of her life was part of the exhibition. Perhaps then she would think about whatever it was she and the vicar had been tiptoeing around.

Besides. She'd seen enough infatuations of a few days' duration to know that it was far too soon to think about Ben in those terms. For all she knew, he'd meet the love of his life when he was paying calls in the village and not give her a second thought.

To her surprise, since her sister was often her most ardent teaser, it was Gemma who came to her rescue. "I suppose we've nettled you enough. Though I hope you will remember this when it comes time for you to scold me about my behavior with Lord Cameron."

"My maid told me she heard the shouting from the laundry," Daphne said with an admiring glance at Gemma. "I must admit I enjoyed hearing that you gave the male editor of a scholarly journal a set down. I've known several in my time who deserved worse."

"Do not encourage her," Sophia said, giving her sister a speaking look. "It might have been cathartic, but it really is not the thing to shout at a gentleman you don't even know. Though I do know your nerves were overset, Gemma, you must know you crossed a line. As did Lord Cameron. It was badly done on both your parts."

"So much for not scolding me," Gemma said under her breath. Aloud she said, "I am sorry for losing my temper. It was not becoming. And I am grateful you arrived when you did."

"And I'm sorry you were so upset," Sophia said, grasping her sister by the hand. "I must confess, I find it difficult to believe that Lord Cameron's manners are so lacking given . . ."

"I thought we weren't going to speak of the Lisle brothers any longer," Daphne cut in. "I really wish someone would ensure that we keep this conversation on track. I don't know if I'm coming or going."

Sophia felt a pang of conscience. Daphne was right. She was being hypocritical.

"Good point, Daphne," she said with a nod. "I broke my own rule."

They were silent for a moment as they concentrated on the delicious fish pie cook had presented for luncheon.

"Where is Serena today?" Sophia asked, noting for the first time that their chaperone—and sister to the Duke of Maitland—was absent from the table. "She would have reined us in before we came to such a pass."

"Jeremy has a cold, poor dear, and Serena is sitting with him while he's feeling poorly," Ivy said with a sympathetic frown. "She's taking a tray in the nursery."

Though the boy was old enough to have been sent away to school, Serena was determined to keep her son at home and away from the often brutal realities of Eton for as long as she could. Sophia couldn't blame her. Especially given the bad behavior the boy had already witnessed from his now deceased father.

"I'm sorry to hear it," Sophia said aloud. "Is there anything we can do?"

"She says not." Ivy shrugged. "I already asked. And Dr. Holmes had a look in on him yesterday when he was here to see you. He says it's nothing to worry about."

Both Lady Serena and Jeremy had become dear to the heiresses in their time at Beauchamp House, and the ladies discussed possible trinkets available in town they might purchase for the child. Nothing too dear, but well suited to divert an ailing child from his misery.

Once they'd settled on a plan, the conversation turned to the exhibition.

"You didn't tell us what the Primbles said about your paintings, Sophia," Gemma said. "Are they going to back you against Morgan?"

"Yes," Sophia said, pleased with that portion of the visit to the Primbles. She filled them in on what the couple had said regarding her place in the exhibition, and their assessment of Ryder as the possible forger.

"Is he the unpleasant fellow who none-too-subtly attempted to determine the amount of each potential dance partner's dowry before he would sign their dance cards?" Gemma asked with a look of disgust. "He is not terrible to look at, but I confess I cannot understand why any of the young ladies present consented to stand up with him."

"He has the unqualified support of his patron." Ivy's mouth pursed in distaste. "Ryder himself might not have wealth or talent, but he has the support of Morgan. And Morgan is not without some degree of influence. Both in Little Seaford, and in some circles in a certain part of London. He may not be a pillar of polite society, but he holds some sway in the middle class. And like it or not, many genteel families with land have a need for the infusion of funds that a connection to Morgan might give them."

If it had been Morgan she and Ben overheard at the ball, perhaps the politician's support of Ryder wasn't as strong as they thought. Without any means of identifying the voices they'd heard, however, it was entirely possible it was someone else who threatened murder. Given her own animus toward Morgan, it would be so much more satisfying to learn he was a criminal. But the truth of the matter was she had no idea. Not with any degree of certainty.

"Did any of you get the feeling that anyone else was particularly interested in Ryder at the ball?" she asked her friends. "Not ladies, but perhaps men who seemed to be taking him under their wing. In a manner similar to the way Morgan did?"

"He seemed to be very friendly with the mayor, Mr. Ivens, and of course Mr. Framingham, but he owns one of the galleries in town, so that's not unusual," Gemma said. "Why do you ask?"

At the mention of Framingham, Sophia's heart began to beat faster. As owner of one of the two galleries in town, Framingham was in a prime position to sell forged paintings. He had the connections in town that would allow him to know exactly what sort of works the newly wealthy middle class were seeking to furnish their homes with. And he knew which artists were least likely to draw suspicion from the authorities. It was much less risky to attempt to sell a forged version of a work by lesser-known Renaissance artists, than, say Tintoretto. And Framingham would know that.

Surely it wouldn't be out of the ordinary if she were to pay a visit to Framingham's gallery while they were in town purchasing things for little Jeremy.

"So," she said, trying to sound casual, "are we all agreed that a trip to the village is in order this afternoon? I should also like to look at the selection of ribbon at White's. My chip bonnet is sadly in need of refurbishing and I'd like a little project to take my mind of this business with Morgan."

To her relief, no one seemed to guess the secondary reason for her enthusiasm for the shopping excursion. And, not too much later, all four ladies were settled in the open carriage, on their way into Little Seaford.

Jeffries was waiting at the door when Ben arrived back at the vicarage from Beauchamp House, accompanied by Cam.

That another of the vicar's brothers had arrived for a visit seemed not to faze him. But the note that had come while Ben was out seemed to be burning the hand that held it.

"This came for you, my lord," he said with a speaking look as he handed it over. "It was tucked into the door jamb. I found it just after you left this morning."

It wasn't unusual for Ben, as the local clergyman, to receive anonymous notes, deliveries of produce as tithe, and even once a cage of chickens. But something about this note must be troubling his butler.

"What's amiss, Jeffries?" he asked, ignoring the smirk on Cam's face. His brother's wandering allowed him to get through life without the responsibility of personal servants. He claimed it was the best way to live, though Ben had his doubts.

"It's just that this arrived without me knowing it, my lord," the butler said in a low, harassed voice. "I always know when someone is delivering something. Even the chickens."

Since the chickens had been rather loud it wasn't exactly a glowing example of the man's all-knowing nature.

"Well, it does happen sometimes," Ben reassured him. "Even the sharpest eye can miss a detail from time to time."

That didn't seem to appease the man, but he took himself off to the kitchens to perhaps vent his frustration on the cook.

"I suppose I'll take myself off, then," Cam said with a wry grin. "When you begin dealing with domestic issues, it's time for me to go back to my vagabond life."

"You just got here," Ben said, not really surprised, but not willing to let his brother off the hook either. "At least Freddie stayed a couple of days when he breezed through."

"I came to confront the man I thought had insulted

me," Cam said with a shrug. "Now that I've discovered he's a lady, I have no more need to be here."

"You can't cozen me, brother. I saw the way you looked at her when she wasn't looking at you." Ben had been amused to see his usually diffident brother fall under the spell of Gemma's spirit. She was lovely— though he was partial to her sister's softer beauty, of course—and Cam had definitely been intrigued.

"And that is exactly why I need to leave," Cam said ruefully. "I might be attracted, but a smart man removes himself from danger before it becomes a real risk. You'd do well to do the same if you know what's good for you."

"Perhaps I'm not so fearful of getting caught," Ben said with a shrug. In fact, he was rather certain he'd found the woman he wanted to spend the rest of his life with.

It took a moment for the realization to sink in.

He blinked.

He wanted to get caught. He wanted to marry her.

Miss Sophia Hastings.

Ben felt the uncanny sensation of rightness that came from knowing his own mind.

He'd only experienced it one other time in his life: when he decided to follow his heart and join the church.

Despite the fact that he was grinning like an idiot, however, his brother was, as per usual, oblivious.

"To each his own," Cam said with a shake of his head. "I'm going to go back to my happy bachelor life and leave you to your little artist. Don't want any of that nonsense rubbing off on me. It's bad enough Archer and Freddie have fallen."

One day, Ben thought wryly as he cuffed his brother on the shoulder. One day Cam would succumb to love's siren song.

However he might try to avoid it.

"The next time you come for a visit, please endeavor not to overset my lady or her sister," he said aloud. Though despite the chiding remark, he was sad to see him go. He missed his brothers, living as he did, away from them.

But Cam didn't seem to mind the scold. "I'll do my best, though you know I've got a particular knack for setting up ladies' backs."

And with an answering clap on his elder brother's shoulder, he took himself off.

When he was gone, Ben took the anonymous note to his study, poured himself a brandy, and broke the seal on the missive.

I HAVE INFORMATION ABOUT THE PAINTINGS. COME
TO FRAMINGHAM GALLERY TODAY AT 3PM
A FRIEND

He'd donned his hat and coat again and was on his way into the village before the brandy settled again inside the cut crystal glass.

Chapter 14

The drive into the village wasn't a long one, but Sophia took the time while Daphne and Ivy were in their own conversation to speak with her sister.

Touching Gemma on the arm, she asked in a low voice, "Are you sure you're well after your contretemps with Lord Cameron this afternoon? He did seem to be remorseful later, but he was quite harsh to begin with."

Gemma, who had been scanning the horizon, likely hoping for a glimpse of the sea, turned to her with a laugh. "Of course, my dear." She gave her a half hug. "It takes more than a dressing down from that sort of man to dim my enthusiasm."

She lifted a dark brow and countered, "I should ask you if you're sanguine that he'll quite likely be your brother-in-law. It's a shame such a self-important prig should be related to a man as delightful as Lord Benedick."

Sophia felt her face burn. "I shouldn't be so quick to assume any sort of permanent match between the vicar and me, Gemma," she said hastily. "We are friends, that is all. If something more should come of our association . . ."

But Gemma was no more ready to believe Sophia's denials than Sophia was prepared to believe Gemma had emerged from that afternoon's argument unscathed. "It's as plain as punch that he's smitten. Why on earth would he have brought both his brothers to visit you in the space of week if he felt otherwise?"

"That was because of the business with the forger," Sophia said with a shake of her head. "At least, that's why he brought Lord Frederick. And we are his closest neighbors so it's hardly a surprise that he would call with his houseguests."

Her stomach flipped at the notion whatever it was between them could lead to something permanent. Of course she was hardly unaware of the logical conclusion of mutual attraction, but then, too, she knew that most meetings of the mind lasted only a few days before one or the other party lost interest and moved on.

"You may pretend to yourself that it's nothing more than good manners that has the vicar paying calls so often," Gemma said with a shake of her head. "But that doesn't explain the way his eyes follow you whenever you're in a room together."

"Since when are you so observant?" Sophia asked pettishly. She wasn't accustomed to Gemma being the one to point out home truths to her and not the other way round.

"You might think me a daydreamer, sister," Gemma chided, "But that doesn't mean I'm entirely without the ability to notice what's right under my nose."

Then, as if unable to keep from admitting the truth, she added, "And Daphne and Ivy are convinced you'll make a match of it. Once they pointed it out, I saw for myself the truth of it."

Sophia gave a frustrated sigh. There were many things

she appreciated about living amongst the most intelligent ladies she'd ever known, but having that intellect turned upon her own life was not one of them.

"Oh, do not take on so," Gemma said, patting her on the hand. "We all quite like him. And it never hurts to have a man of God on one's side in a fight."

That only made Sophia's heart twist. "Gemma," she said in a hushed tone. "What do I know about being a vicar's wife? I'm not even particularly devout. And I certainly know nothing about keeping house or running a village fete, or whatever it is a clergyman's helpmeet is expected to do."

At that confession, her sister's brow furrowed in sympathy. "I'm probably the wrong person to ask, dearest, given that I too know little about the sorts of things other ladies are taught from the time they're small. I cannot regret our unconventional education, but I would not have objected to at least a bit of household management from Mama in addition to the lessons Aunt Dahlia gave us."

At the mention of Dahlia, Sophia's head snapped up. "That reminds me that I've a letter for her in my reticule. I do wish the mail coach ran faster. I should like to know what she thinks about Mr. Morgan's possible involvement in the forgery scheme. She might know whether he has any connections to the art world in Manchester."

Though her mention of Dahlia was indeed sparked by her sister's words, it was also true that Sophia had taken advantage of the opportunity to change the subject. She did have concerns about her suitability as a wife should the attraction with Ben turn to something more serious, but she didn't want to dwell on the matter. Especially when so many other important matters were on her mind.

Gemma seemed to accept the diversion and they

chatted about their aunt for a few moments until the carriage came to a stop in the village.

She waited for Ivy and Daphne to go inside before she
lay a hand on her sister's arm. "I've just remembered I
need to stop in at Framingham's to see if he knows
where in the exhibition hall my paintings will go. I'll only
be a minute."

Gemma rolled her eyes. "I should have known," she
said with sigh. "Why didn't you just say you wanted to
question Framingham?"

"Keep your voice down," Sophia hissed. "I don't want
everyone in the street to know my plans."

"And what are those plans?" Gemma asked in a lowered voice. "You are not a Bow Street Runner, Sophia.
And recall what sort of danger Ivy and Daphne found
themselves in when they began meddling in dangerous
matters. They were almost killed."

Sophia gaped at her sister. "They only began asking
questions because Lady Celeste asked them to. She may
not have known about this particular business, but she
would certainly be against it if she had. Any artist with
integrity would be."

Looking as if she knew that argument was futile,
Gemma threw up her hands. "I give up. You're going to
do what you think best anyway. You always have. Just
promise me that you'll be careful." Her gaze softened.
"You're my only sister and I cannot afford to find another one."

"I promise," Sophia said with an answering smile.
Her sister might be the only person in the world who
could set her back up in mere seconds, but she was also
her dearest friend. "Now, go inside and make my excuses. I'll only be a few minutes."

* * *

In the intervening hour before he was expected at Framingham's shop, Ben paid a call at the home of a local widow, Mrs. Debenham. A sweet-tempered lady of middle years, she'd been left to raise three daughters on her own when her husband died only a year or so ago of influenza.

Though she'd seemed to be coming out of her shell a bit now that her official mourning period was over, he'd noticed her waiting to speak to him after services this past Sunday. But when he'd finally managed to extricate himself from a particularly loquacious elderly parishioner, Mrs. Debenham had been gone.

He'd always been adept at reading people. Even as a child he'd been able to anticipate what his brothers or parents would say or do, sometimes before they themselves seemed to know it. It was a skill that had served him well in his calling. Persuasion and guidance were almost as important in the vicarage as preaching.

So, he'd known something was amiss with Mrs. Debenham, and for the moment, set aside his anticipation of the meeting at Framingham's to focus on his duty as a vicar.

The door was opened by Miss Temple, the widow's spinster sister who had come to live with her after Mr. Debenham's untimely death.

To Ben's concern, her expression when she recognized him was one of relief. "Oh, Vicar, I'm so glad you're here. I told Helen she needed to speak to someone in authority about this."

Before he could ask just what "this" could be, he was ushered into the tidy front parlor of the Debenham house, where he saw Mrs. Debenham seated on a long sofa, a handkerchief crumpled in her hand. She'd obviously been weeping.

On seeing Ben, however, she sat up straighter. Wiping at her face, and sliding a hand over her hair, she said in a thick voice, "Lord Benedick, what a mess you must think me."

She made to rise, but Ben urged her to remain seated. Rather than take a chair, he crouched on his haunches in front of her, and took her hand. "My dear Mrs. Debenham," he said in a calm tone, "whatever can I do to help?"

"Oh, but I—," she protested, shaking her head. "That is to say, I shouldn't—"

"Helen," Miss Temple said in a bracing tone, "Tell him. Someone needs to know what that man did."

At the mention of a man, Ben's heart sank. He knew all too well what indignities could be visited upon the persons of those ladies without male relatives in the house. Especially by those opportunistic men who saw such women as easy prey.

Mrs. Debenham's brown eyes filled with tears at her sister's words. "Oh dear me. I am sorry, Lord Benedick," she said in a broken voice. "It's really not such a calamity as my sister makes out."

Though Miss Temple made a frustrated sound behind them, Ben said nothing, waiting for the widow to speak in her own time.

Once she'd gained her composure, she took in a deep breath and said, "I suppose if you're here, I do need to speak of this with someone. And you've always been kind to me, Lord Benedick. Especially after my husband died."

"Tell him," Miss Temple said, though this time, Ben

noticed a pleading tone in her voice. Whatever had happened, it had truly overset the widow's sister.

"It's a little thing, really," Mrs. Debenham said, her pale complexion reddening a little. "It's just that when I was leaving the stationer's last week I ran into Mr. Morgan and his friend, the artist, Mr. Ryder."

At the mention of Ryder, Ben's focus sharpened.

Aloud he said, "What happened, Mrs. Debenham?" Knowing both Morgan and Ryder were involved, he had no expectation that the matter was a "little thing" as she'd characterized it.

"I had just stepped out into the street, when Mr. Morgan and Mr. Ryder approached. And since we'd been introduced, I greeted them, then made as if to continue on. But Mr. Morgan, well, he stopped me."

Ben's jaw clenched but he said nothing. At the very least, the fact that the encounter took place on a public thoroughfare told him the physical assault he'd feared was unlikely.

"He had spoken to me in the past," she said in a tight voice. "You know how some gentlemen are with widows?"

She didn't wish to say aloud what he'd told her, that much was obvious, but Ben knew well enough the attitude she spoke of.

"He urged Mr. Ryder to continue on without him," she said. "And I guessed he'd attempt to persuade me again. And I was correct. Only this time, he was much more . . . forceful."

"What did he say, Mrs. Debenham?" Ben asked, keeping his voice even with some difficulty.

"He asked me again, and I declined, of course. But then he said that if I continued to refuse him, he would spread it about that I'd consented, and I'd be ruined." Her mouth was tight with anger. "He wanted to frighten me into doing as he wished, Lord Benedick. And he knows how important my reputation is. Especially when I've three young daughters to see well matched in the next few years."

The anger that washed over him was familiar. It was the same kind he dealt with whenever he witnessed the kind of brute cruelty humankind could visit upon one another. More than ever, he wanted to find some connection between Morgan and the forgers so that the industrialist would pay not only for those crimes, but the ones like this against Mrs. Debenham. The poor woman had already been through enough difficulty to last a lifetime. That Morgan had seen fit to heap more upon her with his lewd suggestions and threats was really the outside of enough.

"Your sister was right to urge you to tell me, Mrs. Debenham," he said in a comforting tone. "I hope you will never fear informing me of any difficulties you may have. All the sin in this instance is Morgan's, not yours. And though I know it might be embarrassing to confess such an encounter, such bullying needs to be brought into the light if it is to be combatted."

"Oh, but I hope you won't speak to anyone about it, Vicar," she said with an expression of alarm. "If word should get out . . ."

"Of course I shall tell no one," he assured her, rising to his feet. "But I do beg your permission to have a word with Mr. Morgan on the matter."

Mrs. Debenham swallowed, but nodded as her sister sat down beside her and took her hand. "I would appreciate that, Lord Benedick. Though I do wish it wasn't necessary."

"As do I, my dear," he said with a reassuring nod. "But I find much of the time men like this need only a few choice words to put them in their place. And as frustrating as it may be, they often listen to objections from other men with far more attention than those from ladies."

"He's a brute," Miss Temple said with a scowl. "Trying to pass himself off as a gentleman when he has no more manners than a pig in the pen."

Ben agreed with her, but could hardly say so given his role in the conversation. Instead he only nodded. "He needs to know that such threats are unacceptable."

If necessary, he'd use his father's status as a duke to enforce his rebuke. Ben had few qualms about leveraging the privilege he'd been born with to effect good in the world. He had little enough use for it in his everyday life. Let his accident of birth persuade Morgan to behave himself.

Assured that Mrs. Debenham had been calmed, and confident that her sister would take good care of her, he left the little house and stepped out into the bright light of the main street of Little Seaford.

Sophia waited until the door had closed behind Gemma before crossing to the other side of the street to Framingham's Gallery. Its window had several prints by well-known artists, and a few original paintings by lesser-known ones. But the sign on the door proclaimed the shop to be a purveyor of fine art.

When she stepped through the door, the first thing she noted was that there seemed to be no one in the main gallery. The counter where one would expect Mr. Framingham to position himself was empty.

She rang the bell on the counter, then began to wander the room.

For a gallery in a small coastal village, it boasted

some pieces by several rather well-known artists. But she was not surprised to see some work from the residents of Primrose Green in the mix, some of it quite good—like a landscape by Mr. George Rollins, and a still life by Mrs. Primble herself—and some of it rather mediocre—like an oil on canvas of what appeared to be a depiction of the death of Achilles by Morgan's protégé, Thomas Ryder.

As she often did, Sophia became immersed in the art around her, taking in each brush stroke, examining the scale, perspective, and composition of each work. So engrossed was she that as she stood before Ryder's painting, she was unaware that someone was standing behind her until he spoke.

"What are you doing here?"

Unable to stop herself, Sophia let out a little squeak of surprise at the intrusion and spun around at once to face her accuser.

To her surprise it was not Mr. Framingham, but Thomas Ryder—his dark brow lowered with menace—who stood behind her. His entire mien was one of aggression and for a moment, Sophia feared for her physical safety. He was not a small man, despite his occupation, and though she was no slight thing, he could easily knock her unconscious and carry her away with no one the wiser. At the thought, her heart, already racing, beat faster.

"You are not welcome here," he continued, pointing an accusing finger. "Not after all the trouble you've been causing me. Asking questions at Primrose Green. Sticking your nose where it doesn't belong. Framingham is a friend of mine and I know he would agree."

He wasn't a particularly large man, but there was no mistaking the menace in his tone.

Gaining control of her growing sense of alarm, Sophia imposed a calm she did not feel over herself before she spoke. "Hello, Mr. Ryder," she said, offering her hand. "I don't believe we've been introduced. Though it would appear that you already know who I am."

"Indeed I do, Miss Hastings," Ryder said with a scowl, ignoring her proffered hand. "You're the busybody who doesn't know how to mind her own business."

As he spoke, he stepped closer, forcing Sophia to crowd back against the wall to get away from him. She was grateful she had her walking stick with her, but she was unsure of whether she'd be able to wield it with enough force to do more than stun him. Still, she couldn't let him get away with his threats.

"Forgery is the business of every artist who cares about the integrity of their work. Surely you can see why I would wish to investigate the possibility of such a thing happening here in my own village. You should be interested too, Mr. Ryder," Sophia said calmly. Though her stomach was clenched with anxiety, she maintained a façade of calm.

"I don't know what that's got to do with me," he asked crossly. " And you've got some nerve to call yourself an artist. From what I've heard, you're no more than a provocateur with a paintbrush and a desire to stir up trouble. What I paint is what people wish to buy, to display in their homes, to look at every day and appreciate. What you paint is obscene and no decent person would wish to look at it in an exhibition much less put it in a place of prominence in their home. People like you disgust me."

"You mean artists with original ideas who attempt to provoke thought in their viewers?"

Sophia knew as soon as she said the words that it was

unwise to needle the man, and the flare of genuine rage in his eyes made her cringe backward, though there was nowhere for her to go. She watched in horrified slow motion as his clenched fist rose as if he would strike her. She lifted her walking stick and was about to raise it to block the blow, when she saw someone tackle the artist from behind.

Surprised, she lowered her stick and watched as Ben, his face a mask of barely leashed anger, tussled with Ryder, finally managing to pin the other man's hands behind his back.

"Even a boy in the schoolroom, Ryder, knows that a gentleman does not raise his hand against a lady," Ben said through his teeth as he easily held the scowling artist. "I believe you owe Miss Hastings an apology." Ryder gave them both a mulish glare. "Fine," he said. "My apologies Miss Hastings."

She waited for him to go on, but it appeared that those were the only words of amends he was prepared to make. Even so, Ben let the other man go.

"You should both learn to mind your own business," Ryder said flatly. "This is something that could prove dangerous to both of you. And if you know what's good for you, Miss Hastings, you'll choose not to show your work in the exhibition. Morgan is a powerful man and what he says in the town goes. You'd do well to remember that."

Ben had moved to her side and they watched as Ryder strode away and out the front door of the gallery.

Once he was gone, Sophia felt herself begin to tremble, and with a low curse, Ben pulled her against him and wrapped his arms around her. She buried her face in his shoulder and let him hold her. Taking strength from his nearness and sheer physical presence. They were blocked from view through the window and from the other part of the shop by a large floor-to-ceiling piece that was propped against a pillar.

"I could have killed him with my bare hands when I saw him looming over you," he said into her hair, holding her tightly against him. "I don't think I've ever been that fiercely angry in my entire life."

"Thank goodness you happened by." She had been prepared to use her walking stick against Ryder, but it would have required her to put her full weight on both ankles. And there was no guarantee the injured one would hold up to such stress without the assistance of her cane. "He was prepared to strike me. I could see it in his face. His stance."

Rather than respond, Ben made a low noise that was almost a growl. And without a word he bent his head to hers and took her mouth with a kiss as much a claiming as a caress.

Ben had been telling the truth when he told Sophia he'd never felt such rage.

Coming on the heels of Mrs. Debenham's revelation about the way Morgan had treated her—and knowing that Morgan was the artist's patron—the sight of Sophia in range of Ryder's raised fist had filled him with a primitive desire to hurt the other man. Not to simply stop him from harming Sophia. But to lift him bodily and beat him with his bare fists.

It was a new, and somewhat disturbing bit of self-discovery, and if Sophia hadn't been there to witness the whole thing, he might not have been able to control himself. He wanted to believe his conscience would have been enough to pull him back from the edge, but the truth was that seeing Sophia in peril had flipped some sort of switch within him. And whether it was instinct or some other force, it had been as strong as any he'd ever felt.

And just as instinctive was the need to pull her into his arms. To give comfort, true, but also to prove to them both that this connection between them, new as it may be, was real, and though she might not know it yet, she was his.

At first his kiss was firm, a sort of claiming, and Sophia kissed him back with just as much emotion. But soon the softness of her lips against his and the feel of her curves pressed against him made him gentle the caress. He stroked his tongue over the seam of her lips, asking for entry and when she opened beneath him like a flower, he took the invitation. Her mouth was hot and wet and he bit back a groan when her tongue met his. This was what he'd needed, he realized. Holding her, feeling her life force pressed against him, proving to him in the most physical way that she was safe and alive and his.

They stood together for several long moments, lost in each other. So, it was a surprise when a shout sounded from somewhere beyond them.

"Oh God! No!"

Ben and Sophia pulled away from one another and turned as one toward the direction from which the outburst had come. Sophie started forward, heading further into the shop, and to the source of the noise.

But Ben put a staying hand on her. "You'd better let me go first. We don't know what's going on back there. And with the threats Ryder made and the talk of illegality, it might be dangerous."

Sophia looked as if she wanted to argue, her blue eyes narrow with impatience. But she must have seen the practicality of his words, for she allowed him to step in front of her and lead the way toward the door then into the storage area in the rear of the gallery.

The door itself was ajar, and Ben indicated with a finger to his lips that Sophia should remain quiet while he stepped inside.

She gave a nod and he pressed the door open fully and saw that the storage area was actually being used for that purpose. Stacked against the walls were paintings of all sizes and types; some were framed, some were not, and some appeared to be unfinished. There were also easels, and various other stands for displaying works of art, mostly paintings, but there were some that seemed better suited for sculpture and pottery. It was not particularly tidy, but there seemed to be nothing out of the ordinary for such a storage room.

With one exception.

Just beyond the table inside the door, where it was obvious someone had been working on a framing project, the pieces of an ornate gilded frame lay beside a canvas face down on the surface. And just beyond that, stood Ryder, his head down, staring at the scene on the floor before him.

There was no question in Ben's mind that Framingham—for it was he whose battered body lay bleeding on the floor of his own shop—was dead. No one could lose the amount of blood pooled on the floor beneath him and live.

"Ryder," Ben said, stepping forward, "what happened?"

The other man, who so lately had looked at both Ben and Sophia with undisguised dislike, now seemed relieved to see them. "I don't know. He was like this when I came back here."

Then he seemed to realize that they might not have the most flattering interpretation of his presence there. He raised his hands in a gesture of innocence. "You saw me only minutes ago. He's obviously been bleeding for an hour or more. I didn't do this."

As much as he'd have liked to see the man punished for what he'd done to Sophia, Ben was forced to admit that Ryder was correct. The timing made the possibility highly unlikely.

"We know," he said with a nod. Then, he made his way over to the body of Framingham, and wordlessly knelt beside him. He said a silent prayer that the man's death had been swift and that he'd not felt too much pain, and placing his hand on the dead man's forehead, he said the words that would entrust his soul into the hands of his Creator. "Through the merits of Jesus Christ thine only son our Lord. Amen."

Ryder and Sophia, who had stepped forward to stand beside him, stood watching as Ben closed the dead man's eyes and rose to his feet. "We'll need to alert the authorities," he said to Ryder, who nodded, his face pale as he looked everywhere but at the corpse between them.

"I'll go," he said, obviously eager to get out of the close room.

He was gone before either Ben or Sophia could respond.

Stepping around the body, Ben put an arm around Sophia and gently led her back toward the door and back into the gallery proper. "You shouldn't have come in here," he said. "You didn't need to see that."

But Sophia, though she let him lead her away, wasn't so ready to agree. "Why should you have to see it while I'm sheltered?" she asked, slipping her arm through his. "It must be just as upsetting for you as it is for me."

He couldn't help but smile at her oh-so-rational response. "It's not that it doesn't upset me," he reasoned, "it's that you don't need that scene in your mind. I've seen death. It's one of the most difficult parts of my calling, but a necessary one. And an inevitable part of life."

"But this," he continued, turning to face her, feeling more exhausted than he'd ever been. "This is not inevitable. It's the worst part of what one human being can do to another. And I should have protected you from it."

When she slipped her arms around him it was to offer comfort. And selfishly he took it. He'd seen death before, but what had been done to Framingham was a level of savagery that left him shaken.

"Sophia?" called a female voice from the front of the room. "Are you still here?"

Reluctantly, he pulled away from her and they walked back toward the door, where they found not only Gemma but Ivy and Daphne hovering just inside the entrance.

"Ah," Ivy said with a twinkle in her eyes. "Good afternoon, Vicar. I might have guessed it was you who waylaid Miss Hastings."

But something about both his and Sophia's expressions must have alerted her to the fact that something was very wrong.

"Oh no," she said, her own face turning from teasing to serious. "What's happened?"

"Are you well?" Gemma asked, stepping forward, gazing at her sister as if she could divine the source of Sophia's angst through sheer will. "Did something happen? Did someone harm you?"

Ben would have responded, but Sophia pulled away from him and gave her sister a little hug. "I'm fine," she said, before turning to address the others who were watching with varying degrees of concern. "There's been a . . . that is to say, Mr. Framingham is . . ."

"Framingham has been murdered," Ben cut in, thinking it best to tell the truth of the matter. "We don't know who did it, but it seems that he must have been dead when Sophia first entered the shop. Ryder has gone to alert the authorities. The magistrate, I suppose." It was too late for the doctor to do much good.

"Dear God," Ivy put a hand to her chest. "Another?"

It had only been a few weeks after Ben's arrival in the area that a man had been found murdered in the library at Beauchamp House. These ladies were not entirely unfamiliar with violent death, much as he wished Sophia had been spared this particular encounter.

"Statistically," Daphne said, sounding at once authoritative and worried, "it seems highly unusual that three people so far removed from the criminal underworld should be murdered within the same general area."

"Indeed," Sophia said with a nod to her friend. Ben saw that she gave the other woman a squeeze on the arm. "It is unusual, I think. Right now, though, I think we should probably leave so that when the doctor and the magistrate get here we won't be underfoot."

"Squire Northman will wish to speak to you," Gemma reminded her. They were well acquainted with Northman from his investigation of the previous deaths they'd been connected to.

"Then he can do so at a later time," Ben said firmly. "Let me see you to your carriage. At least I hope you came by carriage." He gave a speaking look in the direction of Sophia's injured ankle. She was leaning heavily on the walking stick at this point and it was no doubt paining her.

"Yes, we brought the carriage," she said wearily. "And I've never been so grateful for it."

The others preceded them from the shop, and Ben took the moment of privacy to squeeze her hand. "I'll come speak to you as soon as I learn anything. Though I may be tied up with Framingham's family for a while this evening. No doubt this will be a surprise to his wife and children. And I need to ensure that they've got sufficient support."

She turned and touched his cheek with her gloved hand. It was no more than that, but he felt it like a more intimate caress. "Take care of yourself," she said softly. "And watch Ryder. He was stunned by the sight of Framingham, but he's not entirely uninvolved, I think."

"Yes, ma'am," he said with a grin. Then, when they'd reached the place where the landau was waiting, he lifted her by the waist and tucked her into the empty seat beside Gemma.

"Keep an eye on her for me, ladies," he said with a tip of his hat.

Sophia looked surprised, but not particularly displeased by his admonition.

And as he watched the coachman flicked the horses with the whip and they drove away.

Chapter 15

After dinner that night, still rattled from the murder of Mr. Framingham and not wanting to be alone, Sophia asked the other ladies to join her for tea in her studio. She wasn't sure why, but she felt as if art itself were under attack. Especially after Thomas Ryder's harsh words about her work, and seeing poor Framingham dead among the paintings and canvases of his workroom. Someone—maybe Ryder, and definitely others—was cheapening the heart and soul of what made art valuable by creating fakes. And though she was certainly in no way comparable to the great artists whose work had been forged, it chilled her to think of a fellow artist carefully stealing every brushstroke, every carefully plotted decision about composition simply to make a profit.

"I don't think I've been up here since you finished your pieces for the exhibition," Ivy said as she and Daphne followed Sophia and Gemma into the studio.

The natural light from the windows and skylights was absent now that the sun had gone down, and the room was somehow cozier in the glow of lamplight. Even so, it was bright enough for Ivy to spot the fallen woman painting from the doorway and she and Daphne made a beeline for it.

"Oh, Sophia," the marchioness said with wonder and sadness in her voice, "it's magnificent."

Sophia never knew how to accept compliments about her work. She liked it, obviously, but there was also a sort of awkwardness that came from confronting the fact that another person—sometimes a stranger, though in this case a friend—was looking at something that had come directly from her soul. It was rather like having one's diary read aloud in a crowded room.

Before she could respond, Ivy continued. "It's heart-wrenching. The contrast between the gaiety of the theatregoers and the utter sadness of the dead woman just steps away. Have you seen something like this? How did you decide to paint it?"

They moved to settle around the low table in the corner where the servants had laid the tea service and a plate of cakes. Sophia's maid had wrapped her ankle in the way the doctor had showed her and because it had swollen again in the wake of the day's activity, she had it propped on an ottoman.

"It was a small article in the *Times*," she answered once they each had a cup and saucer in hand. "Just a paragraph, really, about a woman found dead near the Royal Opera House. No details. Other than to say that she had died of exposure. Something about the juxtaposition of the dead woman and the site of so many of polite society's evening entertainments struck me as particularly shattering. And my imagination did the rest."

"Have you ever been to the Royal Opera House?" Daphne asked, brow furrowed. "I went once during my first season. This is a remarkably accurate depiction." She sounded as if she suspected Sophia of some sort of witchcraft. "Though, there was no dead woman, fallen or otherwise, in that area. At least not that I saw."

Sophia hid a smile. Daphne could be a bit literal at times.

"Our Aunt Dahlia took us to London many times over the years," Gemma said. "Including the Royal Opera House."

"During the day it was galleries and museums and parks," Sophia said with a smile of remembrance, "but in the evenings she took us to the opera, and plays, and fed our minds with great performances."

"She sounds as if she would have got along well with Lady Celeste," Ivy said with a grin. "I wonder if they ever met."

It was something Sophia had thought about before. Her aunt and Celeste had been of an age, and could have attended some of the same entertainments in London when they were young. And they certainly seemed to have similar leanings toward intellectualism and the arts. Still, she had no way of knowing. There had been no mention of her in Celeste's diaries which they'd had to read in order to find out who had killed her.

"I shall write to her and ask," she said aloud, " And until I hear back, I propose we behave as if they did."

She raised her teacup in a toast. "To Dahlia and Celeste—the two ladies who made me what I am today!"

"And the same for me," Gemma said, raising her own cup. Then, Ivy and Daphne followed suit and they drank to the mentors.

"Speaking of Celeste," Ivy said when they'd finished, "I wonder what she would have made of this forgery business. I know what she would have said regarding Morgan and his ridiculous attempts to stop you from showing your work, Sophia. But as a painter herself, she must have

had opinions about forgery and schemes like the one
Lord Frederick alerted his brother to. I know there have
been instances in the world of historical artifacts when
people have attempted to pass off fakes as original frag-
ments of Sappho, for instance. It makes me ill."

It was something Sophia had thought about, especially given that this particular scheme was taking
place in the very village where Celeste had lived. The
Home Office had only timed the forgeries coming out of
Little Seaford to a year ago—several months before the
heiresses had arrived at Beauchamp House, and only
weeks before Celeste's death. Though it was possible
their benefactor had known something was going on, it
was far more likely she was too sick to know or care.

"I feel sure she would have had objections," Sophia
agreed. "But I'm not sure the timing is right. Though I
suppose it is possible the scheme began before the authorities realized it was going on. It seems to have run
too smoothly to be a new endeavor."

"And from what you and Benedick overheard,"
Gemma reminded her, "they don't seem to be loyal to
whichever artist they use to create the forgeries. It's possible there was someone before this latest one."

Which reminded Sophia of something. "But what
happened to Mr. Framingham doesn't make sense given
what we heard. It was clear from the conversation that
they would be eliminating an *artist*. Not an art dealer.
Why was Framingham killed and not Ryder—if he is the
one who is painting the forgeries?"

In the chaos of the afternoon's events, the conversation about the artist had slipped her mind. But now it was
like a sore tooth she couldn't stop poking at.

"I know we're talking about the artist, but I just realized about Framingham," she continued. "Of course we

don't know that he was involved in the scheme at all. It's purely conjecture on our part. But it seems too coincidental that a forgery scheme and the murder of an art dealer would happen in the same village."

"Perhaps Framingham objected to the plan to eliminate the artist?" Daphne, who had been unusually quiet, seemed to be thinking seriously about the matter. "If, as you say, Ryder was there to see him, that means they had some sort of relationship. Perhaps he didn't wish to see Ryder killed or exiled or dealt whatever punishment the men you overheard meant to inflict."

For someone who didn't generally wish to deal in hypotheticals, it was a logical enough explanation for why Framingham might have been killed.

"I believe you might be correct, Daphne," Sophia said with a nod. "And it would explain why Ryder was so overset about the murder. Obviously anyone would be chilled to find a body, but his reaction seemed outsized if the two men were merely acquaintances. Still, we don't know for sure that Ryder is the artist in question. He's unpleasant, to be sure, but he could simply be what he seems: Morgan's protégé. Whatever the case, he and Framingham were connected in some way we don't yet know about, I'm sure of it."

They were silent for a moment as they contemplated the complicated puzzle.

"I still cannot help but think Celeste must have known something," Gemma said, finally. "She had her eye on everything that was happening in this area. She had friends all over the county. The art community among them."

"Unless she left some sort of trail," Sophia said with a shake of her head, "as she did with the quests she left for Ivy and Daphne, I don't see how we'll ever know."

"You're sure there was no mention of it in your letter from her?" Ivy asked. Her own request from Celeste to search for the person who killed her had come via a letter she'd left to be given to her on her arrival at Beauchamp House.

"Or perhaps in the papers you received on your inheritance?" Daphne prodded. Celeste had given Daphne the clues she needed to find a long lost treasure in the letter she received with the news of her being chosen as an heiress.

"No," Sophia assured them. "Nothing like that. Believe me, as soon as I realized how your missives from her contained clues to the mysteries she wished you to solve, I scoured my own letters like mad. Both Gemma and I did. But we found nothing."

"And she gave no letters to Serena to give to you either." Daphne's words were a statement, not a question.

But Ivy was not ready to give up. "With Daphne's puzzle," she said thoughtfully, "she used ciphers hidden within the text of the letter to speak to her. What if she did something similar with you, Sophia?"

"I'm not sure I know what you mean." Sophia was beginning to get a headache. Surely if Celeste had meant to leave her some quest she'd have been straightforward with it as she had done with Ivy and Daphne. She had a feeling they were looking for clues where none existed.

"What if she left your clues in the form of a painting? Or paintings?"

The final clue to help Daphne in her search for a long lost Scottish treasure had been hidden in plain sight in a painting. So, the idea wasn't entirely without merit. "Then where is the painting? There are several stored in one of the cabinets in the corner, but they weren't in any place of prominence when we arrived. I assumed they were simply works that Celeste had chosen not to display in the house. Some lesser known but still valuable pieces by continental artists."

Ivy tilted her head. "Don't large houses usually store things like that in the attics? I know when we were at Kerr House, the housekeeper told me that they rotate pieces on display based on family preference, and in some cases the season. But they're all stored in the attics."

Sophia hadn't actually thought about the paintings in the cabinet since she'd found them on her arrival. Since she shared ownership of the house, she hadn't felt comfortable removing the works of art already on display throughout the rooms, and there was enough storage space already in the studio that she didn't need that particular cabinet.

"It wouldn't hurt to take a look," she said with a shrug. Then, feeling sheepish, she asked, "Could one of you bring them over here? I dislike admitting it, but I cannot contemplate walking even as far as it takes to get to the cabinet."

Gemma gave her a look while Daphne and Ivy went to retrieve the paintings. "I knew you were overdoing it today." Sophia knew her sister's disapproving look all too well.

Then, in a lower voice so the others wouldn't hear her, Gemma continued, "No one will think less of you if you give yourself time to heal, Sophia. You are not Mama. And no one will ever mistake you for her."

At the mention of their mother, who had wielded her imaginary illnesses and time in the sickbed with the precision of a sharpened sword, Sophia felt breathless for a moment. Had she been doing that? Pressing on because she couldn't stand the idea of being assumed to be an exaggerator? It was possible, she acknowledged. Grateful to her sister for pointing it out, she squeezed her hand. "You may be right. I do have a tendency to abhor the sick room because of her. I promise to rest my ankle tomorrow."

Then Ivy and Daphne arrived carrying armloads of canvases which they propped against the ottoman at Sophia's feet.

"This is all of them," Ivy said, slightly breathless from her exertion. "I thought there would be more."

"No," Sophia said, feeling a bit foolish for not realizing the possible significance of the cabinet before now. "I should have known they were special since there weren't that many of them. But I was so thrilled that this studio was to be mine I barely gave them a glance before I shut the cabinet and went about my business."

She picked up the first one in the stack, using both hands because of its size and the heaviness of its gilt frame.

It was clearly a Rubens. It bore all the hallmarks of the Flemish artist's work. A female nude, whose soft, lush body was the central focus of the painting, was seated at a fountain, hunched over to hide her nakedness. But it was her fearful expression as she cringed from the two men crowding into her that told the tale. She knew well how this woman felt—it was the same terror she'd felt that afternoon when Ryder threatened her.

This was, Sophia realized, a painting of the story from the book of Daniel about Susannah, an innocent wife who is spied upon while bathing by two nefarious men who then threaten to falsely say she's been meeting her lover if she doesn't agree to let them have their way with her. She refuses, the men accuse her publicly of having a lover and she is sentenced to death. At the last moment, the young man Daniel appears and demands the men be questioned, and when their stories don't add up, Susannah is declared innocent and freed and the men who slandered her are put to death.

It was a story that always angered Sophia when she thought of just how precarious a woman's virtue could be when men took it into their minds to bring them down. True, Susannah was proved innocent, but she shouldn't have needed to be.

More important than the story depicted in the painting at the moment, however, Sophia realized was the significance of the painting itself.

She knew it was Rubens. It had to be. But it was also, if she recalled correctly, famously missing. There were several versions of *Susannah and the Elders* that were said to have come from either Rubens or his studio. But this particular version was only known because of an engraving of it by another man. The painting itself had been presumed missing for hundreds of years. It certainly wasn't known by the art world to be hidden in a cupboard in Lady Celeste Beauchamp's studio cabinet.

"What is it, Sophia?" Gemma asked, her eyes worried. Clearly Sophia had been quiet for too long.

Instead of answering her, Sophia flipped quickly through the other works leaning against the ottoman.

What she saw made her heart race. She wasn't sure what it meant, but she knew what she saw with her own eyes.

"These are all forgeries," she said, a sense of unreality washing over her. "They are all forgeries of paintings that are known to be missing or lost."

Chapter 16

Ben was bone tired when he left the Framingham house, where he'd spent the better part of the afternoon consoling the grieving wife and children of the murdered man.

It was never easy to console a family who had lost a loved one unexpectedly, but this was different from his experience thus far as a minister. He'd never before had to explain to a wife that her husband had died not by an accident or illness, but by another man's hand. He would never forget as long as he lived the sound of Lucy Framingham's shriek when he informed her that her husband was dead. And then, again when she learned it was murder. He'd been a bit more circumspect with the children, who were too young to understand much beyond the fact that their father had gone to heaven. But their sadness and puzzlement had been, in its way, as affecting as their mother's reaction.

Fortunately, Mrs. Framingham's sister and her husband lived in Little Seaford, and were able to come take control of things in the aftermath of the master of the house's death, and he was able to leave secure in the knowledge that he'd done what he could for them.

And always in the back of his mind as he interacted with the dead man's family was the note he'd received that morning when he and Cam had returned to the vicarage from Beauchamp House.

It was dark as he took the reins of his horse from the stable boy he'd paid to hold him, and almost without intending it, he found himself steering Gabriel toward Beauchamp House. Even if it was just for a moment, he needed to see Sophia before he would be able to sleep tonight. And after witnessing the agony the Framingham family was enduring, he needed to assure himself that she was safe and secure and away from whatever ugliness was lurking in Little Seaford.

Despite the late hour, a groom was at the ready to take Gabriel's reins. Ben was composing his explanation to Greaves for the late call, but was surprised when the butler opened the door before he even reached the landing.

"Lord Benedick," the butler said, bowing. "Is something amiss? Has something happened?"

Belatedly, Ben realized that the household hadn't exactly been a stranger to death and destruction over the last year.

"I apologize for alarming you, Mr. Greaves," he said with genuine regret. "As far as I know, the duke and Lord Kerr are in good health. I am here to see Miss Hastings, I'm afraid."

But the butler's expression did not brighten. "Something has happened to her parents. I'll have both Miss Hastings and Miss Gemma come downstairs and see you in the drawing room."

Dash it, he was making a mull of this. "No, no, nothing like that, Greaves."

Ben rubbed a hand over his face as the butler stared at him.

"I simply wished to assure myself that Miss Hastings is well. That's all. I realize it's unusual, and possibly inappropriate, but you must have heard about what happened in the village today . . ."

He let his voice trial off, hoping the man would see his exhaustion and take pity on him.

To his relief, Greaves' eyes shone with understanding. And something else Ben wasn't able to interpret. "Of course, my lord. Of course. The ladies are in Miss Hastings' art studio at present and I'm sure they will be happy to see you."

At the news Sophia was surrounded by her sister and friends, he almost demurred and left. The prospect of greeting a room full of inquisitive ladies was more than he was ready to face. But nor was he prepared to leave without at the very least laying eyes on Sophia.

So it was that he found himself following the aging butler upstairs to the attic art studio. After Greaves knocked briskly, he stepped inside and announced Ben, and Ben was relieved to see that only Sophia was there. She was on the settee where she'd been when he and Freddie visited her before. Only this time instead of her own paintings she had a stack of unfamiliar ones arrayed on the floor and ottoman next to her.

"Ben," she said, her voice revealing her surprise and a husky note that indicated she might have been napping. "I know you said you'd come speak to me, but I thought you'd been too involved with the magistrate or Mrs. Framingham."

With the silence and discretion that were the hallmarks of a good servant, Greaves slipped out of the room, shutting the door behind him.

Unable to stop himself, Ben gathered her into his

arms, and somehow ended up with Sophia in his lap, his face buried in her neck

"I hope this is all right," he said, leaning his cheek against her bosom. "I just . . . I needed you."

But Sophia didn't protest. She simply held him. And stroked her hand over his back. Offering the comfort he so desperately needed.

"Was it very bad?" she asked softly. "You don't have to tell me. I know it was."

He lifted his head and leaned back against the settee. "I've ministered to the grieving before. Many times. It's never easy, but nor is it entirely without some sort of optimism. Even if it's just that their loved one is no longer suffering. Or will be with God. But I've never had to tell a woman her husband has been murdered."

"I'm so sorry," Sophia said, now leaning her head on his chest. "You're a good man. To do this job that not everyone would be able to do."

He laughed at that. He couldn't help it. "It was the church or the army. And I have no stomach for war. I may have chosen the church because I had some idea that I liked helping people. But it's a bit different in practice than it was in my imagination. I did go with my mother to visit the tenants on my father's estate. But for the most part, they welcomed us. That's not always the case with the vicar. Nor is it as easy as bringing a basket of food and going on my way."

"But that's why it's so admirable," Sophia said, lifting up so that she could look him in the eye. "You know how difficult it is. How thankless it can be. And you do it anyway. You look after the members of your parish—both those who attend services and those who don't—and you do it without seeking thanks or accolades. You do it because it's your job. But also because it's the right thing to do."

He saw the admiration in her eyes, and shook his head. "Don't make a saint of me, Sophia. I'm a man. Nothing more. I do the job I've been called to do. But I am not without flaws. Without sin."

At that she gave a saucy smile, and he was suddenly reminded of the impropriety of their pose. And how good it felt to have her soft curves pressed up against him.

"I never said you were a saint, vicar," she said softly. "In fact, I'm rather hoping you aren't. Because I would like it very much if you kissed me again."

"Would you, indeed?" His gaze went to her lips, pink and full and inviting. He'd have to be a bloody saint to ignore that invitation.

"I would," she said, and before he could make the decision himself, she leaned in and kissed him, just a meeting of mouths. But enough to give him a taste of what was to come. Pulling back just a fraction, she said against his lips, "But I'm happy to do it for you."

His exhaustion, which had so lately hung upon him like a pall, disappeared at the taste of her mouth on his. Curious, and eager to see what she'd do, he let her explore. Savored every nibble of her teeth on his lower lip, then when her tongue dipped into the seam of his lips and prodded for entrance, felt the caress echoed in his groin. Unable to hold back, he opened to her questing mouth and took the lead, lifting his hand to hold her head to his, taking the kiss from an exploration to something more carnal. They molded themselves together, as if any breath of air between their bodies was the difference between life and death. And Ben felt his hunger for her rising, as he cupped her generous breast in his hand, and felt her gasp at the caress.

He would have liked nothing more than to take her here, now, and give them both the release they so desperately needed. He was certain it would be good, and he was sure now—whether Sophia knew it or not—that she was the woman he wanted for his wife. But something about the moment, perhaps that little gasp when he stroked his thumb over the peak of her breast, brought him back to reality. And unfortunately, reality meant that they had to stop.

Reluctantly, with a strength he had doubted he had within himself, he pulled his head back and said her name.

"Sophia." Deprived of his mouth, she'd simply moved on to his neck. "Sophia, stop."

He felt the moment she heard the note of firmness in his voice. She stilled, and pulled back a little to look at him.

"We have to stop," he said, breathing hard even as the words left him. "We must stop now or I won't be able to."

Ben watched as her eyes went from drowsy with passion to a level of alertness that was admirable given the situation.

Wordlessly, she climbed off of him, and sat a few inches away from him. She spent a few seconds smoothing the skirts of her deep blue gown, though they hadn't really gotten to the point where it was an issue.

"I'm sorry," he said, his voice sounding rough to his own ears.

"If you apologize for despoiling me or some other such nonsense, Lord Benedick Lisle," she said in a tone of warning, "I don't know what I'll do. But you won't like it."

He laughed a little at her fierceness, and the hint of frustration in her voice that echoed his own. "I wouldn't dream of it, my dear." He lifted her hand and kissed the center of her palm. "I am sorry we had to stop, but I am not sorry for what just happened."

She was silent for a moment, before she turned to look at him. As if to gauge the truth of his words. What she saw must have satisfied her because she gave a nod of agreement. "Good. Because I'm not sorry for what happened either."

"Then we are in agreement," he said with a smile.

Not quite ready to leave yet, but needing something to spark a change in subject, his eye fell on the paintings that had been strewn around her when he came in. "What are all these?" he asked, indicating with a jerk of his head he meant the artwork. "That doesn't look like one of yours."

At his words, Sophia let out a gasp. "Oh! I almost forgot. Ben, I think these are some of the forgeries. We found them in the cabinet here in the studio. I believe Lady Celeste was purchasing them to keep them off the market."

For the second time that evening, his fatigue evaporated.

"Tell me everything."

Chapter 17

"I'm happy to come with you, my dear," Ivy told Sophia the next morning as they finished up breakfast.

Greaves had just informed the assembled ladies of the house that Squire Northman, the magistrate for this county, had arrived to question Sophia about the murder of Mr. Framingham.

Not long after she told Ben about the cache of forged paintings they'd found in the studio, he'd taken his leave with the promise to come back this morning. He hadn't yet arrived, however.

Even so, Sophia was prepared to answer the man's questions as thoroughly as she could. The memory of the dead man was still fresh in her mind, and she'd even awoken twice in the night in a cold sweat thanks to it.

"I believe I can manage," she told Ivy with a smile. "Though I appreciate the offer. I know both you and Daphne have had your own moments with the Squire."

"I was a suspect at one point," Daphne pointed out, as she buttered her toast. "Northman is not the most pleasant of men, but he is persuadable when the truth is there to lay out before him. I believe he is a bit frightened of Maitland, though. It's a shame he isn't here to go into the interview with you. He was most useful during mine."

Sophia rather thought Maitland had been so fierce with Northman because he was in love with Daphne, but she didn't point that out to her friend.

Instead, she rose, with the aid of her walking stick. "I'm sure it will be routine. I barely knew the man and from all appearances he was already dead while I was in the gallery. So, there's nothing to be concerned about."

She wasn't sure if she was reassuring her friends or herself.

Just as she neared the door of the breakfast room, Gemma came barreling up. "I overslept," she said, slightly breathless and looking as if she'd dressed hastily. It was unusual for the always punctual Gemma to be late for anything. "I haven't missed breakfast, have I?"

"You haven't," Sophia said, hiding her smile at her sister's unusual state. "But I'm off to meet with the magistrate. I'll see you later in the morning."

At the mention of Northman, Gemma's eyes snapped to attention. "Do you wish me to go with you?"

Sophia gave a lusty sigh. "Why is it that everyone thinks I need a keeper with me so that I might answer a few questions from the magistrate? I'm hardly infirm or lacking intellect."

"Of course you aren't, dearest," said Gemma putting a hand on her arm. "But you were overset last night. And the Squire has a tendency to be a bit unscrupulous when he asks his questions. You're the most, well, tender of us. I simply don't wish him to cause you discomfort."

Did they really see her that way? Sophia wondered. It was true perhaps that of the four heiresses she was the most soft-hearted. But she wasn't one to weep at the drop of a hat, or to become tearful at the least provocation. She saw herself as rather practical and unemotional. It was rather jarring to think that her sister and friends saw her any differently.

She was saved from further speculation on the matter by the arrival of Greaves followed by Ben, who despite the late hour of his departure the evening before looked well rested and handsome in his form-fitting trousers and pristine cravat.

"Lord Benedick has arrived, Miss Hastings," said Greaves rather needlessly, given that Sophia could see the man with her own eyes.

"Yes, thank you, Greaves," she told the butler nevertheless. One thing she could count on, at the very least, was Greaves' scrupulous attention to protocol.

"I believe Squire Northman is here to question you?" Ben asked, only a fleeting intensity in his gaze indicating that he remembered as vividly as Sophia did their encounter in the studio the evening before. But the next instance he was all politeness and manners. "May I sit in with you? It will perhaps be easier for him to question us both at the same time. And I can offer you some support."

Sophia purposely ignored the look of smugness on her sister's face, then let Ben take her arm.

In a low voice as they made their way to the drawing room, he asked, "Are you well this morning? Yesterday was quite exhausting and I know your ankle was paining you last night."

Sophia made a noise of impatience. "I wish everyone would stop treating me as if I am made of cotton floss. I am perfectly capable of enduring a trying day. And while my injury still aches a bit, it is nothing I cannot handle."

Her voice rose as she spoke, and to her embarrassment she realized she'd nearly been shouting by the end.

If she was afraid he'd be offended, however, she was mistaken.

Ben laughed and pulled her arm closer to him. "I can see I'll need to have more respect for your strong will, Sophia. I forgot for a moment that you were unlike any other lady of my acquaintance. Forgive me?"

The apology was said so sweetly she couldn't reject it without seeming churlish. "Yes, I forgive you," she said crossly. "And I suppose I'm sorry for ripping up at you. It's just that everyone seems to think I'm some simpering artist who wears her every emotion on her sleeve."

"I don't think that," he said sincerely. "And I daresay your sister and your friends don't think that either. They're just concerned for you after yesterday's ordeal. And they wish to help you. It's what we do for the people we love."

She supposed he was right. Then, realizing what he'd said, she asked, with a sideways look, "Am I unlike the other ladies of your acquaintance?"

"Most certainly," he said without hesitation. Then, in a lower voice, he added, "I don't wish to kiss them until they make the little greedy noises you made last night."

At the reminder of her response to him the night before, and his to her, Sophia felt her entire body suffuse with heat.

Then, as luck would have it, they were at the door to the drawing room.

He gave her a knowing grin, the wretch, before opening the door and ushering her inside.

Squire Northman, a gruff, no-nonsense leader of the local gentry, at whose home Sophia and the other heiresses had dined on a number of occasions, was today in his magistrate guise. That is to say, he was his usual self only more intimidating. He'd been accompanied by his secretary, who, Sophia knew from past experience, took notes during these interviews.

"It's about time, Miss Hastings," he said without preamble as Sophia, followed by Ben, entered the room. "I've been cooling my heels for a quarter of an hour or more. I know you ladies take your time dressing, but this is serious business."

'Good morning to you, too, Mr. Northman," Sophia said without referring to his complaint. "I hope you won't mind, but I've a twisted ankle and will need to sit for this interview."

It was both a way of putting him in the position of behaving like a gentleman rather than a lawman, and also a way for her to get off her ankle, which had begun to throb.

Looking somewhat chastened, the older man nodded. "I didn't mean to be so harsh. M'wife tells me I'm rag-mannered at times. Please sit, Miss Hastings."

As she took a seat in the large wingback chair near the window overlooking the garden, the magistrate turned to Ben, who had been silent thus far.

"Vicar," Northman said with a slight bow. "I'm pleased to see you're here as well. I can question you both about this business and maybe get to the bottom of things."

To Sophia he said as he began to pace before the fire, "I don't mind telling you, Miss Hastings, that I believe there must be something in the water at Beauchamp House, for now it's three of you involved in this sort of thing. I don't hold with ladies getting mixed up in murder. It would be a sight better if the four of you would keep yourselves to yourselves and stay at home with your needlework."

* * *

There was so much to object to in the statement, Sophia wasn't even sure where to begin. She was saved from doing so by Ben, who'd come to stand beside her chair, his hand warm on her shoulder.

"Perhaps you should get to the questions about Framingham rather than giving commentary on the behavior of the Beauchamp House heiresses, Squire," he said with a raised brow. "We all wish to see whoever killed the man caught and punished, do we not?"

Looking frustrated, but resigned, the magistrate gave a slight shrug, then turned to his secretary, who'd been silent throughout the proceedings so far. "Be sure to write all of this down. This is important business."

Not waiting for a response, he turned back to Sophia. "I believe the vicar told me last night, Miss Hastings, that you were in the gallery for some time before you heard the shouts of Mr. Ryder from the storage room?"

Sophia gave him the details of her visit to the gallery—minus the kissing once Ben appeared on the scene—and concluded with finding Ryder standing over the body of Framingham. When she was finished, the magistrate looked, if anything, more grave.

"And you heard nothing before Ryder came upon you alone? No shouts, no crashing around?" Northman asked, his bushy brows lowered with intensity.

She'd gone over the scene again and again in her mind last night, but she could recall no unusual noises or sounds coming from any part of the gallery. "Nothing, Mr. Northman. And if Mr. Ryder had been stabbing Mr. Framingham before he accosted me, then wouldn't he have been bloody?"

The magistrate looked taken aback that she'd mention something so graphic, but reluctantly nodded. "It's unlikely that the person who killed Framingham could have done so and not become . . . messy in the process."

"Do you remember if Ryder came through the front door as you did, Miss Hastings?" Ben asked, turning to look at her. "Is it possible he came from the direction of the storage room and the rear entrance of the gallery?"

Northman looked as if he would object to Ben usurping his duties as questioner, but seemed to think the question was a good one, because he indicated with a wave of his hand that she should answer.

"I can't be sure," Sophia answered truthfully. She'd spent at least an hour last night before finally falling asleep trying to remember the exact details leading up to the discovery of Framingham's body. "I don't recall hearing the front door, but I was also in a bit of a . . . a daze, I suppose you'd call it. I get that way sometimes when I'm engrossed in a painting. I'm still there, my physical presence is still there, but my mind is . . . elsewhere."

Northman gave a grunt, as if this was the sort of nonsense he'd expect from a lady artist.

But Ben gave her shoulder a squeeze. "It's that way with me and reading sometimes. My tutor used to say that he could have shot a pistol in the room and I'd not hear it."

"So you can't know for sure if Ryder was in the back, having words with Framingham before he came upon you, or if he breezed in from the street none the wiser?" Northman demanded. "I can't say as I'm surprised, since it seems to me that the fellow is a bit slippery."

Since Sophia's opinion of the other artist was not much better, she didn't argue. Though she did wonder if they should inform the magistrate about the forgeries.

"Perhaps you know already since you're in contact with the authorities, Squire—" she began, only to be interrupted by Ben.

"—but Ryder is a protégé of Mr. Peter Morgan and both men had dealings with Framingham in relation to the upcoming art exhibition in the village," the vicar finished, his hand on her shoulder squeezing to indicate she should go along. "You should perhaps speak with Mr. Morgan."

It was difficult not to gape at Ben as he spoke, but Sophia managed it.

Just.

Chapter 18

He wasn't sure why, but some instinct warned Ben that telling Northman about the forgery scheme would be risky.

It wasn't simply that they'd possibly discovered a connection between Sophia's benefactor and the fake art—though that was something they'd not been able to examine closely enough yet. Nor was it the fact that they were investigating the forgery scheme under the nose of Northman himself.

But both of these together added up to a compelling reason, so far as he could determine, to keep the information regarding the forgeries to themselves for the time being. He'd once heard his brother's friend the Earl of Mainwaring say that a good investigator had to trust his instincts. Well, if that was the case, then this was Ben trusting his.

Added to that was the fact that he'd paid a call on Morgan that morning to offer the man a strong, albeit somewhat restrained, warning against further intimidation where Mrs. Debenham was concerned. At first the man had attempted to excuse his behavior.

"You're a man of the world, vicar," Morgan had said

with a joviality that made Ben wish fervently he didn't have a duty to eschew physical violence. "Mrs. Debenham is a sweet little thing. You can hardly blame me for being taken with her."

"As a matter of fact, Morgan," he'd said through clenched teeth, "I can blame you. Especially when in the face of the lady's refusal you threatened to ruin her reputation."

If he expected Morgan to respond with anger, he was soon disabused of the notion. "Of course I didn't threaten her. Is that what she said?"

Ben could hardly call the man a liar to his face without there being consequences. And as much as he'd like to put a bullet in him, vicars weren't precisely encouraged to go about dueling. No matter how justified the cause might be. Instead, he said calmly, "She did indeed say that. And I am inclined to believe her. Though, if you deny it, I have no choice but to accept that."

Morgan's eyes narrowed at that, but he didn't say anything in response.

"Of course," Ben continued, "if it were true, then I might be inclined to have a word with my father about the matter. He has a great deal of influence in the government, you understand. And if he were to take an interest in a local political race, like the one here, for example, well, his word in the right ear could make or break a candidacy."

At that the industrialist scowled, and he muttered an imprecation.

"I see I've made myself clear," Ben said with a tilt of his head. "I look forward to hearing from Mrs. Debenham that you've sent her a letter of apology. As well as a donation to the local widows and orphans fund in the name of her late husband."

"Now see here, vicar," Morgan spat out. "You can't make me . . ."

"Do you really wish to face the ire of the Duke of Pemberton, Mr. Morgan?" Ben asked blandly. "I can assure you, my father is many things, but a friend of those who intimidate helpless women, he is not."

The other man's lips tightened, and his eyes blazed with temper.

"Fine," he said tightly. "Now, if you've no more to say, I have work to do."

It had been a satisfying meeting for Ben, but here and now with Sophia and Northman, he was all too aware of the magistrate's friendship with the industrialist. Perhaps Northman had no idea that his friend was a boor and a bully.

But Ben thought that was unlikely. Men like Morgan were the sort who assumed everyone else thought the same way they did.

Aloud, he repeated his assertion that the magistrate should speak with Morgan.

"I know he's a friend of yours, Squire," he said, aware of Sophia's curiosity as if it were a palpable thing. "Morgan may be able to give you more information about both Ryder and Framingham. Perhaps the murder has something to do with the upcoming art exhibition."

He realized his mistake the moment the words left his mouth. And to his frustration, the opening he'd given Northman didn't pass the man unnoticed.

"I believe you are expected to have some paintings in this exhibition, Miss Hastings," the magistrate said, turning his gimlet eye on Sophia.

"Yes," she agreed, remaining poised. But then, he knew she always was when speaking about her art. Sophia was nothing if not knowledgeable about her craft. "I have a few paintings that I plan to show."

"And you had a disagreement with Morgan over the suitability of these paintings, did you not?"

Northman was remarkably well informed about the inner workings of the local art world, Ben thought. But he supposed it was possible that Morgan had confided in him.

"We've never spoken about the matter," Sophia corrected him. "Mr. Morgan has not seen fit to discuss it directly with me. But more to the point, though I am aware of Mr. Morgan's objections, I have heard nothing about Mr. Framingham agreeing with him. Nor have I spoken with the poor man, if it comes to that. So, I'm not sure what my work has to do with what happened yesterday."

"Morgan tells me that he spoke with you, as well, about the matter, Lord Benedick," said Northman. "Is it possible you went to speak with Framingham since he was on the committee organizing the exhibition? To persuade him that Morgan was wrong about your lady friend's paintings?"

"Miss Hastings is a friend, Northman," Ben said tightly. "And I will thank you to be respectful to her. As to whether I spoke with Framingham about the exhibition, I did not. Nor, I believe, did Miss Hastings. As she has already told you."

He'd had just about enough of the man's questions and insinuations. And if he and Sophia were to find any answers regarding the murder or the forgeries, they needed the magistrate to leave.

"If you have no more questions," he said, drawing upon every ounce of hauteur growing up the son of a duke had instilled in him, "I believe Miss Hastings needs to rest now. She is, as you can see, injured, and the events of yesterday were quite distressing for her."

Northman's eyes narrowed for the fraction of a second as if he were trying to see past Ben's outward manner and into his mind. But it was clearly not possible, so he relaxed a little and nodded. "I may need to come back and speak to you again, Miss Hastings."

With an indication to his secretary that they'd finished their business, the magistrate and his minion left the room, closing the door behind them.

When enough time had passed for them to be out of earshot, Sophia turned to Ben with an irritated look. "Why did you stop me from telling him about the forgery? He might be able to help us!"

"And he might just as easily have told us to mind our own business and leave it all to the authorities," he returned, aware even as they spoke about such a serious topic that they were currently alone in the room. Try as he might, it was damned hard to control his baser instincts when he was in her company. Not particularly impressive for a man of the cloth, he knew, but he was, after all, just a man. He might have chosen the church, but that didn't mean he'd lost all feeling below the waist. Certainly not in Sophia's company.

Her huff of frustration brought him back to the matter at hand.

"He could have told us that, yes, but you were asked to look into the matter by the Earl of Mainwaring," she argued. "Does that not make you a colleague of sorts to the magistrate?"

Ben rubbed his neck. "It's not that simple. Mainwaring asked me to look into the matter. It's not as if I've been authorized by the Home Office, or anything like that."

"Well," she said tartly, "if he didn't wish you to investigate the matter properly then he shouldn't have asked in the first place. Though it's entirely possible Framingham was killed for some reason having nothing to do with the forgeries, I cannot help but think otherwise. So, the scheme Mainwaring asked you to look into has become vastly more complicated."

"Of course it has," he answered with a shrug. He prowled across the room to lean his shoulder against the marble mantelpiece. "But that doesn't mean we cannot still unravel it."

"I admire your optimism," she said with a wry look. "So, what do you propose we do next?"

He thought for a moment before he wandered back over to the chair across from hers and lowered his tall frame into it. "I think we need to look at what we know so far."

"All right," she agreed. "First, thanks to your friend Mainwaring, we know that someone has been selling forged paintings through the village of Little Seaford, to the newly rich, to furnish their homes."

"We also know that Peter Morgan," Ben said, leaning back in his chair, "who has lived in the area for about the same timespan as the paintings have been appearing on the market, has many friends among those who might wish to purchase such paintings."

"And at the cliffs, we heard two men, one of whom might have been Morgan," Sophia said, ticking off a third finger, "arranging to get rid of the artist who has been supplying the forgeries."

"An artist we believe to be Ryder."

He watched as Sophia leaned her chin on her hand. "If Ryder is indeed the artist," she began, "then why is it that Framingham is dead?"

"You mean why Framingham and not Ryder?" he asked, curious.

"Yes," she said, lifting her ankle as if it was in pain.

"Here," Ben said gruffly, took her foot gently in his hands, removed her slipper and rested her heel on his thigh. "You should stay off the foot altogether today."

"Not you, too," she said with a scowl. "Acquit me of knowing how to take care of myself, please."

"Of course I know that," he said with a frown. "But you try a bit too hard to be the strongest person in the room. Compared to the other ladies in this house, you might seem like the soft one, but I suspect that's just your beauty giving a false impression, Wallflower. You're beautiful, it's true, but stubborn. And you can flirt and chat and make small talk, but that doesn't mean you're weak or fragile."

She was quiet for a second, arrested by his words. "You purport to know a great deal about me, my lord."

"I make it my business to know . . . people." He'd almost slipped and said *you*, which would not have been appropriate yet. There was still much they needed to resolve before he could think about speaking to her as frankly as he wished to. But soon.

Sophia's gaze rested on him for a moment. As if she were trying to figure him out. Then, as if realizing it was an impossible task, she shook her head a little.

"I believe we were discussing why it is odd that Framingham would turn up dead instead of Ryder," she said, bringing them back to the topic at hand. "Could it be that Framingham was one of the men we overheard?"

That was a possibility. "And Morgan—or whoever it was that we overheard, double crossed him?"

It was entirely possible that there had been a falling out amongst the conspirators.

"Perhaps Framingham no longer wished to sell the forged paintings?" Sophia suggested. "Or wanted a larger cut of the profits?"

Either option was possible. It was also possible that they were overlooking a more straightforward option. "What if Ryder found out that Morgan and Framingham were plotting to get rid of him?"

Sophia's eyes grew wide. "But I thought we'd decided he couldn't have been the killer because his clothes were free of blood?"

"There's nothing to say he didn't hire someone else to kill the fellow, then went to the gallery to check his handiwork," Ben said with a shrug. "And spent a bit of time threatening you to give himself an out."

His jaw clenched at the memory of Ryder standing over her yesterday. It wouldn't disappoint him in the least if they discovered the other man was a murderer and saw him hang for it. He knew the Gospel said to turn the other cheek, but when it came to Sophia he found himself feeling decidedly Old Testament.

"Perhaps we shouldn't spend too much time on the why," Sophia said after a bit of thought. "We can't know the why until we know the who. That will tell us the why."

It was a good point, he had to admit. "Very well. We suspect both Ryder and Morgan. And there are likely others we don't know about."

"There are also the paintings Celeste collected," Sophia reminded him. "I didn't have time to search more thoroughly for any notes or explanations she might have left about them, but knowing how she documented things for Ivy and Daphne, I cannot imagine she left that cache of paintings for me without some kind of clue as to why they were there."

"Then it would seem we have a task before us, Wallflower," he said. And without waiting for her consent, he lifted her into his arms.

"What are you doing?" she squeaked. "I'm perfectly able to walk, Ben. Put me down."

"You are injured and if you won't be so sensible as to stay off your ankle, then I will have to ensure you do so myself." He began walking toward the door of the drawing room.

"Where are you taking me?" she asked, her arms clasped tightly around his neck.

"To your studio," he said as he kicked the door shut behind them. "To search for Celeste's letter to you."

They had reached the second floor landing when Daphne came striding down the hallway toward them.

Sophia felt her cheeks heat as she prepared for the duchess—an unconventional one, but a duchess nonetheless—to comment on the scene of Ben with Sophia in his arms. But to her surprise, when Daphne stopped in her tracks at the sight of them, she laughed.

"Well, isn't this a bit of a scandal," she said with a shake of her head. "Sophia, I hope you know what you're doing."

"We are going to search for a letter from Lady Celeste in my studio," Sophia said with as much dignity as she could muster in her present position. "You are welcome to join us. And Ivy and Gemma as well."

But Daphne didn't seem fooled. "Ivy and Gemma are immersed in the library," she said with a keen look. "I was headed downstairs to post this letter to Maitland. Though I might need to add a few lines, now."

"I hope you'll give the duke my best," Ben said mildly as he shifted a little on his feet. "Is he expected to return soon?"

"In a few days," Daphne said, turning her attention to Ben. "I hope he won't need to give you a stern talking to, Lord Benedick."

Sophia had never wished more for the floor to open beneath her and swallow her up. But that would not help given that Ben would be devoured with her.

"I cannot imagine that he will," he responded with a shrug. "My intentions are entirely honorable, I assure you, Duchess."

At that Sophia turned, needing to see his expression. He looked right back at her, his gaze as steady as a rock.

He was serious, she realized, her heartbeat increasing.

"I am glad to hear it," Daphne said with a nod. "I guessed as much, but it never hurts to get confirmation. I'll just leave you to it, then."

And to Sophia's surprise, she continued her trek downstairs, and left them to continue theirs upstairs.

"What did you mean by that?" she demanded once they were out of earshot. She wished desperately that he would set her on her feet so that she could question him properly. It was difficult to interrogate someone while he was holding you in his arms.

"Just what I said," he returned mildly as they reached the door to her studio. With more ease than seemed fair, he managed to open the door and carry her inside without any trouble.

She waited until he'd placed her gently on the settee she'd spent so much time on these past few days to continue her questions. As if he expected no less, Ben took the chair across from her and leaned forward with his elbows on his knees. Ready for her to go on.

"But, we don't really know one another," she said with a frown. "And my family isn't nearly as aristocratic as yours. Papa is the son of a not very prosperous baronet. And he himself is a solicitor. Not smart at all."

The look he gave her was one of disappointment. "Have I ever indicated to you that I care about any of that?"

"Well, you will care very much when you see how small my marriage portion is," she said with a raised brow. "I know younger sons have to make their own way in the world. And I cannot imagine I'm the sort of wife who will make your position in the clergy comfortable. Surely the archbishop frowns on vicars' wives who call attention to themselves by painting scandalous pictures."

She didn't dare look at him to see if he agreed with her. Part of her was convinced that the idea of their marrying was mad and would lead to scandalous ruin. The other part desperately wanted him to tell her she was being a fool and that he'd marry her no matter what. She wasn't sure which of these parts she wanted to trust at the moment.

"It might surprise you to realize that I am not impoverished and in need of a rich bride to keep me in the style to which I've become accustomed," he said wryly. "Do you suppose I went into the church because my father tossed me out on my ear without a cent to my name? I went into the church because I wished to be of help to people. The politics, the edicts of the archbishop, these hold little interest for me."

That gave her pause. She wasn't sure what she'd thought regarding his financial situation, but she had assumed he needed a bride with a sizeable dowry.

Before she could reply, he continued, "I have made investments with my monthly allowance from the ducal estate which have grown into a respectable fortune. And, though I dislike admitting it lest you think me of the same ilk as Morgan, I own, along with my brothers Freddie and Cam, a cotton mill in Manchester."

Sophia blinked. "I . . . you . . . what?" He could not have shocked her more if he'd just informed her that he turned into a wolf when the moon was full.

"When Freddie came back from France, he had some funds he wanted to invest. He did the research and Cam and I were both looking for something to do with our savings."

"But, how can you do that?" she demanded. She tried to recall that this was Ben, who was so kind to his parishioners, who had comforted the family of the murdered Framingham. Who had kissed her as if she were the most precious gift in the world. But she had questions. How could she not? "How can you put little children to work? And subject them to unhealthy conditions that will ruin their lungs? Eventually kill them?"

"Of course we do not employ children," he said, his mouth tight with displeasure at the idea. "And we offer honest work for a living wage. I do not pretend that ours is morally superior to any other factory in the north, but we have taken steps to ensure that the conditions are as safe as we can make them, and that the children of our workers—most of them women—are offered an education."

Slightly abashed, she said, "I've heard other men, like Morgan, say that it is impossible to run a factory without child labor. How did you manage it?"

"Men who say that are lying to themselves to justify their practices," he said harshly. "It is certainly possible to do it. But it is not without its detractors. And not from where you'd think it. Regularly our managers are accosted by children and their parents demanding that we employ them. Because they need the wages. I've done what I could to ensure that there is someone on staff at the factory to assist those people in whatever way we can. But going against the grain is not without risk."

He meant that in more than one sense, she knew. Marriage between them would not be without risks. Or without its detractors, she knew. She could only imagine what the reaction of the archbishop would be to hearing about *Fallen*. Ben would be demoted or worse.

"I should have known you'd find a way to run a factory in a manner that helped the most people," she said a little sadly. Because there was no way she could ruin this gentle man's professional life by tying his lot to hers.

"I had hoped you knew me better by now," he said carefully. "But," and he smiled crookedly at this, "I tend to forget we've only truly known each other for a few days. For all that we've been acquaintances since I arrived, I don't think I began to actually see or know the real Sophia until I saw your paintings."

If he'd schemed for a hundred years to find a way to reach her heart, he couldn't have found a surer way than through her painting. It was the most direct representation of the hopes and dreams and sorrows and pain she felt in her very soul. And that he could see her now— and she knew it wasn't just easy flattery—was as close to being understood as she'd ever felt.

"I hadn't intended to do this yet," he said, his gaze intent now, as if trying to read her thoughts, "but surely you must know my intentions are honorable. I wouldn't have kissed you without being prepared to pay for them with my hand in marriage. I've never met anyone like you, sweet Sophia. And perhaps I could marry some empty-headed society lady with a large dowry and more hair than wit, but we both know I'd be miserable with that sort of wife. I want you. With all your zeal for reform and need to call attention to the less fortunate in your work. The archbishop might not like it, but to be frank, I don't give a damn."

As he spoke, her heart, already faster than normal, began to pound. Her hands grew damp. And her stomach flipped with nerves.

"Sophia." Ben was on one knee now, and she felt her eyes begin to fill as he took her hand. "Marry me. Make me the happiest of men."

And to her everlasting shame and embarrassment, she fainted.

Chapter 19

Good heavens.

Ben quickly gathered Sophia into his arms and attempted to rouse her from her faint.

He hadn't spent a great deal of time imagining the way his future beloved would respond to his marriage proposal, but he dashed well had not considered that she might fall into a swoon over it!

"Sophia?"

Fortunately for them both, she opened her eyes almost immediately. He watched in mixed concern and amusement as the emotions flitted over her face. First confusion. Then, a smile as she saw him leaning over her—a good sign, surely? Then her eyes widened and a look of horror washed over her.

"Oh no." She shook her head and tried to sit up. Wanting to do whatever it took to make her comfortable, he assisted her to sit up on the settee beside him.

"I cannot believe I did that," she groaned. "I do not faint, Ben. Never. Not even when Tommy Travers spilled punch down the front of my favorite gown at the assembly ball."

She covered her face with both hands. "I am mortified."

"Well, I think the burden of shame lies with me," he said wryly. "I am, after all, the man who managed to make you faint dead away at the notion of marriage to me. If my brothers ever get wind of this, I will never rest easy again."

At that she dropped her hands, and threw her arms around him. "No," she said squeezing him hard. "You mustn't blame yourself or your words. It was a perfectly lovely proposal. I was simply overcome, I think."

She pulled away from him so that he could see the sincerity in her eyes. "You did nothing wrong. I've just had so much excitement these past few days and I haven't really been sleeping well, and I suppose I didn't eat much at breakfast and it all caught up with me."

"Perhaps we should ring for some sandwiches and tea," he said with a practicality he wasn't especially feeling. There was still the matter of his unanswered proposal hanging between them. Though he'd be a churl to bring it up again when she was obviously famished and overset.

"A good idea," Sophia said with a smile. "You always know what to do to make me feel better, Ben."

And to his surprise, she leaned in and kissed him. Then snuggled against his shoulder as if they'd not just enacted a scene from a Restoration farce.

"Do I take that to mean you've accepted my proposal?" he asked, half fear, half hope.

She pulled away from him again and gave him an exasperated look. "You don't honestly believe I fainted from shock and disgust, do you?"

Well when she put it like that . . .

Feeling sheepish, he shrugged. "One doesn't like to presume . . ."

Her laugh was clear and bright and just what he'd needed to hear.

"Of course I accept your proposal, you fool." She shook her head, loosening a few silky strands of brown tresses from her chignon to lightly trace the skin of her neck. "I'm not sure your optimism over the reaction our betrothal will elicit from the church hierarchy is founded, but if you're willing to take a chance on me, then I will take a chance on you."

For the first time in a quarter hour at least, Ben felt himself relax. And with a slight whoop, he pulled her to him and kissed her again. Properly this time, with every ounce of joy and hope and passion he felt when he was with this remarkable woman.

When she came up for air, her cheeks were delightfully pink and her hair was even more disheveled.

Though he would have liked to continue on in that manner, her stomach gave an annoyed growl. "I suppose I'd better send for those sandwiches," he said with a grin.

Just as he pulled the bell, a knock sounded on the door and Gemma called from the doorway, "Sophia, Lord Benedick, I'm afraid there's a bit of a disturbance downstairs and I fear it's something that only you can deal with."

"Come in, Gemma," Sophia called to her sister with a hint of amusement. "We've news."

Cautiously, as if she expected to find them in, at the very least, a passionate kiss, Gemma stepped into the room enough to see that they were both fully clothed with several feet between them.

"Oh," she said, her smile rueful. "I wasn't sure..... that is to say . . ."

"What is going on downstairs?" Sophia asked, clearly wanting to ensure there was no trouble before she made any sort of announcement.

At the reminder, Gemma's smile turned into a frown. "The Bishop of Chichester is downstairs with your father, Lord Benedick. And neither looks particularly happy."

"What?" Ben was not entirely surprised by the arrival of the bishop. He'd expected Morgan's next move in the attempt to discredit Sophia would be to have the bishop rein him in. But he was genuinely shocked to learn his father was here. "Why are they here and not at the vicarage?"

"They said they called there first and learned from your man that you were here." Gemma seemed as nonplussed as he felt. "I've left them downstairs with Daphne and Ivy. I think perhaps it's best to limit their time with Daphne before someone takes offense."

That was an understatement.

Sophia, who had taken all of this in without a word, set about smoothing her hair and righting her gown. Though it wasn't in any sort of disarray that he could see. Using her walking stick, she stood and offered him her arm. "Shall we go downstairs and see what these gentlemen want?"

He'd known he'd have to inform both the church and his parents about the betrothal at some point, but he hadn't supposed it would be quite this soon.

Still, he took her arm. "You're able to get downstairs like that?" he asked. Her eyes showed the memory of how she'd gotten upstairs earlier.

"Yes," she said with prim dignity. "I believe I can make it."

"Then I suppose we should go see what all the fuss is about."

Sophia rather felt as if she were stepping on stage when she and Ben stepped into the drawing room, where Greaves had placed the Duke of Pemberton and the Bishop of Chichester. As she limped in, both men turned to give her polite, but rather searching looks.

To her amusement, the bishop was still holding one of the phallic figurines from the mantle. Which he hastily put back as he stepped forward to greet them.

"Lord Benedick," the church leader said with a regal inclination of his head. "What a surprise it was to find your father was calling upon you here, rather than at the vicarage, as well." He was a tall, reed-thin man with what Sophia imagined was a permanent look of impatience on his long face. "Are you so frequently from home that your parishioners have begun seeking you out here as well? That's hardly proper."

A flash of exasperation crossed the duke's face as he ignored the clergyman and addressed his son. "You're looking well, Benedick. I hope you'll introduce us to your friend?"

At the reminder Ben gave her a look of apology. She imagined he'd been just as nonplussed by the bishop's introduction as she had.

"Miss Sophia Hastings, I'd like you to meet my father, the Duke of Pemberton," he said with a gesture toward the man whom she would have picked from a room full of other peers as his father. Like Ben, and indeed Freddie and Cam as well, the duke was tall with a strong if not particularly bulky build. His dark brown hair was a shade darker than his son's, and he had brown eyes, which must mean that his sons had inherited their blue eyes from their mother. "Papa, this is Miss Sophia Hastings. Her father is the son of Sir Giles Hastings of York. And she is assisting me with a particular matter that the Earl of Mainwaring has asked me to look into. It has to do with art and as Miss Hastings is herself a celebrated oil painter, she has been a valuable resource."

He made no mention of their, admittedly nascent, betrothal, but Sophia felt a pang of disappointment at the omission. Though she supposed that had more to do with the other man who stood waiting for an introduction.

"I'm very pleased to meet you, Miss Hastings," the duke said, bowing over her hand. "Like Gussie, here, I too was surprised to find my son here rather than at the vicarage, but I understand now. How could he possibly stay away when such beauty was here at Beauchamp House?"

It was clear where the Lisle boys had got their charming manners from, Sophia thought with a blush. "You are kind to say so, your grace," she said with a smile.

Then she turned to face the bishop, who was not nearly as pleased with her as the duke seemed to be.

"Your grace," Ben said, his presence at her side giving Sophia a boost of courage as she faced the annoyed ecclesiastical, "Miss Sophia Hastings. Miss Hastings, this is his grace the Bishop of Chichester."

"I had rather hoped to have a word with you alone, Benedick," the clergyman said with a sniff. "Would that be possible?"

"Don't be so stiff-rumped, Gussie," the duke said with a frown. "If Benedick says they're investigating something for the Home Office, then that's what they're doing. Whatever issue you have with him can't be more confidential than that."

If anything the bishop's nose and mouth grew more pinched. "Perhaps, Pemberton, you should mind your own business. And as it happens, since Miss Hastings is the reason for my visit to this Sussex backwater, I believe it would defeat the purpose to counsel your son about her while she's in the room."

"We're both standing right here," Ben reminded them with a little wave. "And as it happens, I have a guess as to what brought you here, Bishop."

"First," the duke said, with a look at Sophia's white-knuckled grip on her walking stick, "I believe we should sit down and discuss this like civilized people."

He offered his arm to Sophia. "Miss Hastings, may I?"

She exchanged a look with Ben, who seemed to shrug with his eyes—something she'd never known possible—and decided it was safe to take the duke's offered arm. Soon she was tucked up in her favorite overstuffed chair near the window with an ottoman at her feet to elevate her ankle.

Once the men were seated in chairs around her, with Ben taking the seat beside hers so they presented a united front, the duke, who seemed to be the unquestionable leader of this meeting, indicated with his hand that his son should continue.

"My guess, your grace," he said to the bishop, "is that you've had a complaint from a member of my parish about Miss Hastings. Perhaps a complaint that I've been spending too much time with her? Or that I recognize her at all given the content of her artwork? Does that sound familiar?"

"That may have been the gist of what I was told," the bishop said with a grudging nod. "And that you've been using your position as vicar to intrude upon matters that do not concern you. I might add that the person who made this complaint is a respected member of the community."

Sophia had little trouble guessing he meant Peter Morgan. And it surprised her not a whit that the bishop thought him respected.

"My son has already explained this, Gussie," said Pemberton, his leg crossed over his knee, perfectly at ease in what must be a difficult meeting for his son. Clearly he was not intimidated by the bishop. That much was obvious by the way he referred to him by what must have been a childhood nickname. "He and Miss Hastings are working together on a matter at the behest of Mainwaring. Whom you and I well know works for the Home Office. If he is able to fulfill his duties as a vicar, then I don't see what the problem is."

"I'm quite able to defend myself, sir," Ben said to his father, who lifted his hands to indicate his son had the floor. "Though, your grace, I do not believe there is anything to defend here. As my father said, Miss Hastings and I are working together on something for Mainwaring. It involves art forgery and more than that I cannot say. But I can assure you that I have not neglected my duties, and having seen Miss Hastings' paintings, I can assure you that they are far from what Morgan claims them to be."

It was all perfectly true, but Sophia couldn't help but feel a bit of frustration at his decision to omit the news of their betrothal. Wouldn't that reassure the vicar about the time they spent together? While she did appreciate that the investigation for the Home Office was perhaps a stronger argument for their closeness, the betrothal would remove the appearance of impropriety at least. Or so she thought.

If anything, the bishop seemed to grow more annoyed. "What business has the Home Office to co-opt my clergymen to perform their nasty little tasks? I've a mind to pay a call on the Home Secretary himself to complain."

None of the others responded to that, which Sophia assumed was a rhetorical question. And if it wasn't, there was no response they could give that would assuage his pique.

"Morgan has done a great deal for this village, Benedick," he continued in a scowl. "In fact, I believe his donations have made the living at Little Seaford one that is no longer the kind of pittance once seen here. You risk him reducing the amount of his tithe by going against him. And of him withdrawing some of his funding for your pet projects like caring for the village poor. Are you prepared to do that?"

Sophia watched as Ben's jaw tightened. She could see that he was holding his temper on a tight leash, indeed.

"Are you suggesting that I cease investigating a matter at my country's behest in order to appease a man who would use donations to the church as a means of getting what he wants?" his words were clipped and cold.

"I warned you about the politics of the church when you came to us, my boy," said the bishop with a shrug. "It is part of the job, no matter how much you dislike it. Of course you must render unto Caesar when necessary, but do not forget what duty you owe to the church and your parish."

He gave a pointed look at Sophia, who felt her back stiffen. "I notice you glossed over Morgan's other accusations regarding Miss Hastings." He did not elaborate, but it was clear from the way his eye roved over her what his meaning was. "Perhaps I should remind you as well that there are certain moral standards to which we expect you to adhere."

At that both Ben and duke stood. "Now see here, Gussie. If you're going to accuse my son of—"

"Don't be tiresome, Pemberton. I'm not accusing him of anything. But there is the appearance of impropriety. And that, I think, is enough to cast doubt on the nature of his relationship with Miss Hastings." The bishop had stood as well. "It might all be perfectly innocent, but it is what his parishioners think that matters. Once he has lost their confidence . . ."

"I doubt very much I've lost anyone's confidence who knows me," Ben said, his anger radiating off him. "And I will not have you cast aspersions of Miss Hastings' good name without so much as a bye-your-leave. It might change your opinion to know that I have only today asked her to be my wife and she has accepted. So, I will ask that you moderate your manner of speaking about her or I will be forced to complain to the archbishop."

At his announcement, Sophia struggled to her feet. "Benedick, you needn't have told him about this now."

She'd wanted him to announce their betrothal before, but now it felt like a play in a chess game. And she could see from the bishop's high color and pursed lips that it hadn't calmed his anger.

"I beg to differ, young lady," the bishop said coldly. "Now is the perfect time, because it tells me that the rumors are true. It is of course, your choice whom you take as a wife, Lord Benedick. But if you choose this route, your career will not be an easy one. You have not shown yourself to be a political man when it comes to rising in the church, but know if you do this that your chances of rising will forever be dimmed."

"Because Miss Hastings and I have been seen in one another's company too frequently?" Ben asked with incredulity.

"Because Miss Hastings paints what more than one of your parishioners has complained to me is obscene. Dead prostitutes? Dying children?" The bishop made a noise of disgust. "It is unfit for a man to paint such scenes. Much less a lady." He said the last word with a degree of skepticism that indicated he doubted her claim to the title.

Sophia clenched her fists in an effort to keep from striking the man. He was, of course, entitled to make judgments based on the content of her art, but to use them as a bludgeon against Ben was inexcusable. His career thus far with the church had been, so far as she knew, blameless. Was he to be censured solely based on the friendship of a few months' duration? She knew of church elders who had carried on affairs of decades duration who had escaped punishment. That Ben would find himself in such a situation because of her was enough to make her want to howl at the unfairness of it.

Like powerful men before him, the bishop also liked to have the last word, apparently, because once he'd said his peace, he swept from the room.

Leaving a pregnant silence behind him.

Chapter 20

"Gussie always was an egotistical fool," said the duke into the silence that fell in the wake of the bishop's departure. Then, turning to Sophia, he offered her his hand. "My dear Miss Hastings, I am very pleased to hear of your betrothal to my son. His mother and I had given up hope that he'd ever choose a bride."

Ben tried to shake off the pall of the bishop's words on him. His anger over the man's criticism of Sophia was foremost in his mind, especially when she herself had been forced to listen to his nonsense. He knew well enough that the church wished its clergymen would marry bland, selfless women who would make good helpmeets and be seen and not heard. But he'd long known that wasn't the kind of match *he* wanted. And certainly after meeting Sophia and seeing her determination to right societal wrongs with her work—something that spoke to his own sympathy for those who by accident of birth were stuck in the lower class—he'd known that she was what he wanted.

That his father, after only a few moments with her, was welcoming her to the family said more than any of the bishop's dismissive speeches.

"Thank you, your grace," Sophia said, though Ben could hear the note of falseness in her voice. "I wonder if you wouldn't mind giving me a few moments alone with your son? We have much to discuss, I think."

Though he was focused on Sophia, Ben couldn't mistake the look of warning his father sent him. He was all too aware of the danger, there, however.

"Certainly, my dear," the duke said with a smile. "I'm in need of a rest after all of Gussie's bombast. I do hope we'll see one another again before I travel on to visit Cam down the coast."

He kissed her on the cheek before bidding Ben a quick goodbye, and then he too was gone.

Leaving Ben and an obviously overset Sophia alone.

He knew something was seriously wrong when he moved to take Sophia's hand and she pulled away.

"Come now," he said in a cajoling tone. "You aren't taking what the bishop said to heart, are you? My father obviously approves, and his opinion is far more important to me than the bishop's is."

She turned from where she'd been facing out the window and he saw that her face was white. "Yes, I do take it to heart when the man who holds the future of your career in the church in his hands claims that a match with me will ruin you. While I am, of course, pleased to have your father's blessing, I cannot help but be troubled by the bishop's censure."

Ah. She was worried for him. "I told you before that I am not dependent upon the church's funding. And unlike the Roman church there isn't really a way for him to defrock me. The worst he can do is scold. Which he has done." He moved closer, reaching out to touch her arm. He was relieved when she didn't pull away.

He ran his hand down her arm until he'd taken her

hand in his. "I'm sorry that I waited until that precise moment to reveal our betrothal, however. It made it look as if I was inventing it on the spot in order to escape his chastisement."

"I doubt it would have made a difference," she said, moving closer to let him hold her against him. "He had already made up his mind about me before he came to Little Seaford. Morgan must have placed a great deal of money in the hands of the right people to get the bishop himself to come to deliver a set down in person."

Relieved that she wasn't angry at him so much as the situation, he took a moment to enjoy the feel of her against him. To smell the fresh lemony fragrance of her hair, and the warmth of her skin.

"I have no doubt that Morgan is quite skilled at the business of paying off those he thinks will be of use to him at some point," he said, stroking a comforting hand over her back. "He is a businessman with a businessman's conviction that money will buy whatever he wants— including the silencing of a critic."

At his words, she stiffened and pulled away. "You don't suppose he contacted the bishop because of what happened with Framingham?"

Ben frowned. "What do you mean?"

"Just that someone must have been worried to silence Framingham permanently," she said with a pointed look. "What if Morgan knew that he'd contacted you before he died? If it was indeed Framingham."

He considered it. He'd wanted—because of the man's behavior with Sophia—the culprit to be Ryder, but it was entirely possible that the murderer was someone else. Someone with more at stake than an itinerant artist did.

Someone who stood to lose an empire if his scheme was uncovered.

"We need to find that note from Lady Celeste," he said with a sense of urgency. If Morgan had either killed Framingham or had him killed, then his next target might be the people who were trying to bring him down. He wasn't worried for his own safety. But if it had been Morgan who sent the bishop information about Sophia, then he just might see Sophia as a threat as well as Ben.

And he would let Peter Morgan harm Sophia over his dead body.

Taking Sophia's hand, he led her upstairs to search for the clue that would lead them to the truth.

In the studio again, Sophia made immediately for the ornate Jacobean cabinet in the corner, where she'd first discovered a collection of documents and diaries relating to Lady Celeste's art dealings. She had given her works as gifts and kept a journal with the title of each painting and the name of the person she'd gifted it to.

As if by agreement, she took a seat and Ben handed her stack after stack of loose pages and other ephemera from the late artist's collection.

"I don't understand why her art papers are so disorganized when the rest of her papers were so very tidy," Sophia said as she opened a letter that seemed to be from an art dealer in Brighton. "Though given the breadth of her interest, I suppose she couldn't do it all."

Ben turned from pulling out a bound journal from the cabinet. "You don't suppose someone has already searched this collection? And that's why it's in such disarray."

The possibility hadn't occurred to her and Sophia thought it over for a moment. Could someone have sneaked into the studio and rifled through Lady Celeste's papers without her knowing about it? It was true there were a couple of months between the lady's death and the arrival of the heiresses. Serena had been here, of course, but she wouldn't have done such a thing.

Then, a thought occurred to her. Someone else in the house might have decided to conceal a letter for her from Lady Celeste. Someone who might think he was protecting her from danger.

"I think I might know who has the letter Lady Celeste left for me," she said with a sigh. If she was right, he would be mortified at being caught out. But there was no time for that now. A man was dead and they needed every bit of information they could gather.

"Who?" Ben asked, his brows drawn.

"Ring the bell pull and we'll find out if I'm right." Sophia said rubbing the spot between her eyes that was beginning to throb.

She hoped she was correct. If she wasn't, then she wasn't sure where they'd be able to search next.

Chapter 21

Greaves himself arrived in answer to the bell, and Ben was struck by the realization that the butler seemed to have a soft spot for Sophia.

It wasn't all that unusual for a butler to respond to a bell from a member of the family, but it did seem that Greaves was, more often than not, the one who came running when Sophia called.

"Miss Hastings," the older man said, offering her a slight bow. Then, turning to offer another to Ben. "How may I be of assistance?"

He seemed to take the presence of Ben in the room as unexceptional, though as an upper servant, Greaves was skilled at keeping his opinions to himself.

"Mr. Greaves," Sophia said from her perch on a high-backed chair near the cabinet they'd been searching, "is there something you'd like to tell me? Perhaps something relating to a note Lady Celeste left with express instructions for me?"

Ben watched fascinated as the man's upright posture sagged a little. Folding his arms over his chest, he leaned back against the cabinet to watch the interaction between Sophia and the major-domo.

"Miss Hastings," Greaves began with a tight-lipped frown, "you must understand it was for your own protection. I cannot imagine Lady Celeste would have wished you to put yourself in the sort of danger both Miss Ivy— that is, the Marchioness of Kerr—and the Duchess of Maitland found themselves in when they followed my late mistress's directives. I know it was not my place, but I . . . that is to say, my affection . . ."

Before he could say more, Sophia stopped him, raising a hand. "Mr. Greaves, how could you?" she asked, looking both disappointed and touched. "You know it's not your place to make decisions like that. Not only has your decision to hold back Lady Celeste's letter or note, or whatever it was, put me in more danger, but it may very well have got Mr. Framingham killed."

At that, the butler flinched. "Of course I never intended to do anything that would harm anyone, Miss Hastings. I was only trying to keep you safe."

"I know that," she said with a sigh. "And I know you have a soft spot for me. But you must always know that more information is better in these situations than less. If I don't know all the facts then how am I to make a rational decision about how to approach this situation? Lady Celeste's letter might contain information that would keep both me and Lord Benedick safe from harm rather than endangering us."

Looking abashed, Greaves nodded. "I only thought to do what would keep you out of danger, Miss Hastings. I knew at the time I was breaking every tenet of my profession. But after what happened to the others, I couldn't stomach the idea of such a thing happening to you." He looked up, his eyes bright with emotion. "I will submit my letter of resignation to Lady Serena in the morning.

I only hope you'll give me time to gather my things and search for a new position."

Sophia, Ben could see, was moved by the butler's confession. It was obvious that she held him in just as much affection as he held her. "I don't think that's necessary," she said briskly. "You were acting out of concern—rather like a father—and as my own father is not here, I cannot help but think that he would heartily approve of your actions. I must warn you, however, that you must, in future, resist the impulse to hide things from the ladies of this house. You are perhaps of a generation that sees ladies as less capable of handling danger or difficulties. But I cannot stress enough that such a notion is wrong-headed."

Greaves closed his eyes for the barest second, letting relief show in the set of his shoulders. Then, before Ben's eyes he pulled himself together and stood up straight and proud. "You are far more generous than I deserve, Miss Hastings," he said stiffly. "I will not make this mistake again. My apologies for allowing my emotions to cloud what I knew to be my duty as a servant."

"And now," Sophia said firmly, "you must bring me the letter or note, or whatever it was, that Lady Celeste left for me. It is imperative that Lord Benedick and I are able to find out just who it is we are looking for. And who killed Mr. Framingham."

With a nod, Greaves bowed again and excused himself to go get the note.

When he was gone, Ben turned to Sophia, who was looking a bit rueful. "I suppose it was obvious the man thinks of you as his special charge," he said gently. "But how did you know he'd taken the letter?"

Shaking her head, Sophia said, "I wasn't positive. But

it suddenly occurred to me that there was one person in the house who would wish more than anyone else to keep me from harm's way. And when I recalled his response to my ankle, I realized that it could be no one else."

"He'd have been sacked in any other household in England," Ben pointed out. He tried to imagine what he'd have done if he learned Jennings was hiding things from him. But the situation was different, he supposed. He was a grown man, and though Sophia was a strong, capable woman, society hadn't yet come to the realization that ladies were able to make their own decisions. Greaves was a product of his upbringing and despite serving as butler to Lady Celeste—who was most certainly not a conventional lady—he must have made the mistake of seeing Sophia as one. Not to mention that his affection for her had made him fearful on her behalf. As Ben well knew—thinking back to his reacting to seeing Ryder's arm raised to her—fear of seeing Sophia harmed could inspire all sorts of rash behavior.

"But this is not any other household in England," Sophia said firmly. "And for all that he's made our task of finding who's behind the forgery and Framingham's murder more difficult, I cannot be angry with him. He's a dear man and has taken excellent care of us all. I believe much of the time there's a tendency to see servants as cold and emotionless. Interchangeable. And I know well enough that there's nothing farther from the truth."

Ben moved to stroke her arm. "You are extraordinary."

As he watched, a blush crept up from her neck and into her cheeks. "I'm nothing special," she responded with a slight smile.

He was calculating whether he had enough time to

kiss her before the butler came back when the man him-self returned.

Presenting a sealed letter to Sophia, Greaves bowed. "Again, I apologize, Miss Hastings. It won't happen again. You have my word."

Taking the proffered missive, Sophia nodded. "I know it won't, Mr. Greaves. Thank you for doing the right thing."

With another bow, the butler began to walk back to the door. He was almost there when Sophia called after him. "Mr. Greaves?"

He turned, "Yes, Miss Hastings?"

"Thank you for looking out for me." She gave him a smile guaranteed to melt the sternest heart. "I don't be-lieve my own father could have done a better job of it."

Ben wasn't certain, but he thought the old man blushed before he gave a brisk nod and slipped from the room.

Once Greaves was gone and the door closed behind him, Sophia slipped her thumb beneath the wax seal bearing the imprint of Lady Celeste's ring.

She was frustrated by Greaves' actions, of course. But she couldn't help but feel that his impulses had come from a desire to protect her. She didn't approve of his de-cision to keep the letter from her, but she couldn't con-demn the man or order him dismissed because he'd acted out of affection and loyalty. It simply wasn't something she could do and remain content with herself.

Ben watched her closely as she unfolded the parch-ment and began to read aloud.

> *My dear Sophia,*
> *I cannot tell you how pleased I am that an artist*
> *of your talent and vision has agreed to come to Beau-*

champ House. You are likely unaware of it, but I attended the exhibition of your work in York two summers ago, and that is what convinced me that I could choose no other painter to join the group of ladies to whom I intended to leave my home. (That your sister is a celebrated naturalist in her own right, and therefore was perfect to round out my quartet of scholars, was a happy coincidence.) Welcome to your new home. I hope that you will find my studio—where I have spent many happy hours engrossed in my own, far less impressive, work—is congenial to your artistic eye and that you will produce more of your wonderful work here.

As with your fellow scholars, I have a task which I believe you in particular are best suited for. In no way am I insisting that you undertake this investigation, but I do believe that if you choose not to, the very artistic world which you cherish so much will suffer. The decision, however, is yours.

Now, the facts. For some time now I've been aware that one of the galleries in the village has been selling forgeries of some very valuable paintings to buyers who are either unaware that the paintings are fake, or don't particularly care. I stumbled upon the matter when I visited Mr. Framingham's gallery one afternoon and came upon the man himself wrapping a painting that looked familiar, while a Mr. Richard Nettles, as he was introduced to me, waited. I had come to pick up one of my own pieces which I'd asked Framingham to frame for me. It was only a quick glimpse, but I was certain I'd either seen the work Framingham was wrapping before—or I'd seen it described. It was Italian, that much I knew. And after consulting one of my collections of art books in the library, I realized that the painting was by Tintoretto. *The Temptation of Eve*, which dated to 1578. But I knew one other detail about the painting that my books didn't. This particular work had been part of a collection of some thirty valuable works of art that were purchased from a French Nobleman who was desperate to buy passage for his family out of France as the revolution raged around them. The purchaser was none other than my father, the fifth Duke of Beauchamp, who was in France on business at the time. You will find enclosed with this note a list of those paintings, which were lost in a shipwreck while crossing the English Channel. My father, was, of course, unharmed as he'd returned to England a month before. He was quite upset over the loss, however, and would often lament it when in his cups.

The realization that this Mr. Nettles had purchased what was surely a forgery was troubling to me, and I approached a friend with ties to the Home Office with the information. That avenue, however, was not productive. So, I endeavored to learn more from Framingham. After a few pointed questions, wherein I hinted that I would like to buy a painting similar to that of Mr. Nettles, I learned the man had been recommended to Framingham by a newcomer to the area, Mr. Peter Morgan. I'd met the man before and found him to be just the sort of bombastic fellow I abhorred, who had no real love for art, but instead saw it as a means of elevating his own stature. I also learned that several more of Morgan's friends had also purchased paintings at his behest. The identity of these paintings confirmed my suspicions. Someone had a list of the paintings that were lost in the Channel and was painting them to order *for the unsuspecting amongst Morgan's set, who doubtless didn't know Michelangelo from Vermeer, much less were able to tell a forgery from the real thing.*

I sent my man of business to each of the homes where the forged paintings were now on display, and one by one, he purchased six of them. These six you will find here in the studio cupboard where I put them for safe-keeping. I did not tell the authorities about the scheme because there was one particular detail that my man learned upon his visits to these middle class homes which made that impossible.

Framingham had told all of the buyers that the paintings in question had come from the collection of an unconventional member of the aristocracy: one Lady Celeste Beauchamp.

That someone has been forging works that my father lost at sea is one thing. That they would attribute the previous ownership of said paintings to his daughter was outrageous. Not only did it make my father look like an insurance cheat, but it also made me out to be complicit in the matter. I could no more report that to the authorities than I could turn myself in to them. Besides, I'd already gone to them with the news and they'd chosen to either ignore me, or conduct their own investigation without informing me of the details.

On top of this, my illness has made it difficult, if not impossible, for me to handle the details and day-to-day investigation into this matter. Which is why, my dear Sophia, I leave it in your capable hands. As a fellow artist, I know you will find the notion of these valuable works of art being reproduced as bold as you please, without concern for the harm it does to the wider world, as abhorrent as I do. And as one of my four heirs, I hope you will see the insult to my good name as an insult that must be answered. I am unable to do so, but I hope that with some assistance, you will.

Feel free to ask my nephews and Serena for assistance should you need it. And please, be careful. I fear that whoever is behind this will not like being exposed for the charlatan he is. I have my suspicions that Morgan may have something to do with it, but right now it is only a suspicion. I hope that you will find some bit of truth that will prove it one way or another. And if it turns out he is innocent, well, I suppose even one wolf cannot be responsible for all the lost sheep in the world.

Be well, my dear girl, and be safe.

Yours in love for the arts,
Lady Celeste Beauchamp

Chapter 22

From behind the letter which she'd been reading, Sophia produced another sheet which was a list of the paintings Lady Celeste had mentioned. At the top of the page was a heading, which read "Items Lost in the sinking of the *Mary Frances*, May 17, 1788, while crossing the channel from Calais to Bristol." Beneath it was a list of some thirty paintings, the titles and artists of which made Sophia's breath catch. These were works that if they hadn't been lost would be worth hundreds of thousands of pounds. At the bottom of the page was the scrawled signature of the fifth Duke of Maitland, who must have written the list, since it was in a different hand.

"Lady Celeste certainly didn't do things by halves," Ben said as he took the list from Sophia and scanned it. "When she left tasks for you all, she made certain they weren't easy ones. I have an imagine of her in my head as a goddess on Mount Olympus crafting labors for Hercules."

He had a point, Sophia had to admit, as she moved to take out the paintings she and the other heiresses had placed back into the cabinet after looking at them earlier in the week. "I can't believe she stumbled onto a scheme like this simply by chance," she said, staring down at a work that rather skillfully recreated a painting by Vermeer called *Girl with a Fan*. It skillfully, faithfully mimicked the famous Dutch painter's use of light and the portrayal of one of several female models he used again and again. How close it was to the original, Sophia couldn't know until she compared it to a print in one of the collections in the library, but she had a feeling it was close. "If she hadn't recalled the list of paintings her father had lost, she would never have put it together that the work she saw being wrapped by Framingham was a forgery at all."

"What I want to know," Ben said thoughtfully, as he held the list, "is who knew about the lost paintings? Was it widely known that the schooner went down with a fortune's worth of artwork on it, or did the family manage to keep it quiet? I know it was likely a coup for the duke to purchase such a collection, but the loss of it would have stung. I can imagine he'd do what he could to keep news of the sinking—or more particularly what went down on it—a secret."

"That's something we'll need to ask Serena, and perhaps Kerr and Maitland when they return from London, about," Sophia said. "They may have heard family stories. Though I believe the duke himself died before they were born."

"If it was kept a secret, then how did Ryder get hold of it?" Ben asked, as usual his jaw tightening at the man's very name. "He had to know which paintings he was meant to recreate. And I think we're no longer in any doubt that he is the one who has been painting them, are we?"

Sophia shook her head. It was possible someone else had been the artist in question, but she'd seen his work during their visit to Primrose Green. And the brush-work, the mixing of colors, it was all very similar to the works she was looking at now. "I think it is him, yes," she said. "And I would very much like to ask him whether he has any conception of the harm his forgeries have done. Not just in Little Seaford, but also in the art world as a whole."

At that, however, Ben shook his head. "Absolutely not," he said with a finality that put her back up. "I will speak to the man if it's necessary. But you are to go no-where near him."

"You are being unreasonable," Sophia pointed out with a scowl. "I can speak to him about the paintings themselves. Artist to artist. And perhaps I can convince him to tell us who else is behind the scheme. Especially when he learns that Morgan was planning to get rid of him."

"And I'm not comfortable with you being in the same room with the fellow," Ben countered. "He raised his hand to you, Sophia, or have you forgotten? I can't speak for my actions if he does such a thing again."

She was at once touched by his concern, and annoyed at his high-handedness. Must all the men in her life in-sist upon protecting her from herself?

Standing, she moved to slip her arms around his neck, and though he was still annoyed, she felt him relax a little at her nearness. "I cannot imagine he would be so foolish as to do something like that again, Ben. He's a forger, not a fool. And if you're with me, he'll have even more incentive to behave."

"Don't think I don't realize what you're doing," he said, even as he slid his hands over her bottom and pulled her closer. "I know when I'm being coaxed, Miss Hastings."

She leaned in and kissed him, just letting her mouth brush across his. "I was Sophia before. Why the formality?"

"I am trying to be a gentleman, Sophia," he said on a sigh as she nibbled over his chin. "And you're making it dashed difficult."

She knew exactly how difficult his struggle was—she felt the evidence of his body's attempt to overcome his mind pressing against her stomach.

"I don't need a gentleman just now, Ben," she whispered against his ear. "I need a man. That's all. Not a vicar. Not a lord. Not a gentleman. Just a man."

Ben felt a shudder run through him as Sophia nipped his earlobe.

She was going to be the death of him.

But there was one particular part of him that came to life whenever she was near, and it was making a very good argument for the opposite.

"I can't just throw you over my shoulder and have my way with you like a barbarian," he said through clenched teeth. "You deserve to be wooed. To be taken in a bed, with proper attention to detail."

His hands stroked over her back as he spoke, however, encouraging her as she kissed a path down his neck.

When she stopped, he almost wept. "Ben," she said in a firm tone. "I know what I want. And I do not care about hearts or flowers. I don't need a proper bed. I only need you. And as shocking as this might be to your delicate sensibilities, I want you."

As she spoke, she met his eyes and he found himself awed again by her ability to cut to the heart of the matter. To get past his reservations and respect for the conventions and to speak the truth of what lay between them. "You're sure?" he asked, his voice husky with desire. "Because I'm willing to wait."

Her mouth quirked into a half smile before she kissed him hard on the mouth. "I know you are and I love you for it. But I am not."

Some recess of his brain where his primitive desires lay took over then, and he lifted her into his arms and carried her over to the settee, which was bathed in afternoon light. Gently settling her onto the sofa, he all but sprinted to the door and turned the lock.

When he returned, he found her sprawled over the deep red velvet of the cushions, her cheeks pink with desire and looking like a sumptuous banquet meant only for him. Never letting his eyes leave her, he shrugged out of his coat and waistcoat and tossed them aside. Then came his cravat, which was a bit more difficult given the slight trembling of his fingers. It went into pile with his coats. His boots took a bit more time, but he removed them with what he considered admirable speed. Turning, he saw that she was gazing appreciatively at him.

"Don't forget to remove your shirt," she said in a sultry tone. "I want to see you."

It was the work of a moment to pull the fine lawn over his head and another minute more before he could gather her against him and reverse their positions on the settee, with him on the bottom, and her sprawled over his chest.

When their mouths met, it was surprisingly gentle. He felt as if he'd been waiting for this moment from their first meeting. Though he hadn't known it at the time. He'd only known then that she was the most beautiful thing he'd ever seen and he wanted her. That thought, like so many that went against his values as a gentleman and a clergyman, had been suppressed. But here, now, he was as fully himself as he could recall feeling in years. With

Sophia, Ben was, as she'd said she wanted, just a man. A man who wanted more than anything in the world to make love to the woman in his arms.

He took his time with her, savoring every soft stroke of her tongue, and answering with parries of his own. Their bodies pressed together, his naked chest against her clothed one, while he explored the rest of her with his hands. While she sighed into his mouth, his hand wandered over the generous curve of her hip, and down over her thigh to gather the loose fabric of her gown and slide it up, inch by inch, until her stockinged leg was exposed and he touched the naked flesh just above her garter.

She gave a gasp against his mouth, then gave a slight tilt of her hips, encouraging him to move his hand up further. At the same time, he used his other hand to pull down the bodice of her gown, exposing the bosom he'd been dreaming of for weeks. Even from the way she was positioned, in the shadows, he could see that her breasts were every bit as beautiful as he'd imagined. Unable to hold back, he bent his head to take one rosy tip gently between his teeth before laving it with his tongue. Sophia gave a gasp of pleasure and writhed a little against him.

Needing to feel her beneath him, he flipped their positions until she was on her back and he was kneeling over her, where he could worship one breast with his mouth while he stroked and caressed the other with his hand. Beneath him, Sophia gave a little cry as he suckled her and he felt her hips buck against him, which was sweet anguish to his cock nestled as it was between her thighs. Taking his hand from her breast, he slipped it beneath her gown and stroked up, up until he reached the heart of her, where the gathering wetness revealed the depth of her desire. He stroked a finger over her clitoris while at the same time giving a decadent suck at her nipple and Sophia almost bucked off the sofa.

"Ben," she gasped, unable to stop her body's response to the caress. "Oh."

He did it again, this time stroking a finger over her opening, then plunging one inside. Then another. Judging by Sophia's little cries of bliss, she was coming undone. And one more stroke had her crying out again and bucking against him in earnest again and again before she finally lay still and panting.

Quickly, efficiently he got her out of her gown, and stockings and undergarments, and when she was lying naked before him, Ben felt his chest constrict at the sight. He had never, in all his life, seen a more beautiful sight.

The eyes she lifted to him were drowsy with pleasure, but she raised her arms to him and he shucked off his breeches and went to her. Finally, at last, skin against skin.

"It might hurt a bit," he warned her, not wanting the realities of their joining to be a surprise to her. As she'd pointed out to Greaves, she deserved to make her own decisions based on the facts. "But I will do all I can to ensure it doesn't last."

"I'm not worried," she said with a smile. "I want you. I want this. Judging by what you just did with your hands, I cannot imagine you're bad at it."

He sent up a prayer of thanks to his years before taking holy orders, where he'd learned quite a bit about bringing as much pleasure as he received. Sex, he'd always considered, was a gift from God. That he was able to share that gift with the woman he loved, was a blessing.

"I'll do my best," he said solemnly, kissing her before he reached between them and pulled her knee up over his hip. Fitting himself against her, he pressed forward thinking of any distraction he could to ignore the hot, wet clasp of her body around his.

Sophia was quiet, as if holding her breath, but he felt her hands clasp his shoulders as he stroked into her. And when he finally, blissfully, seated within her she gave a slow exhale. "No pain," she said softly as they both adjusted to the feel of their joined bodies.

Then, unable to control himself any longer, Ben began to move.

Chapter 23

Sophia wasn't sure what she'd expected the act of love to be like. She'd, of course, learned long ago from naughty books found in her parents' library, and a hidden book of etchings she'd found in the library here at Beauchamp House, what the act entailed. But none of that had captured what it would be like with Ben. With his careful attention to the way she responded to his touch, and the intense look of satisfaction in his eyes as he wrung every last gasp from her while he stroked her with his hands. It was more than anyone could capture on the page, and she was strangely giddy from the emotions it stirred in her.

Now, in what should have been an embarrassingly awkward pose with him braced over her on one arm, she was instead filled with a sense of deepest elation and joy. But as he pulled out of her, and ever so slowly pressed back inside, she felt something else building within her. And her body began to move of its own volition, following him as he pulled away. This was something far more than simple release. As she looked into his eyes, hazy with passion, she felt the bond between them strengthen and wrap them in a cocoon where only they two existed.

His kiss as he plunged into her was needy, desperate. And she answered him caress for caress, stroke for stroke. They moved together in a dance she knew was not unique to them, but it felt as if it was. As if they were the only two people in the world.

And then she couldn't think at all, as his every stroke ignited another small spark within her and she was lost in an explosion of desire, where every touch sent her higher into the flames.

Then, as if knowing she needed it more than anything, Ben slipped a hand between them and touched that sensitive part of her above where they were joined and Sophia felt herself fly higher, like a firework she'd once seen at Vauxhall, shooting into the sky. Her body trembled with the euphoria of it and she was lost. Her body remaining below while her soul flew away into the ether.

Some distant part of her felt his strokes quicken and Ben gave a throaty growl before she felt him stiffen against her. Then, he let out a long sigh and lowered himself on shaky arms to lie fully against her.

It was a moment before she came back to herself. And she was surprised to feel that they were both a little sweaty. Idly she stroked her hand over his naked back as he continued to catch his breath.

"I rather think that was better than advertised," she said with a touch of wonder. The books in her father's library had been rather flowery in their language and she found they hadn't quite captured the truly world-changing effects of what they'd just done. "Someone ought to write a pamphlet."

Ben lifted his head, his eyes full of mirth and a hint of satisfaction she'd not seen in them before. He was more handsome than she'd ever seen him.

"I rather think there are any number of pamphlets, my

dear," he said with a crooked grin. "They just happen to be more common among naughty schoolboys than young ladies of delicate breeding. Otherwise I'm sure you'd have seen them."

"Humph," Sophia said unable to stop herself from ruffling his already disarranged curls. "I think it's preposterous that young men are allowed to see such things and young ladies are kept in ignorance."

"It's hardly something that's encouraged among lads," Ben said, moving so that she was in his lap and he wasn't crushing her. "In fact, at school it was soundly criticized. But I take your point. I imagine a number of young ladies would know better how to protect themselves from randy young lads if they knew what the act entailed."

"I was thinking more along the lines of knowing just how pleasurable it can be," she said with a sheepish smile. "Though there is sense in what you say as well. Either way, I wish I'd known before what I was missing."

He gave a playful groan. "So that you could be off doing this with other men?" he demanded, nipping her ear.

"So that I would have done this with you sooner," she said turning to kiss him. "It's maddening to think of all the months we could have been doing that but were instead sipping tea and chatting about village matters."

Ben gave a laugh that was as carefree as she'd ever heard from him. Perhaps she wasn't alone in the sense of euphoria their coupling had brought.

"I am quite glad you've agreed to marry me, Sophia, otherwise there's no telling what sort of wicked paths you'd lead me down."

"Yes," she agreed. "I will make an honest man of you to keep your reputation from being thoroughly ruined."

At that they must have both recalled the earlier discussion with the bishop, because Sophia saw his smile fade and she knew her own had done so as well.

"I know you said it didn't bother you," she said softly. "But will it bother you very much for the bishop to keep you from advancing?"

He gathered her against him. There was a soft blanket hanging over the back of the settee and he pulled it over them both.

"I want to marry you, no matter what the Bishop of Chichester has to say about it," he said against her hair. "And the sooner the better."

She couldn't help the little sigh of relief that ran through her. Sophia had been prepared to give him up, but it would have been difficult. Still, she didn't wish to come between him and his calling. "You're sure?"

His laugh reverberated through her. "Sophia, do you know why and how I was called to the church?"

"Well, no," she said thoughtfully. "I suppose I just thought you . . . well, I don't know."

He stroked a hand down her bare arm. "I knew from an early age that as the second son, I'd be destined for either the church or the army. It's the tradition in the Lisle family. My Uncle Cedric is a celebrated hero of the Peninsular campaign, but another thing I knew from an early age was that I wasn't cut out for war. And by the time I went to university, Napoleon had been defeated."

"So, you chose the church by default?" Sophia asked, puzzled.

"Not exactly," he said. "It was more a matter of suitability. You see, I was always drawn to helping people. Freddie and Archer are both good with people too, but neither of them is particularly—" he searched for the right word, "—driven to help them, I suppose you'd say. I cannot go through life ignoring the suffering around us, you see. I must do something to help. Even if my assistance isn't necessarily welcomed, I'll at least know I've tried. Given all that, when the time came to choose a direction at university, the church was the logical choice."

She was silent for a moment, her heart full of affection for this dear man who had so much love for humanity.

He mistook her silence for censure, however. "I can see why that might be worrisome for you, I suppose. But I can assure you I would never neglect you, or our family for the sake of—"

She lifted her hand to his face and pulled him down for a kiss. "Of course I don't find it worrisome. What sort of monster would dislike the fact that her betrothed has a good heart?"

"I didn't think you were a monster," he protested. "Just that it was maybe—"

"Hush," she said against his mouth. "You're a dear man and I only hope I can live up to the example you set."

"I'm not a saint, Sophia," he said with a frown. "Far from it."

"For which I am most grateful," she said with a smile as she gestured to them lying together beneath the blanket.

"I want to marry you sooner rather than later," he said firmly.

"And I want to marry you," she said against his chest. "But I must solve this puzzle Lady Celeste has left for me first."

She both felt and heard his laugh. "Of course you do. And I wouldn't think of pulling you away from it. I'm just as invested in finding Framingham's killer as you are. And, in an odd way, I credit the conversation between

Framingham and Morgan we overhead that morning on the cliffs with bringing us together."

It was true, she realized. They'd been drawn to one another before that. But it had taken that shared experience to thrust them together for more than the space of a few hours. "I dislike owing a debt to Peter Morgan," she admitted. "But in this case there's no way around it."

Then, realizing the late hour, they reluctantly dressed and though Sophia objected to it, he wouldn't allow her to walk him downstairs.

"You need to rest," he said, kissing her nose. "And to get off your ankle."

She was loath to admit it, but he was right. It was also likely a good idea not to be seen by the household escorting her lover to the door looking as if she'd just been tumbled. "Fine," she agreed. "But tomorrow we must go see Ryder. It's time for him to admit his role in this."

At that he looked troubled. "I don't disagree, but tomorrow I have to go to London."

"Why?" she thought they'd just agreed that finding Framingham's killer was important.

"Because I need to get a special license," he said frankly. "We will concentrate on the murder of Framingham when I get back in a day or so. But I will not allow you to face any unnecessary censure as a result of your relationship with me. If that means we marry in haste, then so be it. And since the Bishop of Chichester is not particularly pleased with me at the moment, I will instead go to the Archbishop of Canterbury, who happens to be a friend of my father's."

She blew out a breath of frustration. She could argue, but she knew he would win. One thing she was becoming keenly aware of was that Ben Lisle would do whatever it took to protect her. "I suppose it can wait until you return," she said with a shrug. "I can look into the paintings a bit more too. Perhaps find out where they ended up."

He looked concerned. "Do not put yourself in danger," he said. "Please promise me."

As if to emphasize his words, he pulled her to him for a quick kiss.

"I promise," she said, pulling away before they got carried away again. "Now, shoo or your father will suspect me of kidnapping you for ransom."

He rolled his eyes at that. "I rather think he'll suspect we've been up to exactly what we've been up to," he said wryly.

Sophia felt her eyes widen. "I certainly hope not!"

She heard his laugher echo as he strode off toward the stairs.

Left alone in the studio, Sophia collapsed onto the settee and stared off into space.

She was going to marry a vicar, she thought with a grin. Did wonders never cease?

The next morning, after seeing his father off on his trip to visit Cam down the coast, Benedick packed a few things for a short trip into London and set out. It was only a day's journey by horseback and he arrived in town that evening exhausted but determined to meet with both the archbishop and the Earl of Mainwaring.

As he'd traveled, it had occurred to him that Mainwaring hadn't given Freddie the entire story about the forged paintings. Lady Celeste's letter to Sophia, along with the list of paintings that were lost in the Channel crossing, had made several things clear to him. First, that it was likely someone in the government had known from the start that the forgeries were—not coincidentally—copies of items from that list. And secondly, that Mainwaring had known, somehow, of Ben's friendship with Sophia and hoped to capitalize on it to find out what Lady Celeste had known about the forgeries. There was no way that the Home Office could have foreseen that he and Sophia find themselves betrothed, of course, but they were in the business of using connections to learn information.

The way the earl had used Freddie's relationship with his brother to bring Ben into the investigation was a prime example of that.

If it was the case that Mainwaring had known just how much danger Sophia would be in as a result of her connection to Lady Celeste? Well, Ben would have a few choice words for the man. He had no issue with putting his own life on the line, because he'd made the decision to take part in the search for the forgers knowing the risk. But Sophia's position as one of Lady Celeste's heirs was not something she could choose. And as the only painter in the quartet, that meant she was automatically at risk from the men who had undertaken the scheme to fake the paintings that Lady Celeste's father had lost. She was the one most likely to recognize a forged painting when she saw it. And she was the one most likely to receive some word from Celeste about the forgery scheme.

After a bath and a change of clothes in his rooms at Pemberton House, the ducal mansion in Mayfair, he set out for the Mainwaring townhouse.

From the line of carriages leading up to the front entrance, and the lights blazing from the townhouse windows, Ben knew at once that the earl and countess were entertaining. His mother would be horrified to learn he intended to show up without an invitation, but given the closeness of the two families, and the importance of his errand, he ignored the niggle of guilt he felt.

Fortunately, he'd brought and worn evening clothes, so when he presented himself to the butler it was only with a slightly raised brow that the man escorted him to Mainwaring's study to wait for the earl, who was currently with his guests in the drawing room.

It took only a few minutes for Mainwaring, looking not particularly surprised to find Ben in his study, to arrive.

"Ben," said the earl as he stepped inside and shut the door firmly behind him, "I might have known you'd come to beard me in my den at some point. Freddie told me you would have more questions about this forgery business."

The men shook hands and Ben noted that since his marriage, the earl had lost the restless look he'd once worn like a second skin.

"Freddie knows me too well," he responded once the two men had taken seats in the high-backed leather chairs that ranged before the fire. "And, of course, he can't have known at the time that Lady Celeste Beauchamp and her heirs would be so important to your investigation."

To his credit, Mainwaring didn't pretend to misunderstand the implication of Ben's words. "So you've discovered the list of paintings Lady Celeste's father lost in the Channel?"

"Miss Sophia Hastings found the list," Ben corrected. "Which you suspected would happen, I think?

A slight shrug lifted the earl's shoulders. "I knew from both the Marchioness of Kerr's and the Duchess of Maitland's experiences as Lady Celeste's heirs that there was a good chance Lady Celeste had left some sort of puzzle for Miss Hastings as well. It stood to reason that it involved the forgeries she'd been investigating for us before her death."

Ben blinked. "What did you say?"

"Don't tell me none of you has realized yet?" Mainwaring gave a soft laugh. "Given the sheer degree of intellect shared amongst the four Beauchamp House heiresses alone, I would have thought someone would have made the connection. Lady Celeste was one of ours."

It made a mad sort of sense, Ben realized, thinking over the events of the months since Lady Celeste's death. She'd left a series of quests for her heirs to investigate. Her own murder, of course, was personal and the perpetrator had had reasons for wanting her dead that had nothing to do with her work for the government. But the quest she'd sent the Duchess of Maitland on, and the task she'd left for Sophia, were both of interest to the Home Office.

"Did you know she'd left these bits of unfinished business for her heirs to deal with?" he asked carefully. If Maitland had knowingly allowed the Beauchamp House heiresses to put themselves in danger without guidance from the Home Office, he wasn't sure how he'd manage to keep his opinion to himself—longstanding family friendship or no.

"God no!" Mainwaring looked insulted at the very idea. "Celeste made those mad decisions on her own. I did guess that there were more to come after the business with the Duchess of Maitland, and so I sent Freddie to involve you before Miss Hastings got too heavily mixed up in this forgery business. Celeste was the one who realized they were using the list of her father's paintings, and so I left it to her to locate the major players. But she died before that could happen. She collected a few of the forgeries, but was unable to learn who was painting them. We've had our eye on Morgan, of course."

That was a relief, at least, Ben thought, relaxing a little. He'd been prepared to give his brother's friend a dressing down. But given that Lady Celeste seemed to have engineered much of this herself, he could hardly blame Mainwaring for her actions. He might be a spymaster, but he wasn't a mind reader.

"Miss Hastings is heavily involved now," he told the earl pointedly. "Mostly because we both overheard Morgan and the gallery owner Framingham arranging to rid themselves of the artist they'd been using to paint their forgeries. Though I imagine Freddie told you that."

"He did, indeed," Mainwaring agreed. "And of course we know about Framingham's murder now. Do you think Ryder is responsible? I believe he's the one who found the body."

Ben told him about what he and Sophia had witnessed in the gallery the afternoon of the murder, not leaving out the scene between Ryder and Sophia he'd come upon.

The earl's brows rose in surprise when he was finished. "I knew he was a rough customer, but I hadn't realized his thuggery ran to threatening ladies as well. I wonder you didn't plant him a facer then and there."

"I considered it," Ben admitted. "But Miss Hastings reined in my temper. Not for the first time, where Ryder is concerned. Then, of course, we heard the commotion of him finding Framingham's body and the matter was put to the side."

"It sounds as though the lady has become quite the influence in your behavior, Ben," said Mainwaring with a smirk. "Watch out or you'll find yourself, a vicar, caught in the parson's mousetrap."

Ben rolled his eyes at the joke. "How long have you been waiting to use that line?"

"Since you took holy orders, actually," Mainwaring said with a grin. "Given that the swathe you cut through the ladies back in the day rivaled Freddie's, it wasn't unreasonable that you'd one day find yourself snared."

While it was true he hadn't been a saint in the years before he joined the church, Ben wasn't sure it was fair to say he'd been as profligate as Freddie. Still he couldn't exactly defend himself when there was a grain of truth in what the man said.

"As it happens," he said with a grin of his own, "Miss Hastings and I have agreed to make a match of it. Though you needn't look so pleased with yourself. If anyone is responsible for our betrothal, it's Peter Morgan and his insistence upon plotting the demise of his protegé in so public a location."

"Oh, come now," Mainwaring argued. "If I hadn't sent Freddie down to Little Seaford with instructions for you, do you really think you and Miss Hastings would have become so involved in this business?"

"Clearly you've never met the lady," Ben said, "Freddie or no Freddie she'd have found a way to look into the matter. I'm just grateful I was there to curb her impulse to confront Morgan and Ryder on her own."

At the mention of Ryder, Mainwaring raised a finger. "Speaking of Ryder, while I agree that he's a cretin, and up to his eyeballs in this business, I must warn you that the Home Office isn't sure that he's the only artist who's been involved in this business. In fact, we believe Morgan has a partnership with a group of artists. Which makes sense given that the forgeries are of works from artists from different eras and different styles. It would be rare for a single man to master so many different styles with the sort of skill necessary to paint such convincing fakes as these."

The hairs on the back of Ben's neck rose. "A group of artists? Do you have any idea who they might be?"

"There's a couple in the area," Mainwaring said with a shrug. "I believe they've turned a local manor house into a haven for artists? The Primbles?"

Chapter 24

"Primrose Green," Ben said, feeling like a fool for not realizing it before. The Primbles had been so ready to offer up Ryder as the forger amongst them. But if they were working with Morgan, then it would make sense for them to do so. Ryder was just one of many cogs in the wheel of this operation. As such, he was expendable.

"That's the place," Maitland agreed. "Celeste was friendly with the wife, in particular. And even confided about her father's lost collection in her. She never had proof the paintings were coming from Primrose Green, but it would have only taken a bit of investigation on the Primbles' part to get a list of the paintings from the insurance company. And Celeste hadn't told anyone else about the loss."

"Why wouldn't she tell Sophia about this?" Ben asked. "She gave her the list of paintings and told her about how she discovered the forgery scheme, but she left no word about the Primbles or the Home Office involvement in the investigation."

"I can only imagine that she was not in possession of all her faculties at the time she wrote the letter to Sophia," Maitland said with a frown. "Or that she hoped, out of misplaced loyalty to her friends the Primbles, that they were not responsible for the scheme. The last time I spoke to her she was still hoping Ryder was the only forger. Celeste was an intelligent woman, but even she was capable of being swayed by ties of friendship."

"And do you know anything about who murdered Framingham?" Ben asked, suddenly worried that he'd left Sophia in Little Seaford with only the household servants and her fellow heiresses as protection. If the Primbles were involved, they had a houseful of artists whose livelihoods were in danger if their crimes were discovered. Not to mention that Morgan and Ryder were still in the village. What had he been thinking to travel to London at this time?

"Northman has concluded it was likely a thief who was interrupted in the process of attempting to steal from the gallery," Maitland said with a snort. "It's ridiculous, of course, but then Northman is a fool. I think it very likely it was one of his fellow conspirators. Especially given that the man summoned you there to presumably tell you about the whole scheme. So, either Morgan, or the Primbles."

Ben stood.

"What's your hurry, man?" Mainwaring asked, frowning. "We'll have something to connect one of them to Framingham's murder soon. I'm sure of it."

"That's fine for you to say from the comfort of your home in London, Mainwaring," Ben said as he headed for the door. "But Sophia is in Little Seaford with only three other ladies and a houseful of servants to protect her from these people who have already killed once to hide their scheme. Forgive me if I don't share your sanguine view of the situation."

"Damn it," the earl muttered as he stood as well.

"And Maitland and Kerr are in my drawing room. I think. But surely they won't dare to threaten Miss Hastings without provocation."

"Sophia promised me not to confront Ryder while I was gone," Ben said as he stopped for a brief moment in the doorway. "And she knows better than to speak to Morgan alone. But neither of us knew anything about the Primbles' involvement. For all I know she's invited them to dinner at Beauchamp House tonight."

"I knew it!" Gemma said, throwing her arms around her sister's neck upon the news that Sophia had accepted Benedick's proposal.

The sisters were in the library of Beauchamp House, along with Ivy and Daphne, the morning Ben departed for London. Sophia had wanted to give them her news the evening before but she'd been exhausted from the events of the day and had gone to bed early. But today, rested and ready to take on whatever the day brought to her, she'd come to the library after breakfast in her room to do a bit of research on the other artists in the list of lost paintings Celeste had left for her.

When she found Gemma and the others were already immersed in their own research projects in the library, she'd decided to share her news with them. She hadn't considered, however, just how many shrieks of joy and surprise the announcement would elicit.

"From the moment you met I saw sparks," Ivy said with a grin of satisfaction. "I can't wait to tell Quill. He discounted my ability to tell when couples are in love, but this is twice now I've done it."

"Who was your other success story?" Sophia asked, momentarily distracted. She tried to recall her first meeting with Ben and failed. It may have been when they went to discuss Daphne and Maitland's wedding plans, but she couldn't be sure. She'd have to ask him later.

"Daphne and Maitland, of course," Ivy said with a smug smile. "Quill will be quite put out. But I do have a bit of knowledge about the subject, given my study of love poetry."

Gemma frowned. "You can hardly be the only one to see that Maitland was smitten, Ivy, dear. He was gobsmacked from the moment he saw her."

"And he's not exactly one to hold his cards close to his chest," Daphne added with a smirk. "He's a terrible card player."

"Oh, I know Maitland was easy enough to see," Ivy retorted, "But Daphne herself was a different case altogether. And I could tell she was smitten as well. For all that she didn't let anyone know it."

"I was not!" Daphne objected, the telltale flush creeping up into her fair cheeks telling a different story. "I hardly noticed him."

"Dearest," Sophia said to the tall blonde with an affectionate smile, "you must know that's impossible. Your husband might be many things, but easy to ignore is not one of them. Even I noticed him. Any woman who wasn't dead or dying would. He is a handsome man."

By this time the other two had risen from their various study spots and gathered around the Hastings sisters.

"You are right about that, I suppose," Daphne said with a grin. "Maitland is quite good-looking. But so is your vicar."

"There's a reason the church is filled every Sunday since his arrival in the village, Sophia," Gemma agreed. "You've made yourself the most hated woman in Little Seaford by accepting him."

"This calls for a celebration," Ivy said with a grin. She went to the bell pull and when Greaves answered she requested a pot of tea and some celebratory cakes. "You are to congratulate Miss Hastings, Greaves. She has accepted a proposal of marriage from Lord Benedick."

Sophia had been afraid that her easy relationship with the butler might have been ruined by the situation with Lady Celeste's letter, but the man didn't seem to hold a grudge over the scolding she'd given him. And since she was no longer angry about the omission, given his reasons for keeping it from her, she was pleased to see they could go on without further awkwardness.

"I am very pleased for you, Miss Hastings," the butler said with a deep bow. "May I offer my best wishes for your happiness. Lord Benedick is a good man. I hope he will make you very happy."

Touched by the older man's words, Sophia went up on her toes and kissed him on the cheek. "Thank you, Mr. Greaves."

At that the butler turned bright red and murmured something about the tea and beat a hasty retreat.

Some minutes later, the heiresses were once more seated around a tea try and discussing one of Lady Celeste's letters.

Knowing that Greaves' role in keeping the letter away from her would likely poison them against the butler, Sophia had chosen to blame the delay in her receipt of Celeste's letter on her own failure to discover it amongst the documents in the studio.

"How extraordinary of Celeste to leave it up to chance for you to find her letter to you," Ivy said with a frown. "Though I suppose she was ill at the time she decided to do so."

"I think she must have been," Sophia said, sending a

silent apology to the brilliant woman who had done so much to bring them together. "But the good news is that I have it now. And as a result we now know not only that the forgers are purposely recreating lost masterpieces, but also that they attempted to make it look as if Celeste was selling off a collection that her father had falsely claimed lost at sea. Whoever these people are, they are not only trying to profit from forged paintings, but they also sought to ruin Celeste's reputation."

"There are any number of people who must have been unhappy with Celeste and the way she chose to live her life," Gemma said, frowning. "She was outspoken on a number of sensitive topics. Even in Little Seaford she wasn't universally loved, though I believe she counted most of the local families as friends."

"With a few exceptions," Sophia reminded her. "I don't believe she got on very well with Peter Morgan, though by the time he arrived in the village she was already becoming ill. Her description of him in her letter to me is not flattering and she does seem to have suspected him of being involved in some way in the forgery scheme."

"It can hardly be a coincidence that the forged paintings found themselves into the homes of his cronies," Daphne pointed out. "The odds of that happening purely by chance are beyond even my calulatory abilities."

"No, it can't be just by chance," Sophia agreed. "He must be involved. And I think it very likely he had Framingham killed. Perhaps the art dealer was not comfortable with Morgan's scheme to have Ryder killed once he'd become a liability."

"But I don't understand why Ryder is still alive if Morgan had decided to get rid of him," Gemma said, frowning. "Even if he did say he wanted to wait until after the exhibition—presumably to show Ryder as an artist in his own right, and therefore hide his forgery—it would seem that the murder of Framingham made Ryder even more of a liability. He has to know that Morgan is the man behind Framingham's murder."

It was a conundrum, Sophia thought. Then, another possibility occurred to her.

"What if Ryder isn't the forger?" she asked excitedly. "What if we've been looking at the wrong artist this whole time?"

"Explain," Ivy said with a nod.

"It's just that Ben and I have assumed ever since we visited Primrose Green with Lord Frederick that it was Ryder who had forged the paintings. Which made some degree of sense given what we'd overheard Morgan and his accomplice—probably Framingham—say at the cliffs. Ryder is Morgan's protégé. He had plans for the man to be the star of the exhibition. After the exhibition, he would have served his purpose in making Morgan look good. The Primbles were full of stories about how unpleasant Ryder was and his skill at copying other artists. So, we put those facts together and agreed that Ryder was the likely culprit. But there's more than one artist in the area. And Primrose Green has at least a dozen."

"Are you saying the Primbles lied to you all?" Gemma asked, looking shocked.

"The only reason we were predisposed to believe them was Lady Celeste's supposed friendship with Evelyn Primble," Sophia said, "but if we work from what Celeste told us in her letter, about her father's paintings, who among her acquaintance in Little Seaford was she more likely to speak of about her father's lost treasure trove of valuable paintings?"

"Another artist," Ivy said with a look of understanding.

"Celeste confided in her friend about the paintings her father lost and Evelyn took advantage of it."

"Celeste likely could find no proof that it was the Primbles," Sophia said. "If she had she most certainly would have put some clue about them in her letter to me. All I can guess is that she had a suspicion. She knew Morgan was involved without question, given it was his friends who'd bought the forgeries. But beyond that she didn't know."

"Poor Celeste," said Daphne with one of her rare bursts of emotion. "She trusted Evelyn Primble and was betrayed. Again."

The four were silent for a moment as they considered how badly their benefactor had been treated by those in her life. Not only had she been murdered by someone who should have loved her, but her good name had been used to perpetrate a fraud within the very art world she held dear.

"We'll simply need to avenge her," Sophia said, her chin tilted in determination. "And I know just how we can do it."

Chapter 25

As it happened, Ben was able to meet with the arch-bishop just after he left Mainwaring's house. The man was taken aback to be summoned from his bed by his old friend's son, but he'd always had a soft spot for the Duke of Pemberton's boys and though he scolded over the reports he'd had from the Bishop of Chichester, the church leader signed the special license with a flourish.

"Tell your father he owes me a game of whist," he told Ben as he sent him on his way.

Sending a prayer of thanks that his father had happened to attend Eton with the future leader of the Anglican church, Ben returned to the Pemberton town-house, intent on packing his bags for the journey back to Little Seaford.

He was met there by the Marquess of Kerr and the Duke of Maitland, who'd come as soon as their host had informed them of his presence in town.

"Why didn't you tell us what was going on?" Kerr demanded with a scowl. He'd become a friend during Ben's time in Little Seaford, and was clearly annoyed at being left out of the matter. "We can ride back with you in the morning."

"I planned on heading back to the village tonight," Ben said with a warning look. If they needed a night's sleep before traveling then they would do better to remain in London and travel at a more leisurely pace.

"Do you really think that's sensible?" Maitland asked, giving Ben a chiding look. "You've got bags under your eyes I could pack my entire wardrobe in. And your horse is likely exhausted from today's journey. It will do neither of you any good if you have an accident on the journey back."

Ben was about to argue, when Kerr added, "And Sophia is, in all likelihood, safe in her bed by now. If we set out early tomorrow we can arrive in time for luncheon."

He stared at them, thinking. He'd been charging around on the energy his fear for Sophia had given him. But as if it had been conjured out of pure ether, he suddenly felt the weight of fatigue descend upon him like a water-soaked blanket.

"Come, man," said Maitland. "She won't thank you for getting yourself killed. Get some rest before you take to the road again."

With a sigh, Ben scrubbed his hands over his face. "You're right. I'm in no condition for another long ride."

"We'll be here at first light," Kerr assured him, clapping him on the shoulder. "And try not to worry. If Sophia is anything like Ivy, she's up to any rig. Those four are the most determined ladies I've ever me. I'd stake them against Jackson at his best in a prizefight."

Ben had to smile at that. Kerr was probably right.

"Tomorrow," he agreed. "First light."

As promised, the men were on the road by the time the sun came up, Ben on a borrowed mount since his own had needed rest after the previous day's hard ride. After a few stops along the way, they made it into Little Seaford an hour or so after luncheon, and rather than go to the vicarage, Ben accompanied Kerr and Maitland to Beauchamp House.

To his relief, their arrival was met with all four of the ladies of the house pouring into the entryway from the drawing room where they'd been gathered.

"I thought you weren't due back for another few days," Ivy said, throwing herself into Kerr's arms.

As Daphne and Maitland enacted a similar scene a few feet away, Ben sought out Sophia, who pulled him into the drawing room so that their reunion could at least take place in some privacy. (Gemma, who had rolled her eyes at the embracing couples and muttered something about lovesick fools, had made her escape upstairs a few seconds earlier.)

Aware that he likely smelled of horse and the road, Ben nonetheless pulled Sophia into his arms as soon as the door closed behind them. It had been a day and a half since they'd seen one another, but it felt like much longer. And as he kissed her, he felt for the first time what his brother Archer had meant when he described his wife as "home". Sophia was his home. He knew that now as surely as he knew the sun rose in the east.

"I missed you," she said against his cheek as she pulled back a little. "Don't go away for that long again."

He laughed. "I'm not sure I can promise that. Especially given that I spent fourteen of the past twenty-four hours on a horse. A shorter trip to London from Little Seaford hasn't been made, I don't think."

They moved to a large chair where he sat down and pulled her into his lap. "I was afraid I'd come back to find you'd been kidnapped or worse by the Primbles." He rested his chin on the top of her head. "I have news."

She pulled away to look him in the face. "If it's to tell me you think the Primbles are behind the forgery scheme, then I have the same news."

Quickly, they each explained the conclusions they'd come to about the couple who ran the Primrose Green colony, and how they'd come about them.

"Lady Celeste was working for the Home Office?" Sophia asked when Ben was finished. "I should have guessed. This explains so much—not only about her knowledge of the forgery scheme, but also Daphne's search for the Jacobite Cipher and even her suspicions about her own murder. She had an analytical mind and it makes a great deal of sense to think the government would want to take advantage of that."

"It took me by surprise," Ben admitted. "Though I suppose I didn't know her as well as you did."

Sophia frowned at that. "I didn't know her."

"I think you did," he said gently. "You've made a study of her work. You've read her diaries. I think you know her as well as anyone she met during her lifetime. Excepting her family, of course."

That idea seemed to please her and Ben felt a warm glow at the notion.

She laid her cheek against his coat and then sat up again. "You need a bath, sir."

He saw the saucy grin and knew he was in trouble.

"Do I, Miss Hastings?" he drawled. "And how do you propose to make that happen?"

"You'll need to be very quiet," she said with a finger to her lips. "And it will involve a bit of subterfuge."

"Won't your fellow house-mates become suspicious if you suddenly disappear into your bedchamber?" he asked with a raised brow. "Not to mention that my horse is currently in your stables."

She looked disappointed at the news. "The housemates won't be a problem. We likely won't see Ivy and Kerr or Daphne and Maitland downstairs for days. But the horse is a problem."

"Would it make you feel any better if I told you I intended to stay at Beauchamp House to offer you my protection regardless?" he asked.

"Why? Am I in any more danger than I was before?" she asked with a frown. "The Primbles don't know we've realized they're the forgers."

"But they do know that Morgan's scheme with the bishop was unsuccessful," he said. "And I learned in London that Northman has determined Framingham's murder was the result of a robbery gone wrong."

"What?" Sophia asked, her eyes wide. "But that's absurd. Nothing was missing. And no robber would stab a man that many times just because he'd been found out."

"You have a more sensible take on the matter than our magistrate," Ben said wryly. "It's obvious to me that Framingham was killed by one of his conspirators. And to the Home Office, for that matter. But they will let Northman's determination stand for the moment because they don't wish to spook the actual killer. If he feels safe, then perhaps he'll make a mistake."

"Whether it was Morgan and his henchman or the Primbles," Sophia said, a furrow between her brows, "they'll think they've got away with it. I much prefer the notion of them quaking in their boots at the idea of being caught out."

"I know, my dear," he said, kissing her nose. "But we'll need just a few more days of playing along with their scheme before they're brought down for good."

"Oh, I know that," Sophia said with a shrug. "I've already determined the perfect way to make the Primbles confess. And once they're caught, it should be little enough trouble to make them turn on Morgan."

He should have known she'd have a plan. "You'd better tell me all."

She shook her head. "First, a bath. Then, I'll tell you everything."

"You know it's highly inappropriate for us to even discuss such things as bathing. Much less for me, a vicar, to contemplate creeping into your bedchamber to have my wicked way with you."

"You've got a special license in your pocket, haven't you?" she asked with a challenging look.

He patted his breast pocket. "Signed by the archbishop himself."

"Then unless you plan on abandoning me before we can marry, I don't see a problem."

The gossiping tabbies of Little Seaford might think differently, Ben thought wryly. But given that Morgan had already spread rumors about them, staying away from Sophia now would be like shutting the barn door after the horse had got out.

Even so . . .

"As much as I would love to let you have your wicked way with me in your lair, Wallflower," he said with genuine regret, "I cannot do further damage to either of our reputations. And now that Kerr and Maitland are returned I know you'll be safe."

Sophia grumbled under her breath. Something about vicars and propriety.

But he stood firm.

In more ways than one.

Reluctantly, he lifted her from his lap and stood, grateful his coat would cover the evidence of his arousal when he left the room.

Pulling her into his arms, he kissed her thoroughly.

When they were both breathless, he set her away from him. "Now, I must go. I'll come back for dinner if I may?"

The drowsy, just kissed look she gave him was almost enough to make him gainsay his own decision. But he steeled himself against it.

"Yes," she said, with a sigh. "Return for dinner. And we can discuss the plan for routing the Primbles and Morgan."

He left before his desire to pull her into his arms again overcame his good sense.

Once Ben was gone, Sophia went to the library in search of her sister. If she couldn't spend the afternoon in the arms of her betrothed, then she could use it to gather more evidence against the Primbles.

Gemma, as she'd suspected she would be, was curled up in a chair before the fire in the room all the heiresses had decided was their favorite in the house. When Sophia stepped inside, she looked up in surprise.

"I thought you'd be . . ." she seemed to search for the right word.

Sophia gave a shrug. "My vicar has a stronger sense of propriety than I have. And I daresay he has parish business to attend to, though he didn't mention it."

Her sister smiled. "He's a good man, your vicar."

It was a relief to hear her sister say the words. Sophia hadn't really discussed her relationship with Ben with her, and despite her own determination that she'd wed him, she did care what Gemma thought of him. She wouldn't have rejected him if Gemma had done so, of course, but it gave her a sense of inner peace to know that the one person in the world—aside from him—whose opinion truly mattered to her approved.

"He is," she agreed, lowering herself into the chair opposite. "And I have a difficult time believing he's as smitten with me as I am with him."

"Why?" Gemma asked, closing the scientific journal she'd been reading. "It's obvious to everyone that he's smitten. Has been since you first met months ago."

"How did everyone know this but me?" Sophia asked, shaking her head. "I had no idea. It certainly didn't occur to me until he sought me out at Morgan's ball."

"That's because until you injured your ankle you didn't sit still long enough for him to speak to you," Gemma said with a raised brow. "And you were always surrounded by that gaggle of local gentlemen who were trying desperately to catch your interest."

Sophia frowned at that. She hadn't attempted to draw in those men. They simply appeared when she attended a local entertainment. Had they really kept Ben from approaching her?

"Though, I'll add that he himself was busy dodging the lures of every eligible lady in the village," Gemma said. "You're both far too attractive for your own good."

"You make it sound like a liability," Sophia groused. Though in truth, it sometimes was.

"Can you honestly say you don't sometimes wish to fade into the wallpaper?" Gemma asked. "I've seen you juggling gentleman at a ball. And I've seen the look you give when they aren't paying attention."

It was true. Sophia did enjoy lively conversation and always had. But there were times when being the center of attention grew tiresome.

"Then I must be thankful that my turned ankle allowed me the chance to finally slow down." So many things would be different if she'd decided not to take that walk on the shore. "And to let Benedick catch me."

They were quiet for a moment in that comfortable way between sisters.

Then Gemma asked, "What have you decided to do about the Primbles?"

Suddenly, Sophia realized she hadn't shared Ben's news about Lady Celeste with her sister. Quickly she filled Gemma in on Celeste's work for the Home Office, and the role she'd been playing to stop the forgery ring.

"I should have guessed it," Gemma said when she was finished. "It did seem odd that one lady would be involved in so many intrigues, but I suppose I thought she was just interested in many different things. The cipher that Daphne looked for made sense because Lady Celeste was herself interested in puzzles. And the forgeries were in her own village so of course as an artist she'd want to find an answer."

"Now that we know she was officially working with the Home Office, many things make sense," Sophia said. "The clues to her own murder she left for Ivy, the quest she left for Daphne relating to the cipher. And now the forgeries."

"But why didn't she implicate the Primbles in the letter she left you?" Gemma asked.

"We all have blind spots," Sophia said with a frown. "Even someone as brilliant as Lady Celeste."

Still, the fact that her benefactor hadn't named the Primbles specifically bothered her. There was something they were missing as it related to the forgeries. Something that would give them the insight they needed to catch the perpetrators of the fraud.

"I believe I'd like to take a turn in the garden," she said to Gemma. She'd been outdoors since her injury, but that had mostly been in the carriage, and it was no longer paining her now She needed fresh air to clear her head. "Would you like to join me?"

Gemma nodded, and stood up from her chair. "Come," she said, slipping her arm through Sophia's, "let's go see if the sea breeze will give us all the answers."

Moments later, the Hastings sisters were strolling through the garden, which had been designed by Lady Celeste herself. Though it was sunny for spring, there was a chilly breeze and it proved more than Gemma could bear.

"I'm going in to fetch my shawl," she told Sophia once they'd reached the far end of the stand of ornamental trees near the garden's edge. "Shall I bring yours as well?"

Sophia tucked a lock of hair that the wind had blown loose behind her ear. "Yes, please," she said, taking a seat on a stone bench between two lemon trees. She'd brought her walking stick, thankfully, but she still needed occasional breaks for her weakened ankle. "And perhaps my pelisse. I'm not sure my wrap will be enough."

Gemma left with a promise to return in a few minutes. And Sophia, surrounded as she was by the scents of the garden mingled with the sea air, took a moment to simply appreciate her surroundings. It would have been difficult, back when she and her sister had been living with their parents in their respectable, but cramped townhouse in York, to imagine she'd find herself living on the coast in a house that boasted the most breathtakingly lovely library she could have imagined only a few months later. But here she was.

"I've always thought this was a lovely spot."

The voice startled her, and Sophia turned to see Greaves, his hands clasped behind his back staring out at the horizon beyond the boundary of the garden.

"Oh, Greaves," she said, pressing a hand to her chest. "You surprised me."

Something about the man's demeanor made her uncomfortable. But that was likely the residual effect of their quarrel over the letter from Lady Celeste.

"My apologies, Miss Hastings," the servant said with a bow. "That was not my intention."

"Has my sister been delayed?" she asked, wondering why the butler had made it to her side before Gemma.

"I'm afraid Miss Gemma will be unable to rejoin you here for the time being," he said with what sounded like sincere apology. "She's been detained."

"Detained how?" Sophia's heart began to beat faster, though she managed to keep her alarm from showing on her face. "Is she ill?"

"I was forced to give her a bit of sleeping draught in her tea," Greaves said conversationally. "But she'll recover, I assure you. I simply needed her out of the way for a bit."

Sophia was regretting her decision to choose this particular part of the garden for her reflection. With Greaves blocking the path back to the house, and the open stretch of lawn leading to the chalk cliff, she had no options for escape. Not that her ankle would allow her to get far anyway.

"And why is that?" she asked, attempting to sound more authoritative than she felt. "Is there something you wish to tell me?"

To her horror, he stepped closer, and she saw that he'd been holding a bottle and a cloth behind his back. "Miss Hastings, you know I don't wish to harm you. So please, don't fight me."

But Sophia did fight. She tried to block him using her walking stick, but he must have been anticipating it because he ripped it from her hand and threw it aside. Then, with a strength she'd never have expected from the servant she'd come to hold in some affection over the past months, he grasped her by the arm and thrust the sweet smelling cloth in front of her face and she felt herself losing consciousness.

The last thing she heard before she faded was Greaves saying. "I'm that sorry, Miss Hastings. That sorry."

Chapter 26

Despite his attempt to stay away, after a bath, a shave and a change of clothes, Ben found himself on the road back to Beauchamp House some two hours after leaving Sophia and her invitation to visit her chambers.

He was a besotted fool, he thought, as he climbed the steps to the front door, but he didn't much care. As soon as this business with the forgers was over he would marry Sophia and they'd disappear for a bit where no one could find them.

He'd raised his hand to knock when the door was wrenched open from the inside and he found himself face to face with a stern-looking Lord Kerr.

"Good," he said without preamble, pulling Ben into the house and shutting the door behind him. "I was on my way to fetch you."

"What is it?" Ben asked, alarm coursing through him a the other man's manner. "Where is Sophia?"

He'd known he shouldn't have left her here, but his damned sense of propriety had made him go back to the vicarage.

"We don't know," Kerr said, his jaw tight with anger. "And we can't find Greaves either."

At this, Ben went cold. "Damn it."

"What is it?" Kerr asked. "Do you know something?"

Quickly, Ben explained about Greaves withholding the letter Lady Celeste had left for Sophia. "We both thought it odd, but Sophia was convinced he'd done it out of affection for her. To protect her from becoming involved the investigation into the forgeries. But it's possible that was just an excuse when she caught him out. His affection for her seemed genuine, but your guess is as good as mine whether it was an act."

Kerr swore under his breath. "I wish you'd told me about this before. This man has been here with all the ladies for days at a time. And we thought they were safe."

"And it would appear that they were safe," Ben retorted, thrusting a hand through his hair. "With the exception of Sophia."

Following the marquess into the drawing room, he found that the rest of the household—minus Sophia, of course—was gathered there. Gemma, her face pale, was lying on the settee looking much the worse for wear.

"I'm so sorry, Ben," she said when he entered the room. "I shouldn't have left her alone. But I only meant to be gone for a moment."

He hurried to her side. Sophia's sister looked enough like her that it was painful to look at her for a brief moment, then he got hold of himself and took charge. "Where were you? What happened?"

Gemma explained that they'd gone into the garden to get a breath of air and that she'd come inside to fetch their wraps. "When I stepped inside, Greaves was waiting with a tea tray. It had two cups. And he said he'd been on his way out to bring them to us, since it was chilly out. He insisted I drink mine there since I was shivering. And though I was in a hurry, I drank it so he'd let me go."

"And then what happened?" Ben prodded. He needed every bit of information Gemma could give him in order to find Sophia. "Did he say anything else?"

"I think he apologized," she said, shaking her head a little. "And when I started to tremble, he helped me to a chair and told me that Mr. Morgan would see to it that I was compensated."

Compensated? Ben stared. What could that possibly mean?

"I found her in the chair," Ivy offered, from where she stood by Kerr's side. "And she told me that Sophia was in the garden. When I went to look, she was gone. But her walking stick was there, tossed into the shrubbery."

"And there was no sign of where they'd gone?" Ben asked, his blood racing with fear. If Morgan, who had likely had Framingham murdered, was in involved, then there was no telling what he'd do to Sophia.

"None," Ivy said sadly. "But I think we can guess where he's taken her. If Greaves was working for Morgan, then they must be there."

"We need to search the man's rooms," Ben said forcefully, already striding for the door to head down the servants stairs.

"Wait," Maitland said, following. "I'll come with you."

Not waiting to see if he was behind him, Ben kept walking.

Greaves' rooms were small but tidy. He had a small bedroom that was modestly furnished, and a sitting room that was decorated with a far more sophisticated hand than Ben would have suspected of him.

In a place of prominence on the wall, however, was a framed painting that he recognized as one of the works lost in the Channel crossing.

He stepped closer and saw that on the table beside it was a wooden case, such as he'd seen in Sophia's studio, made to hold pigments and paints. An idea came to him. "Do you know if Greaves ever showed an interest in art before Sophia came to Beauchamp House?" he asked Maitland, who'd come into the room behind him.

The duke frowned. "He used to chat with my aunt about her own work," he said thoughtfully. "And I think I recall him saying once that he visited Primrose Green to take lessons on his off day."

They'd assumed because Ryder was the one Morgan had publicly taken under his wing that he must also be the artist the man had hired to forge the paintings. Then, when the Primbles came into the picture, it had seemed that they were the likely suspects since Celeste might have told Evelyn about her father's lost art. No one had considered that there was another person—living in Beauchamp House the whole time—who might also have known about the lost paintings. And whose skill with a brush might be every bit as good at copying as anyone at Primrose Green.

"We have to get to Morgan's mansion," he said, the possibility of why Greaves might take Sophia there sending a shiver of fear through him. "I think that's where he's taken her. And I believe I know why."

Whatever it was that Greaves had used to make her lose consciousness had left Sophia with a dry mouth and a groggy head. She became aware of both as she woke up in the back of a moving cart as it bumped over a bit of rough terrain. Her hands were bound, as were her ankles, and though her head wasn't covered, there was a blanket draped over her whole body that prevented her from seeing where they were headed.

The memory of Greaves overpowering her was disturbing enough, but more troubling was the fact that she had no notion of why he would do such a thing. As with most servants, he'd been good at being always at the ready without revealing much about his own personality. He had always, she'd known, had a soft spot for her. But to her shame, she'd accepted it as just another instance of her outward appearance bringing her undeserved praise. It hadn't occurred to her until he'd kept the letter from Lady Celeste, that his affection might run to something more sinister. Or that it could be a ruse to make her think he was more harmless than he was.

Her mind raced as she tried to remember just what he'd said about his reasons for hiding the letter. But nothing she could recall would have alerted her to the fact that he was planning to kidnap her. He'd said he was trying to keep her safe, and it had seemed at the time that he was sincere. Ben had even thought so.

At the thought of Ben, her gut clenched. What would he do when he discovered she was missing? She wished again that she'd been more forceful about making him stay that afternoon. If he'd been there, she would never have gone into the garden at all. Much less found herself bound and gagged in the back of a cart.

She heard the driver telling the horses to slow, and then the cart rolled to a stop. She waited in fear for Greaves to come for her, but rather than the butler, when the blanket was ripped away she saw two large footmen. One look at the blue and red livery they wore told her exactly where the butler had brought her.

They were at Morgan's mansion.

The larger of the footmen hauled her from the cart and when her ankle refused to hold her weight, he muttered a curse and tossed her over his shoulder like a sack of potatoes. She schooled herself against the indignity of being held against the man's body, especially when the memory of Ben cradling her against his chest was still fresh in her mind. As she bumped against his back, she tried to see details of the house and was strangely relieved to see that at the very least she was correct about the location. Bits of decor and wall hangings, familiar from the ball less than a week ago, told her she was indeed in Morgan's home.

Finally, after what felt like ages, the footmen, and Greaves, who had been walking behind them as if he were any guest being ushered in to see the master of the house, entered what looked from Sophia's upside-down perspective, to be the drawing room.

None too gently, the footman who was carrying her bent forward and deposited her, bottom down, into a chair. As he did so, her elbows went in opposite directions. And she realized that the rope knotted around her wrists wasn't as tight as it had been. Something about the bouncing journey from the cart to the house must have loosened it.

"This one can't stand," he said with a grunt to his master, who stood surveying the newcomers like so much driftwood coming on to shore. "Something wrong with her leg."

And having said his peace, he and his fellow left the room, and shut the door behind them. Clearly, Morgan must ask for many such odd tasks from his servants, she thought grimly. They didn't seem particularly upset or concerned that their master had just had them bring a kidnap victim into his home.

"What have you done, Greaves?" Morgan asked, looking from Sophia to the butler of Beauchamp House, who had come to stand beside her chair.

"I've brought the reason for all your troubles," Greaves said plainly. "It goes against the grain, but now, I want you to do me the courtesy of letting me leave unharmed."

"You damned fool," Morgan growled. "This is the last thing I needed. Do you know how many people will be looking for this woman? She's all but betrothed to the son of the Duke of Pemberton! I wanted her separated from him, but not like this. It's why I sent for the bloody bishop to chastise him. Now you'll lead the authorities right to my door."

"And you see how well your scheme to tell the bishop worked," Greaves returned, unrepentant. "Lord Benedick's kind never thinks authority applies to them. You know how the quality are. It's why I threw my lot in with you, sir. You represent the new way of doing things. Where men rise based on their talent and their determination, not by accident of birth."

"That's as may be, Greaves," Morgan said, his florid face looking, if anything, redder, "but you've got to play within the rules of the game. You can't simply kidnap their women and expect them to go away. We had a good scheme worked out. You're a talented artist, and I appreciate all you've done for us, but your time with this operation is at an end. This only proves it." He gestured to Sophia as if she were a prime example of the butler's failings. "Now I've got to rid myself of both of you. Which will only bring more suspicion my way if I don't take care of it the right way."

Artist? Sophia's brain teemed with the possibilities the industrialist's remark ignited. Was it possible that Greaves was the forger? It seemed impossible, though the man had always seemed to be interested in her work. And had spoken fondly about Lady Celeste's painting. She considered the matter as she continued her attempt to unravel the knot at her wrists.

At his words, Sophia saw Greaves stiffen. "What do you mean? I thought if I brought her to you it would make you see how important I am to you. You may think me too stupid to have realized it, but I know what you and Framingham were planning."

Morgan stopped in the middle of his path to the bell pull. "I'm not sure what you think you know, Greaves . . ."

Then, out of the corner of her eye, Sophia saw the butler bring a pistol from beneath his coat. "I know that you were planning to have me killed," he said coldly, leveling the gun at Morgan's chest. "And I know that I stopped Framingham before he could carry out your orders."

Chapter 27

At the sight of the gun, the color left Morgan's face. "Now see here, Greaves. It wasn't my idea. It was Framingham. He wanted to bring in Ryder because you were too close to the Hastings chit. He thought you wouldn't be able to keep your secret. Especially since we thought Lady Celeste must have left her some word."

Greaves laughed. The sound of it sent a chill down Sophia's spine. "As you can see," he said with a bitter laugh, "I am capable of overcoming my affection for the Hastings chit. Especially when it means a chance to save my own skin. It's remarkable what the threat of death will do to change a man's loyalties."

"What do you intend to do, then?" Morgan asked, looking from Sophia to Greaves. "It sounded as if you thought to buy your safety by bringing her here. Which I can assure you will do just that. I'll leave you be, man. Simply leave her here and go on your way. I'll make sure the authorities never know about your role in the forgery scheme."

But Greaves wasn't appeased by the man's about-face. "I'm afraid it's too late for that, Morgan," he said in a rare bit of discourtesy. "You've made it clear where you see me in the caste system and it is beneath you. You may preach to the masses that everyone is equal and deserves to rise to your level so long as they work hard, but it's all a lie. You care for nothing but your own skin. You set this whole forgery scheme in motion as a way to humiliate your competitors. There was money in it, sure, but you enjoyed knowing that they were paying you large sums for paintings they thought would bring them class, respectability, when in fact they were my paintings. Worth a fraction of what they paid."

"If you're so disgusted by the idea of tricking these rich idiots," Morgan asked with a sneer, "then why were you so eager to take your share of the profits?"

"Because I trusted you had a plan," Greaves said with a shake of his head. Sophia could see that he was just as disillusioned by Morgan as Morgan was contemptuous of him. "I thought you were a man with a vision for how society was supposed to work. I spent the better part of my life working in the houses of people born to rank and wealth. I saw no way out for me. But then you moved to Little Seaford. And I heard you speak about how it was time for a new sort of world. Where folks with determination and talent would run things for a change. And I started to think that my place wasn't fetching and carrying for the rich. It was out there, using my brush, like Miss Hastings here does, to show the world the truth."

Sophia couldn't help her gasp behind the gag.

"It's true, Miss Hastings," the butler said to her, his eyes sad. "I knew as soon as I saw your paintings that I could do the same with my work. But as much as I admire you, you're just another one of them who loves power and privilege. It's obvious by the company you keep. When you marry the vicar you'll be one of them."

So he thought to let Morgan kill her? She wanted to

ask. That was certainly a high price to pay for marrying into an aristocratic family, she thought.

"This way, you'll go before your flame is dimmed by marriage into that family," the butler said kindly.

He really thinks he's helping me, Sophia realized with a start. *That death would be preferable to seeing me marry Ben.*

At that moment, she managed to get her wrists free, and she schooled her features not to show her feeling of triumph. If she didn't get out of this alive, it wouldn't be from lack of trying on her part. She simply needed to wait for the right moment to make her move.

"This little scene is affecting," Morgan said with more bravado than he seemed to be feeling. Sophia could see that the hand that grasped the desk behind him was white from gripping so hard. "But I remind you, Greaves, that I've offered to let you go unharmed. Just leave the lady with me and take yourself off. There will be no repercussions. I give you my word."

"You think your word means a thing to me, Mr. Morgan?" the butler asked, his derision clear despite his polite use of the man's name. "You've proven again and again that you're loyal only to yourself and your own motives."

At that moment, she saw a face in the window of the French door just behind Morgan.

It was Benedick.

Thinking quickly, she decided to create a distraction. With the gag in her mouth it was difficult, but not impossible. Groaning as loudly as she could, she slumped back in her chair, hoping against hope that some remainder of Greaves' affection for her would bring him to her aid.

It worked. The butler glanced from Morgan and then,

still holding the gun trained on the other man, he turned
to see what was amiss with Sophia.

Waiting for her moment, when he leaned over her, she
brought her freed hands forward and pushed against his
chest with all her might.

Ben, accompanied by Kerr and Maitland, decided that it
would be easier to get into the Morgan mansion under
the guise of paying a call than it would be to attempt to
break in. So, Maitland and Kerr drove over in Maitland's
curricle while Ben rode alongside them.

A few coins in the palm of a tinker on the road between Beauchamp House and the Morgan mansion told
them that they were on the right track. Greaves had
driven a cart with a blanket-covered load in the back
about an hour earlier.

Ben planned to request a word with Morgan about his
conversation with the bishop, which he reasoned must
have been something the industrialist was expecting.
That he'd brought his two aristocratic friends with him
would, he hoped, seem like something a duke's son
would do.

Thus it was that they arrived before the ostentatious
manor house, with its overabundance of stone decora-
tions and multiple mullioned windows, as a group. And
when the three men presented themselves at the door,
it was obvious from the look on the butler's face that the
weight of the occasion was not lost on him.

"Your grace," the man said, his eyes wide, "my lords.
It is an honor to welcome you to Morgan Manor."

Playing their roles to the hilt, Maitland lifted his
quizzing glass, and Kerr gave the man a bored look.

"I should like to speak with Morgan immediately,

sir," Maitland said with the air of one who was never gainsaid.

"It's a matter of some importance," Kerr said. "Come man, look lively."

"Mr. Morgan will know what it's about," Ben added. Then, with a speaking look, he added, "It involves a young lady."

At those words the butler blinked. He stared at the vicar for a moment, and Ben was certain that the man had heard the rumors about himself and Sophia.

"Of course, of course." The butler said bowing. "Follow me."

He ushered them down a long hall and into a study that had been painstakingly decorated to resemble the centuries old book rooms in aristocratic ancestral homes. "I'll just let Mr. Morgan know he has visitors. May I bring you some refreshment?"

Maitland was already taking a cigar from the box on the desk and sniffing it. "Just get your master, man. We haven't got all day."

When the butler was finally gone, the three men dropped their poses of aristocratic impatience and moved to the window. They had no way of knowing where in the house Sophia was being held, but they would split up and search in different directions.

Ben had a feeling that Morgan would be just shameless enough to hold her in one of the more public rooms of the house. It was well known that his wife kept to her own apartments—staying as far away from her husband as she could—so there was no danger of anyone but servants coming upon the captive. And given that Morgan was known for demanding absolute loyalty from his staff, that wouldn't make a difference.

"I'll take this floor," he said to the other two men as they peered out the window to the grounds beyond. This side of the house boasted a balcony for every floor. And the views of the sea were something that Morgan was fond of boasting about. The construction of the house in this way was beneficial to their search since it meant that they could see into the rooms on this side of the house, at least, from the balconies.

"I'll go upstairs," Maitland agreed.

"That leaves me with the floor below," Kerr said with a nod.

"Be careful," Ben warned the other two men as they headed for the door. "Morgan is a bully, but he's a dangerous one. And we don't know yet what Greaves' full role in this is. Desperate men do desperate things."

The cousins nodded, then slipped out into the hallway beyond.

Ben turned and, opening the French door leading out to the balcony, he looked in either direction before stepping out and creeping along the outer wall of the house. He moved past two empty rooms before he peeked into a brightly lit drawing room.

The tableau before him made his heart stop.

Sophia, gagged and bound, was seated in a wing chair, just to the left of Greaves, who held a pistol pointed in the direction of a man who had his back to the windows. It was Morgan, Ben could tell. He'd know that arrogant pose anywhere.

He calculated how best to get inside and get the gun out of Greaves' hand. If he did the wrong thing, Sophia could get hurt. He didn't much care, at the moment, whether Morgan was harmed. He was responsible for this entire fiasco as far as Ben was concerned.

The moment Sophia saw him, he felt it in his gut. Her

eyes widened and she glanced at Greaves, then at Morgan. To his surprise, she slid a hand out to show him that her hands were free. Then, just as quickly she pulled it back.

As he watched, Greaves spoke to her. He couldn't hear what the man said, but he knew it was an apology of sorts from the hangdog expression on the butler's face. Then, Morgan said something that made Greaves look coldly at him and raise the gun and point it more firmly at the man.

Sophia must have made a noise then, because Greaves turned to her, and taking advantage of the man's distraction, Ben turned the handle of the French door and slipped inside. Morgan had turned as if to run from the room. He stopped in his tracks upon seeing Ben in the room.

"Vicar!" he said, his surprise evident. "We have to stop this man. He's kidnapped Miss Hastings." Since Sophia had just launched herself at the butler, it wasn't a bad attempt at distraction, but it didn't work.

Ignoring the industrialist, Ben sprinted over to the where Greaves, lying on his back, was trying to evade Sophia's grasp. She was clinging to his head, her bound ankles and legs off to the side of the big man's body like a mermaid's tail.

"Miss Hastings, stop it!" the butler cried, his face a mask of pain as she twisted his ears. The pistol he'd been holding was lying a few feet away on the floor. "I'm trying not to harm you."

"You'd have done a better job of that if you'd not decided to kidnap her," Ben said, lifting Sophia off the man, then pulling him up into a sitting position.

Maitland came in from the hall door then. "I heard the shouting," he said, scanning the room. Seeing Ben tugging Greaves to his feet, he scowled. "Let me take him."

Not arguing, Ben let the duke take over subduing the butler, and moved to help Sophia, who was trying to untie the knot binding her ankles together.

He'd barely finished before she threw her arms around his neck and burst into tears. "I thought I'd never see you again," she snuffled against his neck.

Right there on the floor of Morgan's drawing room, Ben held her tightly and whispered soothing nonsense words into her hair until she calmed.

"I love you," he said, his voice trembling as he realized how close he'd come to losing her. "I'm sorry I wouldn't stay. It was stupid. Priggish of me."

She gave a watery chuckle at that. "I love it when you're priggish. Don't you know that?"

He pulled her to him again. "And I love it when you're wanton, Wallflower."

Her kiss was every bit as enthusiastic as he could have hoped. And it held the promise of decades filled with more of the same.

"I found this one trying to escape out on the balcony."

The Marquess of Kerr's announcement from the French doors where Ben had made his entrance had them turning in that direction.

Kerr had Peter Morgan's arms held behind him, and marched him inside.

"You have no right to hold me," Morgan said with a scowl. "Unhand me."

Ignoring him, Kerr shoved the industrialist over to the where Maitland was finishing up the bonds on Greaves' hands.

"Here," Ben said, reluctantly unwrapping himself from Sophia. Rising, he carried the rope Greaves had used to tie her ankles and used it to bind Morgan.

Turning to his friends, he said, "Have you got these two under control? I'll send for the magistrate."

"Take your lady home," Maitland told him with a nod to Sophia. "I've already had a word with the servants. They might seem loyal to Morgan, but coin is even stronger."

"Thank you," he told the cousins. "I owe you."

"Just take care of Miss Hastings," Kerr said with a grin. "We take our duty to the Beauchamp House heiresses quite seriously."

He returned to Sophia's side. She was sitting on the floor where he'd left her a moment ago.

Without asking if she was able to stand, he pulled her to her feet then into his arms. "Let's go have that bath now, Wallflower."

"But I told you I like your attention to the proprieties," Sophia teased. "If the gossips hear about such a thing we'll be the talk of the village."

"We're already the talk of the village," he said as he made his way carefully down the main staircase. "But I have a feeling the capture of Peter Morgan will eclipse even our notoriety for a time. It's a small window and we have to take advantage of it."

The music of her laughter rang through the cold, marble-covered entryway of Morgan's monstrosity of a house.

Despite Ben's bold words about not caring about gossip, he had little choice but to accept when Kerr suggested they drop him at the vicarage on the way back to Beauchamp House.

Sophia hoped their earlier discussion coupled with the speaking look she gave him before he shut the carriage door behind him was enough to ensure that he doubled back later and found his way to her bedchamber. She wasn't even all that intent upon lovemaking—though of course she enjoyed that too—but instead craved the secure feeling of Ben's arms around her. Especially after the ordeal she'd suffered at the hands of Greaves, whom she'd trusted.

Once she'd bathed, and been fussed over by her maid, who was aghast and not a little overset by the news that Mr. Greaves had been the one to kidnap her, Sophia was seated at her dressing table when a noise at the window made her turn.

To her astonishment, she saw Ben step through the open casement.

"How on earth did you manage that?" she asked in astonishment as he shut the windowed door behind him.

Brushing off the front of his breeches, and then giving the same treatment to his sleeves, which were, she saw, peppered with leaves, he said, "My brothers and I were quite competitive about tree climbing as boys. And fortunately the ornamental trees that line this side of the house are sturdy, and tall enough to give me enough height to grasp the edge of the balcony and pull up."

He stepped forward, and before she could ask any more questions, he pulled her into his arms and kissed her.

"Hello, Miss Hastings," he said in the low voice that never failed to send shivers down her spine. "I did tell you I'd see you again this evening, didn't I?"

"You did," she whispered against his mouth. Slipping her arms around his waist, she reveled in the warmth of his body against hers, the now familiar tingle of desire licking at her insides.

"I'll always keep my promises to you, Sophia," he said in a low voice, his hands caressing her through the fabric of her night rail. She'd been disappointed with the practical nature of her night clothes when deciding on what to wear earlier. But whether it was Ben's proximity or the knowledge that very soon clothing would be forgotten altogether, she soon ceased to care.

She lifted her mouth to meet his, and it felt like the most natural thing in the world to kiss him. To be the one who took his mouth, who opened hers and slipped her tongue against the seam of his lips. And, ever patient, he let her, responding to her overtures with answering heat, but not taking over as she experimented with taking the lead.

Stroking her tongue against his, she soon lost track of who kissed whom, and before long, her hands were tugging at his waistcoat. "Take these off," she muttered against his mouth, surprising a breathy laugh from him.

Without speaking, he lifted her into his arms—and in an echo of the way he'd carried her from the beach only days earlier, he carried her to the bed, which had been turned down, and deposited her gently on the cool sheets.

He made swift work of removing his coat and while he bent to remove his boots, Sophia grasped the bottom of her gown and lifted it over her head. When she turned back from tossing it to the side, she found he was watching her.

His own shirt was gone as well, and for a moment they stared, taking one another in.

It was somehow more exciting to see the muscles and smooth skin she'd already felt beneath her hands. There had been that day in her studio, but this was different. She was far enough away to be able to take it all in. The curling dark gold hair that tapered from between his pectoral muscles—she'd learned about those while studying anatomy for painting—down into a narrow line that disappeared into his breeches.

And beneath that trail, well . . . Sophia swallowed. She might have felt him inside of her once before, but the proud erection there seemed larger than she'd remembered it.

While she watched, Ben—never looking away from her—unbuttoned his falls and shucked out of the breeches.

When he stood naked before her, Sophia felt as if she'd run a mile. Beautiful. It was the first word that came to mind, though not one normally used to describe men.

She must have spoken aloud because almost as soon as she thought it, his lips curled in a knowing smile. "Thank you, my dear," he said as he stalked toward her.

Suddenly overcome with shyness, Sophia scrambled to get beneath the bedclothes. She thought perhaps he'd tease her for it, but Ben slid beneath them too, perhaps sensing that she was less self-assured than she'd at first seemed.

When he took her in his arms, and she felt the overwhelming sensation of skin on skin, she exhaled with such relief that it almost brought her to tears. She clung to him, then, and despite her excitement and arousal, she also felt the fear and rage and disappointment of the ordeal in Morgan's house that evening again.

She must have cried out, because Ben pulled her closer, and made soothing noises as he stroked over her back. "It's all right, Sophia," he whispered against her hair. "You're safe now. I have you."

They lay there together like that for a few moments, just holding onto one another, drawing the most elemental sort of comfort from simply touching. And when he kissed her, the embrace turned fiery again and soon his mouth left hers and trailed down over her jaw and into the hollow just below her ear, where his hot breath made her shiver.

While he kissed her, she let her hands rove over him, stroking down his hard chest, where she stroked a finger over his tight nipples—first one, then the other—and then lower, gliding over the trail of hair she'd only gazed at before.

But before she could stroke the part of him that pressed impatiently against her stomach, his hand circled her wrist and brought her hand up to rest on his shoulder. "Not yet," he said as his tongue flicked out over the tip of her breast. Later."

She wanted to object, but the feel of his mouth, which was now hot and wet and covering her nipple, made rational thought impossible, and she moved both hands to clutch his shoulders as he gave the same treatment to the other side.

"So soft," he whispered against her skin, the vibration of his deep voice against her skin giving her another reason to shiver.

As he caressed her, Sophia's hips had begun to shift restlessly, and that part of her where she needed him most ached. When she felt his fingers there, she almost cried out with relief.

"Yes, please," she said, her head thrashing a little as he teased at her entrance. "Please, Ben, please."

But instead of giving her what she wanted, he pulled away. "What are you—?"

She stopped in mid-question as she felt him slide down the bed and nudge her legs wider with his shoulders.

His mouth was on her before she could even understand what was happening. And the sensation of his hot mouth on the sensitive skin of her core was enough to make her cry out.

It was almost too much to bear. Sophia had never known anything like it, not even the intimacy she'd shared with him in her studio that day. It was as if her whole being had been set alight but the fire made her whole rather than destroying her.

Her hips moved of their own volition now, and when he slipped two fingers inside her while his mouth sucked one particularly sensitive spot, it was simply too much to endure. With a sharp gasp of relief, she felt herself tumble over the precipice, her being suffused with indescribable joy. And for a moment, it felt as if she left the mortal world and reached the heavens.

The feel of Sophia's body climaxing around his fingers was something Ben wouldn't soon forget. He'd guessed this kind of lovemaking would be something she'd take to, but he hadn't been prepared for his own response to her joy in it.

As it was, he was rock hard and though he'd have liked to give her more time to recover, he could barely keep himself from spilling before he moved to brace himself over her and lift her knee to his hip.

"Yes," she said, lifting her arms to him and pulling his mouth down to kiss him. "Yes, now."

And he wasted no time pressing himself into her. By the time he was fully seated his arms were trembling with the effort it took to keep from hammering into her like an untutored youth. When he opened his eyes, however, he saw that Sophia's were open, watching him. It was unlike anything he'd ever felt, this connection. And when he pulled out and then thrust back in, she whimpered. The noise snipped the last remaining thread of control he had, and he could hold back no longer. With a strangled noise, he pulled both her knees up and tilted her hips, which in turn made Sophia gasp at the deeper contact.

Once, twice, three times he pushed into her and on the fourth stroke he felt her clench around him and cry out as her crisis took her. Then, it was only a matter of a dozen or so more before he felt himself fly over the edge with a groan.

He came back to himself and realized he was likely crushing her with his dead weight. But when he made to move to the side, Sophia protested. "Stay," she said clutching him to her. "I like it."

Her shifting hips made him groan at the friction. Clearly his long deprived carnal side was not yet slaked. Even so, he was mindful of her ordeal earlier and reluctantly moved to her side.

When she'd settled against him, their bodies still touching from head to toe, he turned to rub his nose against hers. "We couldn't stay like that forever, you know," he said earnestly. "It would be dashed difficult to wear clothing. And I feel sure my congregation would not approve at all."

As he'd intended, she giggled.

There was something so intoxicating about being here with her like this. He'd been with other women, of course. As a student at university—before he decided on holy orders—he'd behaved like any other randy young man. But in the years since, he'd of necessity curbed his physical desires and channeled them into other activities.

Being with Sophia, though, was different from anything he'd experienced before.

He understood the sacrament of matrimony now in a

way he hadn't before. They might not yet be wed in the church's eyes, but they were man and wife all the same.

"Does it bother you?" she asked, interrupting his reverie. "That we've anticipated our vows?"

"Did it feel as if I was regretting anything just now?" he asked, tilting his head so he could meet her eyes, which were shadowed now with concern.

"No," she said softly, "but sometimes in the moment . . ."

"I don't regret anything I've done with you, Sophia," he said firmly, "because if I know anything about the joy given us to enjoy on earth, then you are the Lord's own gift to me. How can our joy in one another be a sin? We haven't yet wed in the church, but in our hearts we are and have been since that day in your studio."

She exhaled, and Ben felt her physically relax against him. "I felt that too," she said, tucking her face into his neck. "But I was afraid I had sullied you somehow. I've never been particularly devout. And I thought perhaps my own sins might . . . might ruin you."

He touched her face, forcing her to look him in the eye again. "No one is without sin. Not me, not you. No one. I don't need a wife who is perfect. I need a wife who will love me despite my imperfections. Who will let me love her despite hers."

"Did you just tell me I'm not perfect, Ben?" she asked with a mock frown.

"What? Me?" He shook his head. "I suppose I did. But will it make you feel better if I point out my own imperfections?"

She laid her head on his chest and stroked her hand over his chest absently. "I don't think that's necessary. After all, you had to learn all those skills you so aptly demonstrated a few moments ago somewhere."

He stifled a laugh. "Yes, you see. Not so perfect after all. And for all that you seem to think that taking holy orders turned me into some sort of saint, I'm only a man. With the same desires and faults as other men."

As if to prove his point, his body chose that moment to respond to the soft strokes she slid over his chest.

"Thank heavens for that," she said softly. Then, leaning up to kiss him, she said in a tone that made his chest ache, "I love you, Ben. So much more than I thought possible."

"I love you, Sophia," he returned. "Let me show you how much."

There was no more conversation for a long while.

Chapter 28

"I can't believe Greaves was the forger all along," Ivy said the next morning as she buttered her toast.

The four heiresses were at breakfast alone. Maitland and Kerr had gone to speak to Squire Northman about the events of the day before, and Ben had, reluctantly, left Sophia's bed at dawn to return to the vicarage, where he had parish business to attend to.

Their night together had been a revelation for Sophia and she had found herself wondering how she could possibly have gone through her life before without him. Ben was kind and funny and warm, and when she was in his arms she felt as if they were invincible. Alone, apart, they were strong. But together? They could do anything.

Even bring down a forgery scheme that had flummoxed the Home Office for almost a year.

"The clues were there," Sophia said with a shake of her head. "We just didn't know to look for them."

"Maitland told me that Lady Celeste took a real interest in Greaves' painting," Daphne said, looking sad. "She told him once that Greaves had real talent, but no imagination. Which is why he was so good at copying masterpieces, I suppose."

"I must confess that it never occurred to me," Sophia admitted, her own feelings of guilt still lingering despite Ben's reassurances that she was not to blame. "He took an interest in my work, but I thought that was all it was. I had no notion that he had ambitions of his own. And I was far too wedded to the notion that Ryder and then the Primbles must be responsible for the forgeries. I fell into the habit of seeing what he wished me to see. A servant."

"He fooled us all," Gemma said, patting her hand. "Even Lady Celeste. When I think of how brilliant she was, how much she managed to foresee before her untimely death, it's maddening to think of how she missed the turncoat living under her very own roof."

"I wonder what the authorities will do to him," Ivy said with a shiver. "If he did in fact kill Mr. Framingham, then it's likely he'll face hanging."

"We'll know more when the men come back from seeing the magistrate," Sophia said. "I suppose the Home Office will need to speak to both Greaves and Morgan before anything can go forward. Ben said that they had suspicions that the money from the forgeries was being sent by Morgan to a group of Bonapartists."

"What on Earth for?" Gemma asked, aghast. "Haven't we spent enough years at war? Why would they wish for such carnage again?"

It was the same question Sophia had asked Ben, whose response had been galling.

"Because in addition to cotton mills," she told them, "Morgan also owns several factories which manufacture supplies for the military."

Daphne said a word that was not appropriate for mixed company.

"For once," Ivy said to her, "I agree with you. What a horrid man. To think that he would try to foment war simply for the purposes of lining his own pockets."

"It's despicable," Sophia agreed. "I just shudder to think what would have happened if Ben and I hadn't overheard his conversation with Framingham at the ball. We might never have become interested in the forgeries at all."

Ben had told her last night that the industrialist's crimes hadn't stopped at treason either. She'd been horrified to learn what Morgan had done to Mrs. Debenham. As if his other crimes weren't disgusting enough, he'd attempted to intimidate the widow into a liaison.

"Speaking of," Gemma said with a frown. "Why did Greaves give you the letter from Lady Celeste? Surely it would have been in his best interest to keep that information from you as long as possible."

Sophia shrugged. "I'm not really sure. All I can think is that he knew I was looking into the matter anyway. And that Lady Celeste's letter cast suspicions on the Primbles since she and Evelyn were such good friends. I wondered if he had read the letter before he gave it to me. I decided he must have. The seal did look odd. He must have melted it then re-sealed it. Lady Celeste had several seals in her study. It would have been easy enough for Greaves to get hold of it and melt some wax."

"It's all so hard to believe," Ivy said. "Such a great many mysteries left behind by Lady Celeste. And even though they were all left unsolved, I cannot think we would have even known about them if she hadn't gone to such lengths to leave us the clues."

"She was a remarkable woman," Sophia agreed.

"And so are you, Sophia," said Gemma with a smile. "I can't wait to see your paintings at the exhibition next week."

"Now that Morgan is out of the way you'll be able to show them without objection, right?" Daphne asked.

"I believe so," Sophia said. "I shall have to speak to the Primbles, of course, though I believe they will allow it. It was always Morgan's attempts to influence the committee that stood in my way."

Just then, the sound of the front door alerted them to the fact that the gentlemen had returned.

Daphne and Ivy rose and went to investigate, leaving Gemma and Sophia at the table.

"I am happy for you," Gemma told her sister with a grin. "Even if knowing Lord Benedick spent the night here has stripped away my last vestige of maidenly innocence."

"Oh, please," Sophia said with roll of her eyes. "You are as prone to fits of virginal blushes as I am."

"You wound me," Gemma replied before ruining the effect by sticking out her tongue.

Their teasing was interrupted by the entrance of Serena, who was followed closely behind by Ben whose cheekbones were suspiciously pink.

"Gemma," said Serena in a suspiciously calm voice, "would you leave the three of us alone for a moment?"

Gemma bit back a giggle, before giving her sister a wide-eyed look. Aloud she said, "Of course."

When she was gone, Serena shut the door behind her and Ben went to sit beside Sophia. Under the table, he took her hand in his and laced their fingers together. Exhaling gustily, Serena took the chair opposite the couple and poured herself a cup of tea. "I believe we had a wager, Sophia," she said in a suspiciously calm voice.

Sophia relaxed a little, and squeezed Ben's hand. "We did. Any of my paintings you want."

After taking a sip of tea, Serena settled her cup back on its saucer. She turned her attention to the vicar and shook her head. "I thought if I could count on anyone to conduct himself with propriety, Lord Benedick, it would be the vicar. I hope the two of you are satisfied. I've now proven myself to be the least effective chaperone in Sussex. Possibly all of England."

"Don't say that, dearest," Sophia said with a frown. "It's a silly antiquated notion in any event. I'm my own person and responsible for my own actions. One hardly expects you to sit with a shotgun outside our bedchambers."

Clearing his throat, Ben added, "I take full responsibility for the lapse in propriety, Lady Serena. And I promise you that we will be wed as soon as possible by special license.

"Don't you dare take responsibility for me, Ben," Sophia said hotly, pulling her hand from his. "You hardly forced yourself on me."

"But I should have been strong enough to resist," he countered in a heated whisper. "Let me take the blame."

"I certainly will n—"

"Children, please!" Serena said sharply. "It doesn't matter which of you seduced the other. What matters is that you marry soon enough to preserve both your reputations. Which I am happy to learn is your plan, Lord Benedick. In that, at least, we are in agreement."

"I am pleased to hear you approve, Lady Serena," Ben said with a nod. "And I can assure you, in your role as guardian, that I love Sophia and will do my utmost to make her happy."

"Why must you be so sweet," Sophia said pettishly.

"I wasn't finished being cross with you over your high-handedness."

She kissed him on the cheek to take away the sting of her words, and then slipped her hand back into his.

"Completely without remorse," Serena said with a laugh. "I don't know why I'm surprised since neither my cousin and Ivy, nor my brother and Daphne showed an inkling of regret either."

"It's difficult to feel sorry when you can't stop smiling," Sophia said grinning.

"Come give me a hug, then," Serena said, opening her arms, and Sophia and Ben rose and crossed to the other side of the table to exchange embraces with Lady Serena.

"I'm pleased for you, my dear," she told Sophia as she held her close. "Be happy, that is all I ask."

To Ben, she said, "I will keep you to your promise, you know."

Then, giving them one last shake of the head, she told Sophia. "Instead of one of your paintings that is already finished, I have a special request."

"Anything," Sophia said, blinking back tears of joy and gratitude.

"I should like a portrait of Jem, if you feel up to it. I know as the baronet, he should have an official portrait, but I should feel better knowing his likeness is in the hands of someone who knows and loves him."

"I would be honored," Sophia said, clasping her hand to her chest. "Truly."

"Good," Serena responded with a smile. "Now I'll leave you alone. But please recall that servants are quite observant and that the walls in this house are not quite as thick as everyone seems to think."

With that closing remark, she left them, shutting the door behind her.

Almost as soon as the door clicked shut, both Sophia and Ben burst into peals of laughter. When Sophia grasped onto his arm to hold herself up, he pulled her close and soon their giggles turned into kisses.

"I missed you," he said in a low voice that played over her spine like a bow on a violin string, echoing his fingers doing the same thing. "It took every ounce of strength to leave you sleeping this morning and go back to the vicarage."

"I missed you too," she said, tucking her head into the crook of his neck. "Were you able to send for the vicar in Bexhill?"

"Yes," he said with a broad smile. "I asked him to come tomorrow. Unless something unforeseen happens, by dinnertime tomorrow we'll be wed."

Sophia gave a squeal of excitement. "I can't wait."

"You're sure you don't wish to wait for our families?" he asked, his tone serious. "I'm eager to say our vows too, but I am happy to wait if you wish it."

Kissing her on the nose, he added, "I will do whatever you wish."

"You will?" she asked, her voice going soft.

"Perhaps you haven't noticed yet, Miss Hastings," he said with mock solemnity, "but I am utterly devoted to you."

"You are?"

To prove how charmed she was by this, she took his mouth and it was some minutes before they spoke again.

"Miss Hastings, please," Ben said with mock severity when they came up for air. "Whatever will the neighbors think?"

"That I'm pleased at the idea of marrying you?" she asked, feeling her heart swell with so much love she could hardly bear it. "Because I am."

"So, is that a no on waiting for our families?" he asked a moment later.

"We can celebrate with them later," Sophia said, her whole being suffused with love. "For now I want you all to myself."

If his kiss was any indication, Ben most heartily approved of the notion.

Epilogue

"I don't know, Miss Hastings," said the mayor with a shake of his head. Then, catching his mistake, he said, "I mean Lady Benedick. I do apologize. It's hard for me to remember your good news. What I mean is that, I don't know, Lady Benedick, how I feel about this painting. If you'll pardon me for the admission. It just doesn't seem proper."

They were standing in the empty exhibition hall, where Sophia's painting, *Fallen,* was hanging high on the wall above a landscape by one of the Primrose Green artists and beside a mediocre still life of some fruit by the butcher's wife. It was hardly the most illustrious showing for an artist of Sophia's caliber. But given the work that she'd had to put forth in order to get it here, she wasn't complaining.

Now, in the quiet before the doors were opened to the local populace, she had come to take one last look and had found the mayor standing transfixed before it.

"I agree that the subject matter is rather difficult, Mr. Mayor," she said carefully. She preferred not to receive criticism of her works directly from the mouths of her audience. It was much easier to make the decision about whether or not to pay attention when it came in the form of a newspaper column or a magazine review. "But I think anything that makes people think must be accounted a good thing, do you not?"

He turned to her, his bushy brows furrowed. "I . . ." Then, as if the sun had suddenly clarified things he laughed. "Goodness me, no. I don't mean the dead lady there." He pointed a beefy finger to the figure of the dead prostitute at the edge of the painting. "I meant that we should divide 'em up by type. Your painting is very good. But it's got people in it. I think we ought to have a section for people and a section for fruits and a section for trees and the like."

She turned to look at him, arrested by his placid acceptance of the fact that her painting—an indictment on the disposable manner in which men in the upper classes treated women—upset many of the proprieties laid out by polite society, and instead was troubled that it was placed between fruit and a stand of trees.

"I'm afraid that's not up to me," she said, relieved to be able to say so. "You should bring it up with Mrs. Primble. I believe she's over there by the refreshment table."

With a nod, the mayor shambled off to share his concern with the chair of the committee. She gave one last look upward, and was startled to feel a hand at the small of her back. As caresses went, it was subtle, and likely no one would have seen it given its speed. But she knew who it was without turning.

"Lady Benedick, have I told you today that you're talented beyond measure?" Ben asked from where he stood just close enough behind her so that she could feel his warmth.

"I believe you told me that this morning," she said, remembering just how much his praise of that talent in

particular had pleased her. She was still a relative novice, but she was eager to gain more proficiency. And he
seemed quite happy with the frequency with which she
insisted upon practicing.

"And so I did," his voice got that roughness that told
her he was remembering that morning's activities too.
"And so you are. Talented at any number of things."

"Why, thank you, Vicar," she said with a coy smile.

"Minx," he said with an answering grin.

Then, changing the subject, he asked, "What was the
mayor saying to you? He looked very concerned. I was
worried he might be upset by your work."

When she told him what the mayor's pressing concern
had been, he threw his head back and laughed.

"It's not that funny," she said with a chiding tone.

"Oh, I disagree," he said, reaching out to squeeze her
hand. "I've been dreading this day for you. Because I
know how talented you are, and how exquisite your work
is. But I didn't trust the good people of Little Seaford to
appreciate it. So, imagine my relief when the worst our
mayor has to say about it is that it's been misplaced."

Her heart constricted. "You've been worried for me?"
She fell in love with him all over again in that moment.

"Of course I have," he said, with a frown. "I want
every minute of your every day to be a pleasure. I know
that's not possible. But I want it for you nonetheless."

Not caring who saw them, she wrapped her arms
around his neck and kissed him.

Since it was a public venue—and no matter how they
might feel about one another, they did have a certain
level of propriety to maintain—she quickly withdrew
and settled for slipping her arm into his for the moment.

"I almost forgot," he said when they'd stepped further
down the line of paintings. Reaching into his coat, he

withdrew a letter. "This came for you, and Serena asked me to give it to you."

Recognizing Aunt Dahlia's handwriting, Sophia quickly unfolded the missive and scanned the crabbed writing for the highlights. But one line in particular leapt out at her and she gasped.

At almost the same moment, there was a commotion at the door to the exhibition hall.

"I am well able to walk on my own, young man," said Miss Dahlia Hastings, still dressed for travel as she entered the large room flanked by the Duke of Maitland and Daphne. "I am hardly so old and infirm that I cannot cross a threshold without assistance. Now, tell me where I can find my nieces, if you please."

Suppressing a laugh, Sophia pulled Ben toward where a sheepish-looking Maitland waited with Daphne and Aunt Dahlia.

"You did seem to stumble when you climbed down from the carriage," Daphne said in her blunt fashion. "I think maybe you are wrong about yourself."

"Aunt Dahlia," Sophia said before her aunt could respond in her own blistering fashion to the duchess, "What a surprise. I only just now received your letter."

The old woman's face softened for just a fraction when she saw her niece. "Finally," she said with a nod. "Someone with sense. I am happy to see you, my dear child."

Ignoring the hand her aunt offered, Sophia hugged her. Aunt Dahlia might not be particularly demonstrative, but she was not opposed to affection. "It's good to see you. I have news."

Stepping back a little stiffly, her aunt pinned her with a narrow gaze. "If you mean the news that you have up and married a vicar without so much as a by-your-leave, young lady," she said with a scowl, "I've already heard it. It was the first thing your sister told me when I saw her at Celeste's house. Your parents will be none too pleased, I can tell you. Your Mama was hoping—despite your attempts to dissuade her—on a viscount at the least. Still, you might have married a blacksmith as you threatened to do. I'll never forget the look on her face."

Sophia took the opportunity to speak while her aunt drew breath.

"There was no time to let them know, you see, and—"

But her aunt had already turned to Ben, who bowed over her wrinkled, beringed hand. "Miss Hastings," he said with the typical Lisle charm, "I am so pleased to meet the strong lady who helped shape my dear Sophia into the jewel she is today."

Turning to Sophia, Aunt Dahlia said in a stage whisper, "I can see why you rushed this one to the altar, my gel. Vicar or no, he's a charmer, isn't he?"

Sophia exchanged a mirth-filled glance with her husband.

"But make no mistake, young man," Dahlia said to him, "you've married one of the most intelligent, principled, talented young ladies in this great nation. And custom and propriety be damned, if you prove to be a rapscallion I will help her leave you behind. Duke's son or no."

Instead of arguing, Ben kept his expression grave and only said, "Yes, ma'am. If I prove to be a rapscallion I shall do all I can to help you."

Dahlia gave a bark of laughter. "Impertinent, too, I see? Well, I suppose you'll rub along well enough together then."

Then, as if she'd done what she came to do, she turned to Maitland and Daphne, who had waited behind her like retainers. "You may take me back to Beauchamp

House now. I've seen m'niece and it's clear she won't be able to leave this place for a while." She gestured to the doorway where curious exhibition goers were beginning to trickle in.

"I shall see you and your vicar at dinner, Sophia," she said with a regal nod before turning to offer her arm to a bemused Maitland, who pulled a face, but escorted her out as his gentlemanly training dictated.

"Why do I feel like I've just survived a typhoon?" Ben asked as he and Sophia watched them leave.

"Because you have," Sophia said with a shake of her head. "You most assuredly have."

"I see where you get your backbone from," he said with a grin. "Will you be like that at her age? Shall I prepare myself to be ordered about?"

"Most assuredly," she nodded. "Prepare yourself."

"I'm prepared for anything so long as you're with me," he told her, turning to face her fully, taking her hands in his. "Together, we are unstoppable."

"I love you, Reverend Lord Benedick Lisle." She looked up into his dear, handsome, sweet face, her heart full with love for him.

"Not as much as I love you, Lady Benedick," he said kissing her nose. "And just so you know, I also have a deep appreciation for your intellect and your work as an artist. Just in case that gives you some sort of extra appreciation for me."

"I don't need any extras from you, Ben." She pulled him down, until his mouth was hovering a breath from hers. "You're perfect just as you are."

His eyes softened, in that way they only did when he was looking at her.

"So are you, Wallflower," he said closing the distance between them. "So much more than perfect."

Don't miss the next Studies in Scandal novel
from Manda Collins

One

for the

Rogue

Coming soon from St. Martin's Paperbacks